Five Days of Christmas Spice

Mercy Denton

FIVE DAYS OF CHRISTMAS SPICE BY MERCY DENTON

Second edition

Ebook ISBN: 978-1-997661-04-7

Paperback ISBN: 978-1-7380914-2-3

Contents

AUTHOR'S NOTE

Welcome to the Sinful Delights Series! I hope you enjoy Noel and Holly's story in Five Days of Christmas Spice.

This series is about instant attraction, exploring desires and taking chances on love. This book has been painstakingly and lovingly edited by human eyes by patient humans who are too good to me and all my extra commas. It's worth mentioning that this book takes place in Canada and is written in Canadian English and some words may look different to you.

Five Days of Christmas Spice is about exploring kinks in a safe space with a partner who respects consent and boundaries and includes: light bondage, pup play, orgasm control and public play. I hope you enjoy the read!

Merry Kinkmas,

Mercy Denton

1

"You don't want to go see the kinky resort next to your grandmother's farmhouse?" Patricia Smythe, my best work friend, grabs my phone out of my hand.

My cheeks heat.

Patricia levels me with the same look she uses on reporters when a story won't bend her way.

"This is what happens when you ply me with drink." I snatch my phone back, wishing I had kept my mouth shut. "I spill my secrets."

It's the day before Christmas Eve. Twinkling lights decorate her mantel, and the smell of her spiced candles surrounds us in her cozy living room.

We don't get much time outside of work together, and it's a nice change of scenery instead of one of our executive offices, and our hair is definitely down.

"Good drink, too." Patricia holds the bottle of Blanton's Single Barrel Bourbon to the light. "Beats the orchid I sent her."

I arch an eyebrow. "Are you going to tell me who that's from?"

"I haven't had that much to drink." Patricia smiles, wagging a finger at me. I'm a talent manager at one of the country's top firms. Patricia is a PR executive. Her team often cleans up after my actor clients when the press turns on them.

"Worth a try," I smirk.

"Don't try to change the subject. Why won't you go scope this place out?"

I don't want to talk about this, but Patricia's expression is open and judgment-free, her short, black, curly hair untamed, falling in ringlets to her chin, her brown eyes curious behind her red-framed glasses.

"The guy from the consortium that owns V,ixen's Paradise keeps bugging my cousin to sell. We've told them no. What's there to go look at?"

Even the thought of Gran Deb's farmhouse knots my stomach and drowns me in sentiment as if I can smell the cinnamon and nutmeg in her kitchen and see her tree glowing in the huge front room window. I haven't been back in years because it's not the same.

"The fact that this place is a kept secret in a small town outside of Toronto makes me curious. Maybe I can hire their PR person."

"Patricia!" I giggle. "We have no interest in selling the land. I don't need to go see a chintzy resort."

"How do you know it's chintzy?"

I bring up photos on my phone. The outside picture shows a manicured lawn and a huge old farmhouse with one or two additions, and the interior shot is of a luxurious, well-outfitted dungeon.

The kind with spanking benches and X crosses.

I flip my phone down and toss it on the table.

"I assume the place is falling apart and cold and drafty with bad towels." I curl my feet under me on her corduroy couch.

"You don't know until you go look. Why won't you guys sell?"

"It's been in the family for generations. We don't want to sell it." The words come out too sharp, and I wince.

"But your cousin and your parents don't want to live there?"

"No. My mom and stepdad are happy in their St. Augustine condo. My cousin, with her five kids and two budgies, has no interest in living in the middle of nowhere. Neither do I."

"Farming is hard. If nobody wants to live there, why don't you look into renting the place to this consortium?"

I shrug. I don't want to deal with the Brennon Consortium, but truthfully, I've left my cousin, Stella, to handle it for too long, which is unfair.

"Yeah, maybe I should take a look at it. It's been years since I've been there." I take a sip of my booze, the gnawing guilt making me reconsider.

"You could bring Phil." Patricia waggles her eyebrows.

Ha! I sputter out my booze.

"He's way too vanilla for that. Going to Cozumel is enough excitement." I say it lightly, but the truth bites. Phil and I have been doing the same Cozumel trip for three years, like clockwork. Safe. Predictable.

"It is *exciting*! I'd love to go somewhere warm for Christmas!"

"Then why don't you book a resort and take Jared?"

Patricia lets out a bark of laughter and gets up from her chair, still chuckling. From the fridge, she pulls out a fruit and cheese board.

"He hates sand. We're going to visit friends on New Year's Eve. Speaking of adult-only places, we're going to a kink party. Patricia flashes me a cat-got-the-canary-grin.

"No way!" We've never talked about anything like this before.

Guess the bourbon loosened her tongue tonight, too.

"Yep. Christmas with my parents, then we're leaving for Vancouver the next day. When are you leaving for Cozumel?"

"Tomorrow."

"On Christmas Eve?" Patricia winces and gives me a look as if I told her the most famous pop star on her roster joined a convent.

"It's when Phil booked it." I should be relieved the trip's off my plate. I'd have booked it two days earlier but I stomp down my annoyance.

"Okay, well, he doesn't have great time management skills. Or he enjoys a crowd."

"That's a positive way to put it," I mutter.

And these days, I spend a lot of time counting up Phil's positives.

"Present time." Patricia dives under her tree and picks up a gold-wrapped package with a green bow. "Open."

I balance the gift in my hands, admiring the perfectly tied bow. Smiling at my friend, I tear away the shiny paper and reveal a clothing box. Carefully, I deal with the tape and get it open.

My breath catches. Nestled in soft pink tissue paper is a gold cardigan. I pick it up, the fabric soft and luxurious in my hands.

"Patricia! It's gorgeous!"

The gold material shimmers in the soft lighting of Patricia and Jared's contemporary house.

"It's handmade. The artist is local. One of my clients finds the most unique things, and I jumped on them for the intel."

"If I can get one of my actors to wear this, this artist would have so much work." I carefully settle the sweater in the box and put it aside. "Thanks so much."

"My pleasure. I thought it was light enough to pack, and you could wear it on the flight to Cozumel."

I reach for the bottle on the table and pour us a half measure. I raise my glass to my friend's. "You're always so thoughtful. It's perfect."

"Good," Patricia's lips quirk. "I had to come up with something that wasn't wine. How many bottles did you get this year?"

"We're not competing!" I laugh.

Patricia grins. "Come on, I beat last year's record."

I spread brie on a cracker, hiding a grin. "The last count? Ninety-six bottles of red and fourteen bottles of white. Two bottles of ice wine."

"Impressive haul!"

"Yeah, we keep it in the office closet and give it out to clients when they sign a deal. I only took one bottle home."

I shouldn't, but I slip into pitch mode anyway.

"Speaking of clients we've signed, I was hoping we could get Mr. Durand some friendly press while he's taking his adorable toddler skating?"

Patricia shakes her head and laughs. "Holly, this isn't business. We can discuss it on the fifth of January when you're sun-tanned and back from Cozumel."

"I'm just saying the toddler is adorable, and I know they're going to be skating at the Victoria Park Iceway around three o'clock on Boxing Day."

"Naughty, Holly." Patricia reaches for her cell and quickly taps out a text. "No promises."

"Hey, I didn't expect any." I lift my hands, trying to convey innocence. "Only putting a bug in your ear. I know the press loves him and wants to get as much from him before he heads back to L.A."

"Consider the bug placed," Patricia drains her glass. "You know I adore your gift. Thank you."

My gift to Patricia had been a pair of orchestra tickets for a Bach performance.

"You're welcome." I check my watch. "Guess I have to get ready for Christmas at the beach."

"Did you want to do something different for Christmas this year?"

I swallow past an unexpected lump in my throat. Christmas has always been complicated.

"Phil's family doesn't really get together, and mine gets together for Thanksgiving. When I was a kid, it was perfect. You know?"

A memory of Gran's farmhouse floats through my mind. The house all cozy with the scent of sugar in the air and snow piled on the roof, the fields piled high with snow. The thought of the Brennon Consortium wanting to buy it leaves a sour taste in my mouth.

"I think Christmas is like that when you're a kid, and if it is, you're lucky." Patricia squeezes my arm.

"Yeah, I think you're right." My throat tightens with tears, but I push them away. And because neither of us can stay away, we spend the next half-hour talking about work until I realize how late it is, and I have to get on a plane.

"My Uber should be here any moment. Thanks for sharing your liquor, the dinner, and the gorgeous sweater."

"You're welcome for the sweater, and you know I'll share any time. We have to do this again." Patricia hugs me. "Tell me how Cozumel is and if you change your mind about going to Vixen's Paradise!"

A security alarm elicits a double beep. Patricia's face lights up. "Jared's home!"

I gather my things and follow her downstairs.

"Hello, ladies," Jared Smythe, all six-foot-something and built like a defenceman, stomps the snow off his boots and flashes a pearly white grin at his wife.

"I'm so happy to be home!" He lifts Patricia around the waist, and they lock lips. It's a Hallmark movie on the doorstep. Those tears threaten to spill, and I push them away. Phil isn't into giving lots of affection, but he's steady, solid. And that's what I want, even if it feels boring.

"Hey, Jared! Merry Christmas."

"Merry Christmas. Can I give you a lift?"

"No, there's my Uber, but thanks." I hug Patricia. "See you in the new year."

"Merry Christmas, Holly!" Patricia waves as I rush down the snowy steps.

"Hi, hope I didn't keep you waiting," I say as I slide into the backseat.

"Not even a minute," the driver flashes a grin. "You're going to Saskatchewan Drive?"

"Yes, that's me."

As the car rolls out of the driveway, I see Jared kiss Patricia through the still-open door. My heart twists with a twinge of envy. Solid is fine. Phil is *fine.* He's steady, remembers to take out the garbage, and gives me space. But watching my friends makes me ache a little for passion, even if it's reckless.

I tell myself it's okay. The lump in my throat grows bigger, and I end up sniffling through the rest of the drive.

2

NOEL

The sharp wail of a baby cuts through the airport's din.

Everywhere I look, people are hugging and kissing goodbye or hello, Santa hats are everywhere, and it's enough to make me wish I had stayed home.

I push down the lump in my throat, irritation heating my skin.

Lots of people don't have anyone special to spend the holidays with, and *it's fine*.

I dodge a cluster of women cooing over a baby and shake my head.

At least I don't have kids.

Claire didn't want any.

That thought just adds to my mood, and I sidestep the *cooing* and *ahhing*, dashing down the corridor to my gate.

Travelers are standing shoulder to shoulder, and people are sitting in all the chairs.

On Christmas Eve, what did I expect?

My phone vibrates in my pocket. I answer, leaning against the window.

"Yeah?"

Glancing outside, I see thick snowflakes covering the tarmac, and I hope the weather doesn't cause any delays.

"Why are you so hard to get a hold of?"

"Why do you have to call me so often?" It's my younger brother, Evan, and he excels at being a pain in my ass.

Someone bumps into me, and I turn to see a man with a toddler, waving in apology.

"We are trying to make sure you're okay, Noel. Give us some slack."

I probably shouldn't ride them so hard, but what kind of older brother would I be if I didn't?

"No snow out your way?"

"Nope, it's a balmy ten Celsius. The sun is shining."

I think it was October the last time we saw anything above zero.

Weather is a safe topic, which is why small talk often starts there.

I'm tired of telling them how I am and reassuring them I'm fine.

I *didn't* drink too much the night before.

I *didn't* buy a new car or go on a property-buying binge.

Like I did that one time, when I bought six properties for sale in the middle of nowhere in Ontario.

And I didn't do something completely rash, like return to working for a firm.

"Evan, it's the third year without her. I'm not great, but I won't abandon ship."

I reflexively clench my fist as if I could stop the pain that's still an open wound deep in my solar plexus.

"Good to hear, Noel," Evan's tone has lost its usual snark.

I know my brothers have a hard time watching me deal with my grief.

"I am going to see good friends at the end of this flight, and I enjoy checking on my pet project. I'll see you on New Year's Eve."

Vixen's Paradise may have come to life on a whim, but I left the day-to-day operations with the two people I trust most in the world, outside of my brothers. And it was Evan who convinced me to bring my half-formed idea to life.

"Okay, I'll see your ugly mug soon. Are you going to join the party?"

I turn from the window, my gaze drawn to the commotion on the floor.

In the crowded room, a woman on her knees frantically shuffles clothes from shopping bags into her small carry-on.

Her long auburn hair falls past her arm as she clutches a pair of flip-flops.

"Noel?" Evan barks my name, impatience clear in his tone.

"Sorry. No, I will not join in."

"It's okay if you do."

I close my eyes against the icy grip of grief because it's a weird mix of guilt, this kindling of need I have, and knowing I can't bring it to my wife.

Other than a string of lousy one-night stands, I haven't slept with anyone since Claire passed three Christmases ago. And forget indulging in play.

"I'll see you in a few days." I end the call before Evan can say another word, and I lose my cool.

A man hands the suitcase-packer a stray sun hat that escaped her pile, and she looks up, flashing a smile. Her face transforms into a soft glow.

But as soon as she returns to packing, her expression hardens again.

My bag digs into my shoulder, and I adjust the strap.

Claire didn't like to fly, but she wouldn't have repacked a suitcase in the middle of an airport.

Her anxiety wouldn't allow it.

She would, however, have made friends with the people sitting next to her and made sure I had a cup of coffee.

Damn, I miss her.

There's something self-assured about the woman kneeling on the floor.

The set of her shoulders, the confident way her fingers fly across the items, the force field of "I don't care, I'm packing this bag in the middle of the airport" — it holds my attention and makes my dick stir.

Maybe it's because I've lost some swagger and some self-confidence that my gaze is glued to her. It reminds me of the hotshot corporate lawyer I once was.

I used to strut into rooms, untouchable and unaffordable to all but a select few, knowing a gorgeous woman waited for me at home.

Until my wife was snatched away by something as ordinary as the flu.

I give myself a shake, determined to enjoy this festive season.

Rosa and Axel will make sure I don't wallow, and I'm eager to check on the resort.

Old friends are coming to stay, and I'm looking forward to seeing them.

I miss having a woman beside me as much as I miss having one in my bed.

But commitment isn't for me.

Grief has wounded my heart too much to allow it.

The announcement to board comes, and I hang back, gauging the line.

The gate seems to have passengers from a previous flight because the plane doesn't look packed.

A wave of longing stirs through my veins because I want to talk to this woman.

My stomach twists.

It feels weird to admit the attraction I feel.

But I tell myself that a conversation doesn't mean putting a ring on her finger.

3

HOLLY

"Excuse me? Can I have another coffee?" I call to the back of the flight attendant.

I furiously grab napkins from my purse and wipe the spilled java off the tray.

I'm not even supposed to be on this plane, but at least it's half-empty, and I tuned everything out by listening to a playlist.

"I don't think she heard you." The rich, smooth voice comes from a man seated in the aisle seat of the next row over.

He's in an empty row. I'm also in the aisle seat, and a teenager is dozing silently against the window seat next to me.

The man extends a handful of napkins, and I take them.

"Thanks. I guess someone's not happy working on Christmas Eve."

"You can't blame her." The man smiles, and my pulse races.

His smile is a gold star on his attractive face, making his chocolate eyes shine.

Yeah, I could relate to being somewhere you don't want to be because I am not landing in Cozumel with Phil beside me.

Instead, I'm on my way to the middle of nowhere.

Because this morning, when I was waiting for Phil to pull up in his Volvo, a text buzzed on my phone.

Sorry, Holly, it's time for us to end things. Merry Christmas, Phil.

I stopped myself from hurling the phone into the bushes beside my condo entrance, but didn't feel upset.

No, I felt fury.

The kind of fury that heated my blood and made me see stars.

Quickly, I ran through my options.

After I booked a flight to Toronto, I hopped in an Uber, and here I am.

I know things between Phil and me were getting stale.

Anger heats my skin, and I gulp back a mouthful of water.

Phil works for an accounting firm. Which is fine; someone needs to crunch numbers.

But I have a roster of world-class actors, producers, and directors.

I don't want to be a snob, but honestly? I'm out of Phil's league.

Stella tried to tell me, but I wouldn't listen, wanting to create something good.

Something solid.

Something I thought would last.

"I don't think she's bringing you another coffee. Maybe she needs a beach vacay," the man across the aisle says with a smile that shows off two impressive dimples.

"That's where I was supposed to be," I mumble before I can hold the words back.

Desperately, I want to get off this plane.

Checking my watch, I'm relieved to see we should land in twenty minutes.

Then I have to find a way to Vixen's Paradise, and to the tiny town outside of Toronto where the resort is located, next to my Gran's.

I swallow the lump in my throat.

"How come you aren't?" His tone is friendly and curious, but my emotional state takes it as an assault, and my skin crawls with irritation at the question.

"I decided to do something more adventurous."

"Oh? Like what?" He leans forward, his hand stretching across the aisle as if to brush my arm, but he pulls it back to the armrest as he catches me noticing.

I choke back a giggle, wondering how this clean-cut man in an expensive suit will react if I tell him I'm going to be spending Christmas at a kinky adults-only hotel.

Yeah, they call themselves a resort, but I've been to resorts, and some were nothing more than dressed-up hotels.

I don't have high hopes.

But the man still looks at me as if he's genuinely curious.

He has a slight smirk as if he's daring me to answer him.

"I'm spending Christmas in the town of Creekside. You've probably driven through it."

"Oh, I've done more than drive through it. There's a world-famous chef in that town. It's a picturesque village that'll make the perfect Christmas card. Would you believe I'm also headed there?" His tone is all smooth purr as he smirks.

I laugh, shaking my head. "No. This isn't some corny movie."

"Why does it have to be corny? You don't believe in coincidences?" He leans forward to me, amusement clear on his face.

I notice how clean and well-trimmed his fingernails are, his expensive shoes. "No."

"Do you believe in fate?"

I shake my head. I believe in hard work and well-laid plans.

He flashes me a smile that I could lose myself in and shrugs. "It's true. My brothers and I own a hotel about thirty minutes from the village."

There are lots...okay, not lots, but several other B&B's and places to stay in Creekside. There's no way we're going to the same place. But my heart races, like it's thrilled at that possibility.

"Why are you going there for Christmas?" I can't help but be curious.

"There is never time off when you own a hotel, but it's a good chance for me to look over the property. What do you do?" The corners of his eyes crinkle slightly.

He's attractive. Okay, he's super-hot, and my libido is taking notice.

I bite my lip.

Most of the time, telling men I work as an entertainment agent usually leads to them asking if I could make them a star.

"I work in sales," I spit out.

"You must be very good at it." The look he gives me makes my cheeks heat.

"Why do you say that?"

"A beautiful woman like you, brimming with confidence? Whatever you sell, I'd buy it."

"Screen covers." The words tumble out of my mouth, and I cringe inwardly.

If I had said "vacuum cleaners," it would be more credible, but sometimes thinking fast on your feet leads to screen covers.

"How interesting." His tone is dry and his smile is wider, as if he's holding back a laugh.

Does he believe me? I don't care.

The seatbelt light chimes on, and a muffled captain's announcement follows.

I presume it's announcing that we're starting our descent, but I can't make out the words.

"Would you have dinner with me at the hotel?" This time, he touches my arm. It's a firm, warm touch, just enough to spark little shivers across my skin.

"How do I know you're going to the same hotel as I am?" I say the words cooly but inside my pulse is racing like a running herd of wild animals.

"You said you decided to do something adventurous. There's only one hotel that offers any kind of adventure in that small town. Add having dinner with me to your adventure list." He flashes me a smile, and I can't help but laugh at his flirting.

It might be ridiculous, corny, but the way he's looking at me is making me squirm in my seat.

"At the chintzy hotel? I don't know. I kind of booked it to get away." I say, shrugging a shoulder, being all nonchalant despite the heat that's coursing through my body.

"Why did you come if you think it's going to be...'chintzy'?" He cocks an eyebrow at me, and it makes me shift in my seat.

"You know what they say about curiosity." I say, shrugging.

I need time to get my head together and decide what I want to do next.

"If you don't want to eat with me, I'll respect your privacy, but I have a car picking me up, and you're welcome to ride along."

He looks so earnest and hopeful that I can't say no—and I don't want to—and besides, it's just dinner, right?

I'm blushing furiously, heat crawling up my neck.

My mouth opens, ready to take the words back, but the teenager beside me shifts and pushes against my arm.

Grateful for the excuse, I gently lift her head and let her settle again, buying myself a moment to breathe.

And where I'm supposed to be right now and why I'm not, makes me say, fuck it.

"I'll take you up on it. I'd love to have dinner," I say. "What's your name?"

"Noel Brennon. Who do I have the pleasure of meeting?"

Brennon. Is he part of the Brennon Consortium?

My stomach lurches, mind spinning as if this could all be some elaborate setup.

Patricia would roll her eyes and remind me I've watched too many murder-mystery movies.

Still, when you represent one of Hollywood's top villain actors, it's hard not to see sinister motives everywhere.

And yet...one glance at Noel's steady gaze, and I'm caught between yanking back my yes and leaning into this spark of attraction.

"Holly Burkholder." I run towards the spark.

"Nice to meet you, Holly. I can't wait to have dinner with you." His eyes darken, banked with heat, and heat pricks my neck.

The teenager next to me stirs, pressing into my arm, and I try to rouse her.

It buys me a moment to break eye contact with Noel and try—unsuccessfully—to compose myself.

My chest feels too tight, my pulse too loud.

The plane finally dips onto the runway, wheels screeching against asphalt.

The instant our seat belts click free, Noel is at my side.

His enormous frame looms like a wall of heat and yummy muscles, close enough that his cologne teases my senses, warm woodsy spice threading through recycled cabin air.

"Do you have a bag besides your carry-on?" His voice is low, almost intimate.

"Yes." My answer comes out breathier than I'd like.

"I'll walk you to baggage claim to get it."

I gently shake the teenager's shoulder, nudging her awake.

"We've landed," I murmur. My voice feels steadier when it's not directed at Noel.

Her eyes blink open. "Thanks."

Dinner with the person who wants to take Gran's farm.

I should have said no, but I don't want to back out.

But...

I want to go to dinner with a man who might appreciate me, and by how Noel's gaze drank me in, I think dinner with him would fit that brief.

With my carry-on in hand, I wait for the rows before ours to empty.

Noel steps behind me, and his nearness makes me keep my eyes straight ahead as we follow the line of people through the crowded airport.

The contents of my bag won't do much for Ontario's snowy cold.

I had packed for the sun, but did what I could with the airport gift shops, and I'll have to make do with the bikinis and flip-flops.

"This way," Noel points me in the opposite direction from where I was going.

The airport buzzes with excitement, and carolers' voices join the background music from somewhere ahead.

At the baggage carousel, I wait impatiently.

Noel is beside me, silent, but impossible to ignore.

My eyes linger on the strong line of his jaw, the dark stubble making him look rugged in a way that sends heat down my spine.

His thick black hair begs to be touched, and those broad shoulders and chest leave no doubt that he could lift me without effort.

He's a head or two taller than my five-ten, and I feel almost small next to him.

My lavender suitcase spits out on the carousel, and I grab it. "Where to?"

"This way," Noel reaches for my bag.

"That's okay, I've got it."

"I insist." Noel covers his hand over mine, and my pulse races.

I stare at his perfectly formed cupid's bow, take in his muscled arms, and my tummy flip-flops, strung tight with nerves.

Maybe this isn't a great idea.

I had my run with controlling men before, and I don't want to go back to that kind of relationship.

That's why Phil was good for me. He never controlled anything and let me lead.

"I'm only being a gentleman, Holly. If you're uncomfortable with me touching your bag, it's all yours," Noel says, his tone gentle.

He takes his hand away, and all I want to do is grab it back.

"No, it's okay. It's nice of you to get my bag, thank you."

"You're welcome."

Walking through the crowded airport with Noel beside me, attraction makes my blood sizzle.

When was the last time someone I didn't pay carried my bag? Phil would pick up something if I asked, but he wouldn't carry my bag because he knew I could do it.

We'd spent increasingly less time together in the last six months, which I know didn't feed the relationship.

"Out this way. The dark-blue Range Rover at the end is our ride," Noel's smooth voice breaks into my thoughts.

He holds the door for me, and I allow myself to be guided to the vehicle on the snowy sidewalk.

A driver steps out of the vehicle. "Good evening, Mr. Brennon."

"Hi Martin, thanks for coming. Did you have a good Hanukkah?"

"It was great. My brother and his family came down. How was your flight?"

Noel places his hand on my back, and I allow myself to be guided into the cushy leather seats.

"Good, thanks. Straight to the property, please," Noel settles in beside me.

"You got it." Martin picks up my bag and puts it in the trunk.

Noel closes his door and stretches his long legs out.

"How long are you staying at Vixen's Paradise for?"

Cloying nerves take my voice away.

For a second, I'm frozen.

This was a stupid idea, getting in a car with a man I don't know. Didn't my mother warn me about this? And this whole trip.

I should have turned back on the doorstep and gone home to my empty condo.

I could have worked through the holidays or caught a flight to St. Augustine.

But the Brennon group has been calling my cousin Stella for nine months about selling our grandmother's land.

I kept telling her I'd look into it, and honestly, it went to the bottom of the list because I didn't want to think about it.

I couldn't think about a place that held so many wonderful memories against the backdrop of my parents' marriage falling apart.

"Holly?" Noel places a hand on my arm. "Are you okay?"

"Sorry, I got lost in my thoughts. I'm heading back home to Edmonton on the thirtieth."

"And mere curiosity made you book into our fine resort?"

A snort escapes before I can stop myself.

Noel raises that cool eyebrow again. His mouth twitches, revealing a dimple.

"You don't think our resort is fine?"

"I don't know what to expect. After my beach plan didn't work out, I wanted to do something just for me on my Christmas holiday."

"And you thought going somewhere you could explore kinky fantasies was just the thing?" His gaze is making me squirm, and I look out the window, shaking off his intensity.

But his words echo in my mind.

Until I told Noel, I hadn't realized that I wanted something just for me.

"Vixen's Paradise had availability when I made the reservation. On Christmas Eve, a lot of places don't."

"Most people who come are interested and eager. You sound as if you expect it to be awful."

My nerves flutter under his perceptive gaze. "I've learned to keep my expectations low."

"Afraid of being disappointed?"

"Used to being disappointed," I spit out the words, feeling tears prick my eyes.

Noel places a hand on my knee, and my breath catches, the simple touch sparking a rush of warmth that's almost too intimate for this moment.

"I challenge you to walk in with an open mind. Vixen's Paradise is designed to be a safe place for people to be themselves and engage in activities they might not do in their regular lives. Do you have something on your kinky bucket list?" His tone is light, almost teasing, like he's daring me to answer, but his eyes are locked on mine, watching for my reaction.

"Maybe," I admit, taken aback by this conversation. At one time, I wanted to engage in all the kinky things.

But I got burned. Climbing back from that wound took me years.

My eyes feel heavy, and I stifle a yawn.

"We'll talk more about it at dinner. Do you want a blanket? We're about forty-five minutes away if you want to nap?"

"I won't nap, but I have an email I have to return." I dig my phone out of my bag.

"Of course. I won't interrupt you," Noel says. He takes an iPad from his briefcase and puts on a pair of headphones.

I smile in thanks, grateful for the excuse to hide in work.

In this enclosed space, with this man making my belly flutter and pulse race, it's a distraction I don't want.

He makes me feel things I haven't in a long time...like I did before Phil.

And that's what scares me most.

Because casual sex, maybe even some kinky play with no strings attached, might be exactly what I need.

Or it might be the very thing that breaks me again.

4

NOEL

Sitting next to Holly is a test of my self-restraint. There's something about her.

The attraction is immediate, undeniable, and I can't wait for dinner with her tonight.

But then the acidic taste of guilt rises in the back of my throat, sharp and bitter, like I've swallowed something sour.

My stomach tightens, and the warmth of the car suddenly feels too hot.

I swipe at my phone, tapping through emails, forcing myself to focus, to keep my hands to myself

Claire wouldn't have wanted me to stop living; I know that.

What makes coming to Vixen's Paradise bearable for Christmas is that it's a project I poured my heart and soul into, and it's something outside of my life with Claire.

As the Range Rover turns down the long country road, Holly peers out the window, watching the property with the farmhouse next door to us roll by.

"It's like a Christmas card," Holly says as we pull into the driveway that's lined with evergreens, their boughs heavy with fresh snow.

"My favourite part of Vixen's Paradise is arriving at it."

"The building is beautiful...like an old country farmhouse but rich."

"We try for an aesthetic," I grin, and she smiles, and my chest tightens.

I look away before I do something ridiculous, like pull her closer and kiss the smile off her lips.

Strands of gold lights cover the large estate, and you can see a Christmas tree in the large window from the drive.

The property sits on land that stretches forever.

And because it's Christmas, the old-fashioned sleigh that Axel found adds that nostalgic touch.

"It's beautiful." She almost sounds surprised, and I chuckle.

"I hope you are surprised and delighted by your stay with us, Holly." She glances at me and then quickly looks away, and I want to know what she's thinking.

I also want to know what she's hiding because I know she's not in screen protector sales, and few people find Vixen's Paradise on a whim.

They come because we cater to the experiences they can't get elsewhere.

"I'm curious to see the inside."

"Let's go."

I wave off Martin and open my door, waiting for Holly to step out.

"Thanks for the ride." She gives me a smile that lights up her eyes but bites her lip, and I want to run my thumb across it, to take her in my arms and soothe her worries.

"Mr. Brennon, I'll bring your bags to your room."

"Thanks, Shawn." I wave to the staff member.

He's dressed for the season in a black coat trimmed with red piping and pushing a luggage cart.

"This is Holly. She's a guest and has a room booked." I set her bag on the cart next to mine.

"Your bags will be waiting for you, Holly."

"Thanks," Holly says.

Shawn waves and marches ahead of us, whistling, and I offer Holly my arm.

"Welcome to Vixen's Paradise." My heart skips a beat because I want this woman—this stranger that I met on a plane—to like it.

She wraps her fingers around my biceps and glances down at her boots.

"These boots were outrageously priced but worth it," she says as we follow the path to the front door.

"You are very adventurous." I smile as I say it, wondering about her back story, and why she made a detour from her destination that required flip-flops to one that required more layers.

Holly laughs, a high, sparkling sound I want to hear more of. "Let's just say I was overdue."

"Come on in and tell me what you think." I open the door for her, and she walks through, and I close it behind us.

"Oh wow," she breathes.

Pride stirs in my chest. My team and I have worked tirelessly to make Vixen's Paradise something special. Twinkling lights and glass decorations hang from garlands above the walls.

"Welcome!" Rosa steps from behind her desk at the front.

"Thank you," Holly moves from the hallway, taking it all in while I lean down and kiss Rosa's cheek.

"That Dom of yours is taking good care of you. You're looking well." My heart gives a pang as I hug my wife's best friend.

She touches the collar at her throat, and I see Holly's eyes go wide, as if what this place is has hit her.

"He is taking care of me and of Vixen's Paradise." Rosa beams at me. "I'm glad you came for Christmas, Noel."

"Me too."

When it came to choosing the people to run the day-to-day operations of Vixen's Paradise, Axel and Rosa were my pick.

They were in the middle of dealing with a loss of their own, and bringing this place to life helped to heal them.

"Holly, this is Rosa. She runs the place."

"Noel likes to exaggerate," Rosa says. "I have your room key right here." She passes it to Holly, but Holly's cheeks turn a bright red and her eyebrows rise to her hairline.

"Is that a clitoris?" Holly gestures to the thick garland draped along the wall.

I laugh, taking a step closer to her without thinking about it.

"Yes, we like to keep it on theme. There's a glass dick beside it." I take a step closer to her, and she meets my eyes, blushing, and the heat rises between us.

"I'm not opposed to a beautiful dick." She leans up and runs her fingers along the glass ornament, and I bite the inside of my cheek.

Blood roars through my ears, and her green eyes swim with heat, and I want this woman.

Desperately.

My phone chooses that moment to interrupt, and it's a supplier I need to talk to.

"Holly, I'm going to leave you in Rosa's capable hands, and I'll see you for dinner."

"See you then, Noel. Thanks for the ride."

My feet are heavy as I reach for the door behind the reception desk that leads to my private apartment, as if I have to force them away from Holly.

5

HOLLY

Noel leaves, and I exhale, though I'm disappointed that he's gone. The attraction between us is there, and I decided to touch the flame.

But it's overwhelming, making my head spin and questioning my choice to come to Vixen's Paradise, enough to make my head spin.

"Let me give you a tour. Follow me to the Parlour." Rosa gives me a kind smile, and I follow behind her to a door.

"This is where I like to mention that guests' clothing is optional throughout the space. You signed that acknowledgement when you booked. Our Parlour is a space where guests may come to socialize and relax."

"It's so soothing." I take in the scene. It's a large, warm room with deep-chestnut hardwood floors and textured walls.

A man with a bushy beard casually lounges on a sofa, his hand resting on the shoulder of a man sitting on the floor, with his back to the sofa.

The simple gesture is so intimate that tears well in my eyes. I didn't have that with Phil, and I'm not sure I've ever had that kind of casual intimacy.

Near the window, two women are lying on a chaise lounge, their feet intertwined. Behind them, a man and a woman are working on a jigsaw puzzle at a small table.

Red candles on the mantle glow, and a piano sits at the other end of the room.

"That is the point." Rosa smiles and leads me to the dining room.

"In here is our dining room. Of course, we're also happy to provide room service."

The dining room, with its soft-cream walls and the fireplace at the centre, has tables with seating for two and four.

A table on a raised platform in the room's far corner makes me curious.

"Beautiful." I run my hand along the wooden door frame. It's a place you want to linger in, and anticipation buzzes through me, thinking of dinner with Noel.

"We think so." Rosa straightens out a table setting and brushes by me. Her perfume lingers as she passes, light and musky, reminding me that this whole place hums with sensuality.

"Down this hall are a games room, a library, and if you watch your step—"

I look down to see a low step as the hallway veers off in a curve.

"This leads to our full-service spa. Do you recall that one treatment is included with your stay?"

"Yes, a nice touch." A stay at Vixen's Paradise is pricey, but these added touches make it worth it.

"And you know all guests are free to take part in as little or as much of the open dungeon times as they like. This way." Rosa turns sharply into a dimly lit hallway. "It's quiet today, and no guests have requested the dungeon."

Rosa opens the pair of gold-framed doors, revealing a vast space with sunlight pouring in from the oval-shaped windows that line one side of the room.

"This couldn't have been original to the house?" I throw out small talk as I take in the luxurious play area.

"No, this was part of the extension built when Vixen's Paradise opened."

I didn't want to like it. But it literally stops me in my tracks, and I can think of at least four people on my roster list that would kill to film in here.

The navy walls with the tall windows give it the feel of being in a place of worship without being ornate. My breath catches as I take in the well-made equipment.

Spanking benches, a St. Andrew's cross, a cage in the corner—all of it tugs at my heart, and I feel an ache, knowing what I missed, burying myself in a vanilla relationship for the last three years.

I need kink.

I want to be placed over that spanking bench or cuffed to that bondage table because being a submissive is part of who I am.

The thought alone has heat licking up my neck, my thighs pressing together with longing.

I miss letting go and yielding.

All day, I chase contracts, negotiating deals that change people's lives.

My throat grows dry with the longing to submit.

To submit so I can turn my work brain off and simply rest in my own self.

Every piece of equipment gleams.

"We have everything you can imagine for purchase to enhance your time in our play space."

"It's gorgeous." I didn't want to like this place. But I can't fault it.

"If you're done here, I'll show you the spa area. It's down this hallway."

I pull myself away from the dungeon, my mouth dry, my heart thudding with the possibilities, wondering if I could let go enough to indulge here.

It's been a long time since I've played with a Dom, since I let myself give in to my dark desires.

For the last three years, I did everything I could to stay in a bland relationship because I craved stability.

I bite the inside of my cheek as Rosa leads me into the spa area. It's just as stunning as the rest of the place, and suddenly my palms are sweating. I want to get away from here.

Phil broke up with me. I didn't even get the chance to end it with him on my terms.

It's ridiculous, but it makes me angry. I tried to be everything he wanted, and he's the one who got to walk away?

"The only thing left to see on this level is the whiskey tasting room. To get to it, we need to go outside through these doors." Rosa points to an exit.

"Maybe later. I want to go to my room."

"Of course."

I follow Rosa, retracing our steps, passing guests bundled for the weather on their way outside, and follow my host up the staircase to another long hallway, the plush carpet clean, the low afternoon sunlight lighting our way.

"You are in room five, at the end of the hall." Rosa passes me a keycard.

"Thanks for showing me around. I can tell how much you love this place." I slip the room key into the reader.

"Yes, I do. Everything you need is here. Please call down if I can assist you."

"Thanks."

Rosa smiles, and I step into the room.

The room is gorgeous. The walls are the softest tone of mauve, and the king-size bed has big fluffy duvets and mauve pillows, urging me to take that nap Noel had mentioned in the car.

I open the door to the left and see a bathroom done in chrome and marble, with a simple shower. There's no need for a tub when there's a clawfoot under the windows. A small seating area is on the other side of the window. The room is spacious and elegant.

I glance out the window but can't see Gran's property from here. My room faces the other direction.

My bags are by the closet, and I kneel on the carpet to open the rugged zipper.

From here, I can see there are hooks above the bed and hard points on the headboard perfect for bondage play.

I swallow past the lump in my throat as I unzip the bag to see bikinis, short skirts, beach hats, and flowy dresses.

The reality that I am not in Cozumel hits me.

I had packed a couple of evening dresses for the upscale beachside restaurant, and these, along with the stuff I bought at the airport, are going to have to do.

The room is so perfect it's hard to explain why I feel cheated by my expectation of the place being lackluster.

I want a cup of tea, and after searching the closet and the cabinet by the television and not finding even a coffeemaker, I grab the little phone by the bed, punching the button that says "desk."

"How can I help you, Miss Burkholder?"

"You said my room has everything I need."

"That's correct. If you need something special, I can find it for you."

My face is hot, a mix of anger and sadness bubbling through me, my emotions as unchecked as the sea.

"I want a cup of tea, but there isn't a kettle."

"If you look to the left, the door—"

"I did, and it's not there!" Tears fall on my cheeks, and I know I'm being unreasonable. I set the phone down, trembling.

I can't believe I just unleashed on Rosa. That's not my style, but I lost control of my emotions, and I have to apologize.

My hand is on the door when there's a knock.

"What is it?" I yank the door open.

"You're giving me plenty of reasons to spank you, but I haven't even had dinner with you yet."

Noel arches an eyebrow at me, and my stomach somersaults to the floor. He's taken off his suit jacket and changed into a fresh shirt that he has rolled up, exposing his forearms.

Catching sight of those muscled arms makes me blush, further embarrassed by my outburst with Rosa, and my mouth waters at the threat of a spanking.

"Spank me?" I stumble back, surprised. "We need to talk about that."

"Yes, we do." Noel tilts his head, as if he's indulging me, but it's kind of cute and it diffuses my angst and makes me smile.

He brushes past me into the room, the scent of cedar cologne wafting over me.

An almost electric awareness crawls across my skin.

"Why are you here?"

"I heard you yell through the phone at Rosa."

"Do you check in with all your guests?"

"Only the most perplexing ones." Noel's mouth quirks to one side.

Great, now the super-hot guy is going to think I'm an emotional wreck. Isn't that what I fight against every day? I can't show emotion in the office, or they'll think I can't do my job.

"I was on my way to apologize to her."

Noel takes two steps, and he's swallowed up all my space.

He presses a finger against my mouth, his touch firm.

It sends a tremble through me, and my gaze drops to his shiny black shoes to keep from melting.

"Everyone can have one bad moment, and it's Christmas. You're forgiven. You're not the first guest to yell at Rosa. She can handle it."

His warm palm slides against my cheek, caressing me softly. The heat seeps into me, untying the knot in my chest, making it hard to breathe.

"I'm usually better behaved."

"I don't doubt it." Noel takes his hand away, and I stop myself from catching it, holding it there.

His eyes search mine, and a shiver rolls up my spine.

My day started with being dumped by a man, and now here I am with this stranger.

But he doesn't feel like a stranger.

"I'm okay," I whisper.

"Good." He brushes by me, pausing beside the bathroom.

"Here." He pulls open a pair of doors that were set in so cleverly they blended with the wall.

"I didn't see it." My voice wobbles, to my horror, and I inhale a steadying breath.

The door opens, revealing a shelf with a pod coffee maker and a tea kettle.

"This is a little fridge." Noel opens the door of the tiny fridge.

"I missed it."

Noel fills the kettle in the bathroom and plugs it in.

"What type of tea do you like?"

"Anything decaf right now."

"May I suggest hibiscus?"

"Thank you." I cross my arms in front of my chest, leaning against the wall.

Noel takes a saucer and a china cup from the shelf and, from a canister, measures out loose tea into a tea ball.

"May I make another suggestion?"

"You seem to do that a lot."

"Yeah, I can't help it," Noel says, waggling his eyebrows, and I laugh, some of my tension eased.

"What do you suggest?"

"You take a bath and a nap before I knock on your door again. I'm happy to start the tub for you."

His deep-brown eyes pin me in place, and I suck in a breath of air. This feels so intimate, but I'm not going to say no.

"Good. Now take this." Noel presses the warm mug into my hands, and I follow him to the tub, taking a seat on the bench seat under the window.

Noel turns the taps on, and the steam from the hot water rises.

"There are all kinds of different oils and salts. What do you like?"

"Whatever." I shrug.

"Let's go with mulled wine oil. It's going to turn the water a pretty shade of red." He cocks an eyebrow, sending flutters to my core. "Like the colour your pretty ass will be after I spank it."

"You really want to spank me?" My voice rises on the word, making me want to disappear.

He opens the jar, and red liquid flows into the water.

When he looks up at me again, the hungry look in his eyes makes it clear that he wants me. "I want to do more than spank you, but that's a good start."

My thighs press together, my pulse races as I join him at the tub.

Heat pools between my legs as I swish my hand through the water. "We'll talk about that later."

"I'm looking forward to it," Noel hesitates, as if he wants to reach out and touch me, but he takes a step back.

"You're welcome, Holly. I'll see you at seven."

"I'll be a calmer woman," I promise.

He gazes at me across the tub with a look so full of heat and naked want that wetness pools between my legs.

"I like a storm every now and then."I bring the teacup to my lips to hide my smile. "Good."Noel winks and strides out of the room, closing the door behind him. The silence he leaves behind feels charged, my skin prickling as if he's still here. Now I'm disappointed that he didn't stay and watch me get undressed.I set my tea on the tray by the tub, slip my clothes off, and sink into the steaming red bath with a sigh as the warm water soothes my tired muscles. This is the kind of Christmas I could get used to.

6

NOEL

In my private apartment, fresh from the shower, I throw off a dress shirt and grab another, only to snatch the first one back off the bed and shove it on. My fingers fumble with the cuff, taking several tries before the button slips through.

I rake a dollop of styling product through my hair, my stomach knotted tight with nerves.

The attraction between Holly and me crackled to a high heat, and it took all of my willpower to leave her room with my balls about to burst.

I jerked off in the shower, thinking of how much I wanted to watch as she lowered herself in the tub, wondering what her breasts look like bare and under the water. The release left me hollow and emotionally empty because what is she doing to me?

Tonight, I want to fan the flames of those sparks between us and see where it goes.

Would she agree to a scene with me?

Not since Claire passed have I indulged in kink, and how much I want to break my drought with Holly charges my veins with anticipation.

And that starts with dinner.

What about Claire? My chest tightens with that familiar ache of loss.

But my brothers are right. This is okay.

Not like I'm asking her to marry me, but if I don't leave this room, I'm going to lose my nerve.

Closing my door to my private loft space with a bang, I take the stairs two at a time and enter Vixen's Paradise through the door behind the reception desk.

The noise of guests' laughter and soft whimpers and notes from the piano hit me instantly along with the scents of cinnamon and vanilla wafting through the air.

Homey, luxurious, and kinky; that's the vibe of Vixen's Paradise.

Rushing to the stairs, I stop mid-step as I see Holly coming towards me, and I feel as if a deer in the middle of the forest has rammed into me.

Damn.

Her mouth curves in a smile, her green eyes are like shiny gems, and that dress...

"Something wrong?" Holly asks, stepping off the last stair.

"No, I'm just frozen to the spot with how that dress clings to your curves in the most delicious way."

Her eyes widen, and she throws her head back, startled into laughter.

"Good evening, Noel." Her voice is sultry and smooth.

Fuck, what would it sound like around my cock?

I offer her my arm, and she blushes as she takes it.

"Are you hungry?"

She tilts her face toward me, and at the hollow of her neck, her pulse flutters. Heat licks through my veins.

I want to wrap my arm around her waist, but I keep it to a polite touch.

"Yes, I am." The floral scent of her perfume teases my nostrils, and my dick twitches as she brushes against my side as I lead her to the dining room.

"The place is festive," Holly says.

"We like a theme."

I guide her through the softly lit dining room, the air warm with laughter and the scent of pine. Every table gleams with glass candleholders shaped like Christmas trees, their flickering light catching in the evergreen boughs that frame each centerpiece.

I stop on the way to our table and say hello to guests I recognize from past visits.

"This is beautiful," Holly says, her eyes scanning the room.

"Still not the chintzy hotel you expected?" I tease.

"Not even a little."

Stopping at the table tucked into the corner, I pull out her chair.

Her brows lift in surprise, a slow smile curving her glossy lips, and she brushes her skirt before she sits down.

"How was your bath?" I ask as I take my seat.

"Delightful," Holly murmurs, fidgeting with the table setting.

"I'm pleased." I take her hand in mine, rubbing the soft skin with my thumb.

"Are you so easily pleased?" Holly asks, her eyes light with mirth.

I lean forward, eager to participate in this conversation. "It doesn't take much to please me. I like a woman who is open about her needs."

Adorable spots of red splash onto her cheeks.

"In my experience, that makes you a rare man." Her tone is detached and cool.

I have a racing urge to plunge through her defenses until I have this woman figured out. I can't say no to a challenge.

"Would you like to elaborate?" I'm curious whether she'll tell me more.

"Good evening, Mr. Brennon. What can I get you to drink?" Lori, one of our servers, interrupts us.

"I'd like a whiskey neat. Holly?"

"Same, please."

"Thanks, Lori."

Holly takes a sip of water and regards me coolly.

"You were saying?" I sweep my thumb over the pulse point of her wrist, and she shifts forward in her chair.

"No. You asked me whether I wanted to elaborate. I was considering it."

Laughter breaks from my chest, and I can't help but grin. I like this woman a lot.

"My brothers and I created this place for consenting adults to indulge in anything their minds can come up with. I enjoy playing with a woman who knows what she wants."

"And not how much she can take?" Holly spits the words, her voice sharp.

The urge to wrap her in my arms and soothe away the hurt in her tone overwhelms me. I want to promise I'll never be the one to cause it.

"I'm not into making a partner suffer or dishing out pain, Holly. At least not unless it's the agreed-upon, consensual kind. I'm more into how much pleasure I can wring out of a woman until she's screaming for mercy."

"Noel, I..." She stops as Lori interrupts with our drinks, setting them down quietly before leaving us.

"Cheers to Christmas," I say, raising my glass, my gaze never leaving Holly's.

"Cheers to unexpected stops," Holly says, clinking her glass next to mine.

"It's been a while for me...since I've played. My college boyfriend left me pretty shaky with kink. He took things too far and ignored my safeword." She stares at the flickering candle and shifts in her seat.

"He sounds awful. I'm sorry you had a terrible experience." The whiskey is smooth on my tongue as I sip it.

Holly sits forward, fidgets with the place settings. "I got over it and moved on but left the kinky stuff to the side. When my Christmas plans changed..." her voice breaks slightly, she lifts her chin and the fierce expression in her gaze makes me lean forward. "I decided to come here and see what this place offered."

Her confidence is sexy as hell, and my cock presses hard against my zipper.

The air between us arcs with an electricity that charges my blood with need.

"I'm glad you did." I seriously want to kiss her.

"You might regret saying that," Holly says, and a cloud comes over her expression.

"What do you mean?" I give her fingers a gentle squeeze.

She shakes it away, giving me a teasing smile.

"Here we are!" Lori says, setting a plate down in front of us. Another server, Martha, helps her.

"Potato waffle with smoked salmon, fig with goat cheese, and a cucumber prawn cocktail cup," Lori explains. "Enjoy!"

"Chef has outdone himself as usual. Thanks, Lori," I say, as my servers head off to another table.

"This looks amazing," Holly says.

"What would you like to try first?"

"The salmon."

"Allow me." I lift the delicate bite from the plate, holding it to her mouth. "Open."

The pulse at the hollow of her throat jumps. I wait to see if she'll give in to this little test of surrender. Her mouth opens; arousal tightens low in my gut.

I hold the canapé just shy of her mouth until she leans forward, lips parting. Her tongue flicks the edge of my finger as she takes the bite, a soft sound escaping her throat.

Pressing my fingertip against her bottom lip, holding it there while she swallows.

"That is a perfect bite."

I pop the other potato thing into my mouth. "We pride ourselves on service, Holly."

"Is the service having dinner with all your guests?" Her little smirk is delightful, the cool tone scathing.

If Holly spends her days selling screen protectors, I'm Mr. Claus.

"This is the first time I have had dinner with a guest. It must be Christmas in the air."

The tension breaks with her ringing laughter, and I move my chair closer to her, so we're not across from each other but beside each other.

Her leg brushes against mine, and she lays her hand on top of mine.

"What do you usually do for Christmas?"

I bristle. The question momentarily catches me off guard because I have done my best to ignore Christmas for the past three years.

"The holidays are always busy for the hotel industry."

"Now who isn't answering the question?" Holly reaches out for the cucumber cup and drinks, tilting her head, exposing the hollow of her throat that I desperately want to trace with my tongue.

"My brothers and I attend a New Year's Eve party at our restaurant, Sinful Bites, and then we all try to take the next three days off and hang out."

"Are you close to your brothers?"

"Yes, we are. They drive me crazy and keep me sane," I say, laughing. "What about you, any siblings?"

"No siblings." Holly glances away. "My boyfriend of three years broke up with me. Right before I was supposed to get on the flight with him to Cozumel."

A wave of fury simmers through me at the cruelty of this act. How could this guy dump this gorgeous woman right before Christmas?

"He's an ass," I say.

"Thank you. I should have broken up with him long before now."

"Why didn't you?" I gently walk my fingers along her arm.

She lifts her glass, her hand trembling just slightly, then takes a sip. "I thought what he offered me was enough."

"And what was that?" I touch her again, feeling her pulse jump under her skin. All I want to do is reassure this woman that she's worth more than the douche who broke up with her.

"Predictability and safety." She pauses, her eyes fluttering to meet mine. "Vanilla life."

Lori approaches us, and I raise my hand, stalling her. "We need more time, please."

"Of course, Mr. Brennon." Lori leaves us.

Holly stares at me, frozen momentarily, then sips her whiskey.

"And that's what you wanted?"

"What I thought I wanted." Her shoulders rise, and I feel the tension rolling off her like an icy breeze. "When I was in university, I thought I would be married by now. I'm twenty-nine."

"Funny how life doesn't work on our timeline." I say, staring into her eyes, wanting to pull her onto my lap and kiss the curve of her neck.

I want to kiss her shiny lips until they're puffy and gentle and learn her essence.

She wraps her foot around my ankle, and the blood roars in my head.

"Where did you go to school?" I toss out to break the tension.

A red flush spatters across her cheeks. "U of T for my medieval studies degree. Waterloo for law."

"You're a lawyer?" I knew this woman was a professional from the moment I saw her.

"No. I have a law degree, but I chose another field."

"Screen protector sales." I can't help but smile.

"Nothing wrong with sales," Holly says, smirking. "Men are often intimidated by me. That's why I broke up with my first serious boyfriend, the bad Dom. He stopped me from writing the LSAT, saying he wanted to be a lawyer, not married to one. The breakup caused me to miss a year."

I force myself to relax because I want Holly to keep talking, but that kind of trumped-up macho bullshit bothers me.

Before I gave it up, I was a corporate lawyer and encountered that type often.

"He was a dominant. We attended kink events together, and I thought after he broke my heart I didn't want that anymore. And I didn't want to chance it. He messed up my head." She brushes her hair behind her ears and sits up straighter.

"That sounds awful. You're incredible for getting through that and going on to law school."

She glances up at me under a curtain of long lashes.

"A full year later, I wrote the LSAT and got accepted to Waterloo."

I could soak in this woman's confidence all night. The LSAT, the entrance exam to law school, is challenging for many. I know guys who failed it several times. That Holly picked herself up and went for it is super impressive.

"Yeah. But I thought, Phil... I thought I could be vanilla."

"Then you realized you couldn't?" I keep my voice soft.

I thought going to work and providing for Claire was enough, and I was a lucky bastard that she was open to indulging in my kinks.

"Yes." Her voice is a whisper, but she stares at me as if challenging me to leave.

"I came here this Christmas to escape and to reconnect with my old life. I lost my wife three years ago."

I hate saying those words. I hate the icy shiver of grief that worms its way into my body.

"That must make your Christmas suck." Holly squeezes my hand and, under the table, she touches my foot with the toe of her shoe.

I love her honesty, and it makes me laugh.

"Yeah, it does, but this place and our kinky restaurant are a haven from life, and I wanted to take a few days to indulge. You asked me whether I eat dinner with all of our guests. You're not an ordinary guest, Holly."

"I get special treatment?" Her tone is all husky.

"From the moment I saw you in the airport..." I let the sentence hang, and she leans in closer to me, slides a hand on my thigh.

"I'm glad I said yes to taking that ride with a stranger." She picks up her glass and takes a sip, watching me cooly as if she's waiting for me to make the next move.

"Yeah? I'm glad I invited the beautiful stranger to take the ride with me."

"Yeah? I want to touch the handsome man I rode with," she waggles her eyebrows.

"I'll accept that invitation," I say, my pulse leaping.

She laughs, and her hand keeps running up and down my thigh. My cock throbs against my zipper, and I want to issue another kind of invitation.

"Coming here is the distraction I need. Christmas can be lonely." Holly's arm brushes against mine.

"What if I offer to be your distraction for the next five days?" I lift her hand to my mouth and kiss it.

She giggles, and her hot breath blows across my knuckles.

"What do you have in mind?" Her hot gaze sears into me. I pick up my whiskey and throw back the rest of it, needing courage as the din of the dining room fades and it's just the two of us.

"For the next five days, we play, indulge our kinks with each other, and enjoy each other's company."

Her eyes widen in surprise, her mouth forming a little *O*, and she pulls her hand away.

Great, I've fucked this up. But then she straightens her shoulders and juts out her chin.

"I am not into impact play, nothing that marks. I like it light and fluffy with a touch of pain —only a touch, and I will not apologize for that."

This gorgeous woman shouldn't have to apologize for a single thing, though I wonder what her asshole ex-Dom did to her. But I don't need to know the details to respect her boundaries.

"Light and fluffy is exactly what I need. What about spanking?" I take my fork and feed her another bite, watching her brow furrow slightly as she works out her thoughts.

She accepts my bite of food, slowly chewing and swallowing, and I like that she's patient and takes her time.

Everyone has a different range of what they consider to be a touch of pain, and I want to know her limits.

She shifts in her seat in the most appealing way, giving me my answer.

"Over your knee?" She shifts again, eyes glinting. "I don't hate the idea."

"I can work with that."

"Good." She nods as if the deal is sealed. "What do you like?"

"To give pleasure and praise. To have my way with a woman who tells me what she wants. That's what I like."

She fidgets with her table settings. "You asked me if there was anything on my kinky bucket list."

"Yes?" I brush my hand along her arm, my cock hard as a rock.

"I thought...please don't think it's ridiculous."

Her confidence when it's on full display is dazzling. Her vulnerability reels me right into my protector side, and I want to hold her.

"Holly, I've been in the lifestyle for fifteen years. I was a Dom to my wife, and we tried a lot of things. The things I've seen at Sinful Bites have made me immune. The dungeon here is designed to cater to a lot of different tastes. I won't judge you." I lean back, trying to make myself as non-threatening as possible.

"Pet...pup play." The words tumble from her lips, barely above a whisper, her eyes downcast, her cheeks blooming with pink.

My pulse kicks hard. I want to cup her chin, make her look at me, but instead I give her the words she needs. "Good girl."

"I've never told anyone that before."

"I'm so thrilled you trust me. I can make that happen for you. Can you agree to give me these five days? Five days of Kinkmas?"

Her laugh is the perfect thing to break the tension.

"Kinkmas?" Her eyebrows shoot up to her hairline.

"Yes, Kinkmas." I reach out and lightly run my fingertips along her arm.

"What happens at the end of five days?"

Looking into her glowing eyes, I know I want her past these five days, but I'm not sure if my grieving heart can move on to a new future.

"What do you want to happen?" It's my voice that is all husky and low, and I want to take her into my lap, but I resist, even with my cock throbbing.

"I am not looking for commitments, Noel. A chance to let go and play? That I can do."

Pushing down my fractured emotions, I lace my fingers through hers, lean forward and trace her jaw gently with my thumb. She shudders under my touch, her long sweeping eyelashes fluttering closed.

Five days.

An opportunity for me to lock up my grief and concentrate on the now. I am going to give Holly the best kinky five days I know how to.

"I'm not looking for a long-term commitment, but I'm open to remaining friends, maybe more."

It's the only thing I can give her right now.

She squeezes my thigh, and all the blood rushes to my cock.

"You need to know that I don't like honorifics. I like being called a good girl. I like praise and pup or puppy or pet when we're playing, but I don't...I don't want to call you sir or master or be called sub...or anything like that."

A sour taste coats my mouth, and I hope Holly's first boyfriend is alone with a shriveled dick somewhere.

"I can't wait to hear my name from your lips tonight."

"Tonight?" Her hand freezes on my leg.

Yes, because I want to show her that she can trust me, and I want to start erasing her past experiences and replacing them with good ones.

"Why wait?" I rub my thumb along the webbing of her right hand.

"Does this make it the first day of Kinkmas?" Her voice is all sultry with desire, and I want to lick the hollow of her throat.

"Tonight... is a compatibility test. Kinkmas is five days—it's one night and five days—and they're going to be as dazzling as your smile, Holly. Is it okay if I order?" I want to switch gears for a moment to give her time to absorb everything we've discussed.

"Yes." She reaches for her water.

I turn to wave to Lori and notice the dining room is emptied of guests. She comes over, and I place the order, and Holly shifts slightly away from me as if she too noticed the empty space, and the passion haze we were glued in broke.

"Was it hard to get people to work here?"

Ah, business is a safe topic and a break from the vulnerability she shared.

"We offer a full salary, great benefits, and an above-industry package. Obviously, it helps if our staff is familiar with the lifestyle, but if they can be discreet and comfortable with it, that helps. Are you going to tell me what you do?"

"What would be the fun in that?" She tilts her head to the side.

"Maybe I'll unwrap that secret like a bow with my tongue."

Her green eyes sparkle as she leans forward, showing me a bit of her cleavage. "You could try, Noel."

I reach under the table, placing a hand on her knee. "If I didn't want you to have stamina, I'd insist on skipping dinner."

"Are you impatient?"

"To taste you? Yes, Holly, I am."

She rewards me with another dazzling smile, and my heart lurches.

What am I doing? Having fun. Indulging. Everything I set out to do when I decided to spend Christmas at Vixen's Paradise.

"I'm on birth control and was tested for STIs last month. I...wondered if Phil was cheating on me."

"I'm sorry your relationship was unfulfilling."

She squares her shoulders, her green gaze cutting through me. "I'm starting to get mad at myself for staying that long. But a new year's in sight, right?"

Servers set fresh plates down in front of us.

I break off a piece of the mushroom with my fork and hold it to her mouth. She closes her eyes, opens her mouth, closes it, and makes a sound of pleasure that I want to hear her hum around my cock.

Damn, it has been a long time since I fed a woman.

Pleasure ripples through me as I continue to feed her small bites, enjoying how her lips close around my fork, how she takes her time chewing and swallowing.

"Can we be done with dinner, Noel?"

Her knee brushes mine under the table, a deliberate touch that sends a charge through me.

With how my cock is throbbing in my pants, it's a great idea.

"Yes, Holly." I throw my napkin on the table, stand, and offer her my arm.

I led us out of the empty dining room. At the bottom of the stairs, I stop and rest my hands lightly on her shoulders, feeling the warmth of her skin through her dress. "I need to grab a few things from my room. I want you waiting for me."

She arches a brow, tilts her chin, a knowing smile curving one corner of her mouth. "Undressed?"

The sight shoots straight through me. I want to haul her upstairs and never let her out of reach.

"Exactly." My knuckles find the line of her jaw. I ignore the guilt that threatens to pull me under.

"Don't leave me waiting too long, Noel." She brushes a quick touch down my row of buttons, and I swallow, the heat of her fingertips searing me through my shirt.

"I wouldn't dream of it." I press a quick kiss to her cheek, and she gives me a wave, turns and walks upstairs.

I stay there, watching as her dress rides up her ass slightly as she climbs each stair before giving myself a mental shake to get going and prepare for our night.

7

HOLLY

My heart races as I climb each step.

Forcing myself not to look back, even though I can feel his gaze lingering on me like a ray of heat, I keep my shoulders straight and hold my head high.

But inside, my thoughts are a mess of self-doubt while my body hums with anticipation.

Dinner with Noel wasn't what I expected, but it left me wanting more. It feels good to have a man look at me like he does —with want in his eyes.

It feels freeing, like the tension I carried in my body and my pent-up emotions from this last year all melted away because I spat out my innermost desire.

He didn't laugh in my face.

After my last relationship with a Dom, I didn't think I'd ever give it a chance again. But five days of kinky play, with no attachments, is a safe way to dip my toes in the water again.

I'm not the twenty-something-year-old who got lost under a big personality and pretty promises.

I'm almost thirty, successful in my male-dominated field. My ability to read people is far better than it was back then.

Maybe I need to tell myself these things, cloak myself in reassurances that this is okay, that I am *allowed* to go and play and have my sexual needs met as I step out of my dress and hang it in the closet.

Catching sight of myself in the mirror, I pause. I'm not shy, and I like the curve of my hips. The muscles I've worked hard to put on at the gym give my body strength. My C-cup breasts have always been okay, not too big and not too small, and I walk across the room as if I am trying on my nakedness for size to get comfortable in it before Noel arrives.

I know he'll expect me to be waiting on the bed.

I'm not a brat by nature. But I don't want to do what is expected, and I want to see how he'll react when he opens the door and finds me...not on the bed.

Sitting on the window bench, I cross my legs, willing myself to project the calm I want to broadcast.

This is okay, even though I'm nervous.

Idly, I try to recall the last time Phil and I had sex, but it doesn't matter. Am I okay if tonight ends in sex?

Honestly, I'm not sure. That might be too much of a jump for my need to be cautious. But I want to run my hands down Noel's chest, feel how hard his muscles are, get close enough to breathe in his scent of cedar and musk, something I caught sitting next to him on the drive here that I can't get out of my memory bank.

Noel makes me feel good, and it's not a pretense. He genuinely seems like he's what he's told me so far: a man looking to indulge and offering me a way to do the same if I choose.

The window against my back is cool, and I press against it; it steadies my nerves.

A sharp knock on the door comes before I decide I've had enough of sitting in place. My mouth grows dry with the canopy of nerves, but I want to do this and am ready.

"It's open." Despite my nerves, my tone is cool and steady.

I sit still, with my hands on my knees, my right leg over my left. Just casually sitting here on Christmas Eve like it's my tradition to be naked in my room.

The door opens with a slight click. Noel enters the room, pushing a cart. He closes the door, turning towards the bed.

I smirk as his eyebrows rise, and he strides past the bed.

"Good evening, Holly. I'm ready for dessert, are you?"

"Depends on what you brought."

He smiles as he catches sight of me, his austere features softening, and he runs a hand through his black wavy hair and then it drops to his side, he leans forward as if he's going to touch me but stays there, his eyes linger on my breasts, drinking them in.

"I did expect you on the bed."

"I like being a surprise."

He strides slowly, crossing the room to me. It's his turn to pretend to be casual, and he shoves his hands in his pockets, walks around the tub and stops when he's right in front of me.

I stay still under his roaming gaze that heats me from head to toe even as my mouth goes dry with anticipation.

"You're beautiful, Holly, much prettier than any ornament I've ever seen."

My face heats at his words, and my pulse races, charging my entire body with anticipation; a flush breaks out up my neck.

"What have you brought?" I ask. I want him to touch me, and for a moment, his hand reaches for my shoulder, but he lets it drop by his side.

I bite my lip, wondering if he's nervous or is having doubts or if we're taking our time. I'm patient because suddenly, here, naked with this stranger, I want the offer he put on the table.

He ever so slightly brushes my shoulder before going to his cart.

"Whipped cream." He holds out a steel bowl piled high. "I thought I could make you dessert."

He sets the bowl on the table by the tub.

"I'm not opposed to the idea." My voice comes out thickly.

Noel takes off his cufflinks, dropping them on the table by the bowl of whipped cream, and rolls up his shirt sleeves.

"I don't know if we covered everything at dinner. I admit that I'm out of practice negotiating a scene."

Something warm flutters from my core. The admission he utters kind of turns me on because it's sexy to find a man who admits not knowing every damn thing, a man who even admits to second-guessing himself.

It makes what we are doing more human and normal, somehow.

"Sometimes things can be over-negotiated, don't you think?" I'm really in the mood to be surprised, and I have no doubt that this man will honour my words, whether it's a no or a safeword.

"That's true. I propose this: I will do nothing to you without your enthusiastic consent. I want you to say 'yes.' As in, 'yes, you can lick the whipped cream off my naked body.'"

I try to swallow, cough, and force the words past the roar of my beating heart.

"That could be one of Vixen's Paradise's theme weeks."

The resort seems to have plenty of them. I lean forward, aware that my nipples have pebbled. Negotiating is a heady high; the thrill floods my system with adrenaline, and it's addictive.

That's why I've made a name for myself in my chosen career. I put in the hours necessary to keep reaching for the thrill that a new contract brings.

"You've read about our theme weeks?" Noel cocks an eyebrow.

"It has to be a great draw. I did find it amusing that the week after Valentine's Day is 'Bring the spark back' week."

"That one is my brother Evan's idea. Many couples have found it a great way to reset their marriage." A shadow crosses his face, and I shift on the bench, wanting to change the tone back to play and fun.

"What else have you noticed about our fair establishment?" He takes a step back, and I wonder if he's nervous, but I realize I'm happy for a longer pause.

"You treat your staff exceptionally well."

"It's a cornerstone of our business. Every property we own is held to the same high standards."

"It is warm, evoking an old-time feel, but everything is clean and perfectly set. It doesn't feel cluttered."

"Not chintzy?" Noel smirks, tilting his head.

"Not at all."

"Spread your legs as wide as you can." The command is cool, like the window against my back. The stare he gives me is sizzling.

"Yes, Noel." I don't hesitate because the confident way he shifted from casual acquaintance to Dom doesn't feel forced, but the next step in the game we've agreed to play.

"What's your safeword, Holly?" His voice drops to a low murmur, sending a shiver down my spine. The command in his tone makes my pulse race, the thought of yielding to him in this way—of being completely under his control—filling me with a heady mix of fear and desire.

My mouth goes bone dry at his rich timbre.

"Bells," I spit out. It's the first thing that pops into my head.

"It fits the theme," Noel says. "Tell me what you want me to do with this whipped cream."

He holds the bowl up as if he's holding a holy relic.

"Lick the whipped cream off my body, Noel."

"You're a beautiful woman, Holly, and you know it." He takes the spoon from the bowl and kneels right in front of me.

"I don't shy away from it." I shrug, trying for nonchalance, but I'm quivering in anticipation. He slowly presses the cold metal spoon against the top of my breast, and I gasp at the sudden chill. It's a sharp contrast to the heat pooling low in my belly, my skin reacting to the pressure of the spoon as it trails down my body, leaving a wet, cool line in its wake. The whipped cream flows in one long line; a dollop slides down my breast to my nipple.

"Good." Noel drips whipped cream on my other breast. He sets the bowl aside, then grabs hold of my hips, his hands firmly pressing into me.

His dark eyes smoulder. He leans forward, his mouth hotly presses against my breast. He sucks my nipple and I gasp, my body instinctively arching forward, desperate for more. The heat of his mouth sends a pulse of pleasure straight to my core.

I can't help but grind my hips against the bench, wanting more friction.

Noel makes a guttural sound around my breast before he switches sides and flicks his tongue over my other nipple.

My belly tightens, and I'm instantly wet as my nerve endings wake up from their long neglect. Noel sucks my nipple between his teeth then soothes it, his tongue laps around it until I whimper.

I hiss but want more of his mouth on me. I thread my fingers through his silky hair. It's odd to touch a man who isn't Phil, but also thrilling. My head swoons as I pull him closer, wanting more.

He lifts his mouth from my nipple and licks my sensitive skin, his tongue following the path of whipped cream.

I'm lost in the hot, prickly sensations of his lips sealing against my flesh. He switches sides, sucking in my nipple harshly, as if he can't get enough.

"Oh!" I cry out, needy with want.

He swirls his tongue around my beaded nipple, pulling it to the roof of his mouth. My pussy is throbbing, and I'm soaked between my legs.

His breath is hot as he lifts from my nipple, licking and lapping the whipped cream.

"So tasty." He smiles, leaning forward, but doesn't kiss me.

He spreads my thighs even further apart. I gasp at the sudden coolness of the air.

"I can smell your arousal, and I want to taste you."

"Yes, please! I want your mouth on my pussy."

My keening tone surprises me, but Noel's smile eases my nerves.

"Perfect."

He gently swirls a finger through my pussy lips and spreads them open.

"No coming, Holly. I want you to give control of your orgasms to me for Kinkmas. Can you do that?"

The request sends a shiver of fear up my spine, but his touch on my lips is gentle and teasing. He's waiting for my reply.

If I give him this, is it too close to the territory I want to avoid, or is this a new path with a new man? It's also only a game for five days.

"Do you think you've earned such a present?" My voice is thick with desire.

"I'm going to make sure I do."

His thumb presses on my clit, ripping a laugh from my throat.

"What do you say?"

"You can have my orgasms, but it may mean I keep my secrets."

He throws his head back and laughs. "Maybe if I am very good at enjoying my present, you'll tell me what you keep so tightly wrapped."

The intensity in his dark eyes shoots my heart into a steady drumbeat against my chest.

"Stay still, Holly, while I explore this beautiful pussy. Be a good girl and let me eat my present."

"Yes, Noel." The words come out in a whisper.

The moment his tongue flicks across my clit, my body jolts, a wave of heat flooding me so fast I can't catch my breath. His tongue moves with purpose, driving me higher and higher, until the tension snaps like a taut string, and I'm lost in a storm of pleasure.

My hips lift off the bench wanting more.

"Noel, I have to come! I have to!" I screech the words as he licks my clit. His tongue darts out of his mouth in fast, quick-fire strokes. The heat from my core envelops my entire body, setting it aflame.

In reply, he licks the side of my clit, little flicks of his tongue at a rapid-fire speed, and it makes me pant.

"I need to come, please!" The sensations solidify, a wave about to break open, and I know I can't hold back this orgasm.

His mouth seals around my clit, and he sucks as if extracting all the juice from an orange.

"Noel!" The wave breaks, and I scream his name, blazing shudders rolling through me as I float away from myself on a crest of pleasure that brings tears to my eyes.

Lifting his head, Noel smiles, caressing my face with his palm. "Delicious. I need another taste."

"You can't!" I reach for him, and my hand closes around his shoulder as the aftershocks ribbon through me.

"You agreed to give me your orgasms. Do you want to stop?"

My body hums with hot liquid satisfaction, but my head feels floaty. He's staring at me intently, steadying my reply.

"No, I'm good to continue."

"I'm so pleased that you gave me your trust, Holly. That you're playing this game with me." He palms my breast and gently squeezes it.

"I am, too," I exhale, shuddering, and gently drag my hand across his jaw.

Noel grabs my hand and sets it on my thigh. "I want that second taste. Ready?"

"Yes, Noel. Give me what you've got."

"Gorgeous, Holly." He presses a finger to my lips, slowly tracing the outline. Without lifting his finger, he traces a line down my collarbone, over my breast, and down my tummy to my mound. He bends his head. I spread my legs.

He licks my inner thighs; his warm tongue in this sensitive area sets off a new wave of sparks, and I grab at his shoulders.

"I like that!"

He takes his time licking every inch of my inner thigh, then swiftly moves to my clit. I grab his head, and for a moment, I wish he'd throw me down on the bed, but that's a little too fast for both of us.

I settle back against the window, my body warm now, and get lost in his licks and laps, enjoying the picture of this strong man kneeling between my legs, giving me pleasure.

He increases his rhythm faster and harder. His tongue strikes my clit, his nose presses right to my seam.

"Noel!"

I'm gone, flying high. I squirm on the seat, closing my eyes tightly. Hot tears fall down my face, and I gasp for breath.

"Come here, Holly." Noel moves beside me on the bench and wraps an arm around me. "Making you fall apart in pleasure is the best Christmas I've had in a long time." His voice is thick with emotion.

He lifts me up and pulls me onto his lap. His fingers trace the back of my neck softly, his breath hot against my ear.

"You're perfect," he murmurs, his voice thick with emotion. The intensity of his touch is a slow burn that makes my heart flutter, even as my body vibrates with the aftershocks of our play.

I cup his face, and this time he doesn't stop me. "I needed that. Thanks." It's an odd thing to say, but I want to say something to express that he's brought me relief for the first time in so long, connecting me to my body's wants that I've ignored.

I reach for the bowl of whipped cream. Scooping a dollop onto my finger, I dabble some on his lips.

He stares at me, his eyes wide, and before I lose my nerve, I kiss him.

He tastes of mint and sweetness from the whipped cream, and I twine his tongue with mine. A growl emanates from his lips, and he grabs my head and takes control of the kiss, his tongue dominating mine.

He groans, and I bask in the high of making this man utter that sound and yield to his exploring tongue, his soft lips against mine.

"Merry Christmas Eve, Holly." He drapes an arm around me, pulling me tight against him.

"Merry Christmas Eve, Noel."

His expression tightens. "Would you like to go further or leave it for tonight?"

My body feels languid and heavy, my head floating with the after-effects of our intimacy, but my thoughts are a knotted mess.

"I want to leave it here. But I feel you didn't get a turn."

"Sweet Holly." He kisses my cheek gently. "Giving you pleasure is enough for me."

Noel gently lifts me off his lap, sets me standing before him and takes my hands, pulls me down to him, and brushes my lips with a tender kiss.

I let out a moan, my nipples beaded, and his kiss turns hungrier. He strokes my tongue with his and kisses me roughly, cupping my nape.

With a groan, he breaks it off.

"I'll see you tomorrow for the first day of Kinkmas."

"I'm not sending you out into the cold on Christmas Eve, am I?" Half of me wants to ask him to stay, but I need the space to process what we just did.

"No, Holly." He runs his knuckles along my cheekbone, and I shudder, his touch setting off a needy throb between my legs.

Past boyfriends claimed that I needed too much alone time. But with my job, being alone sometimes is the only way I can decompress, and I guess it's become a habit.

"Good night, Noel. Thanks for…" Words fail me for a moment, and then I decide to say it. "The orgasms."

He chuckles. "Goodnight, Holly. I'll see you tomorrow. Sweet dreams, gorgeous girl." He presses a soft kiss to my lips before leaving me to my thoughts.

8

NOEL

DECEMBER 25TH, FIRST DAY OF KINKMAS

"You got laid last night. That's what you're telling us?" I can tell by the high-top tables behind him that Evan is in Sinful Bites. He waggles his eyebrows as he sips his coffee, and his brown eyes, so much like mine, have that mischievous glint I know so well.

"Knock it off, Evan." Theo, my middle brother, levels a stare at Evan.

Theo resembles our mother: sandy-brown hair and light-grey eyes. He's at our parents' house, hanging out in the garage. I see our dad's hockey sticks behind him.

"What?" Evan leans back in his desk chair.

"You're being obnoxious," Hunter says.

Hunter, the youngest Brennon brother, sits with arms crossed over his muscled chest. I have no idea where he is. It's a white wall behind him. His beard is full, and he looks like he needs coffee.

Hunter comes and goes as he pleases, and I'm touched he showed up.

Even though I want to mute them and leave this Zoom meeting, Evan insisted we have one this Christmas morning.

I'm totally blaming the lack of sleep I got last night and the lack of coffee I got this morning on Holly. And that has me smiling like a loon.

My brothers drive me nuts, but I'm damn grateful for them. Our family is pretty tight, and I know I wouldn't have gotten through these last three years if it weren't for them driving me crazy.

"Noel, if you found a way to make your Christmas happy by meeting this woman, I think that's a good thing. You don't have to sleep with her," Theo says. Theo's tone is his usual seriousness.

"Thanks, Theo," I say.

"Yeah, but the man's not dead," Evan says.

His quick mouth and quick temper often get him into trouble. Theo sits back in his chair, Hunter leans forward, and Evan goes off screen for a moment.

"I have things to do. Check in with you guys later," I say.

"Hey, I'm an ass. Sorry." Evan comes back in the frame, holding up a potted lavender tree. "Look, I put this in the entryway. I know Claire loved them."

She loved our garden and, for Christmas, would give everyone a plant of some kind. In the first year Sinful Bites opened, Claire decorated the space with lavender trees. Evan freaked out, saying that their smell would compete with the food. Claire shrugged and moved her trees to the entranceway.

"The man does have a heart," Theo mumbles.

"It's fine. I know I've been a widow for three years now." A lump rises in my throat because it's three years to the day.

"Isn't this the usual bowl of cheer? If Noel is shacking up with one of his guests or plans on it, I'm for it. Later, boys. See you in the New Year." Hunter waves before he logs off.

"I have things to do. Merry Christmas," I say.

"Merry Christmas," my brothers echo back.

I stride across the room and glance out the window. From my private loft slash office space, it's a white blanket of fresh snow covering the fields across.

I wanted to come to Vixen's Paradise not only to see Rosa and Axel and to check on the place but also because this is a place that my wife hadn't been to. Grief made me buy up all the properties and follow in Evan's footsteps, opening a luxury hotel serving kinky tastes. The properties were mostly abandoned or on the way to being left destitute. The banks owned several, and people who were ready to move on were looking to sell, so it was good timing on my part.

All except for Winterhaven Farms, the property next to us. The owner hasn't returned Evan's calls in a while. When I first bought this property, Evan dealt with a lot of the administration stuff because I was still in my cloud of grief.

Vowing to call the owners myself after the holidays, I change from my sweats into a pair of pressed grey slacks and a light-blue dress shirt, missing that I once had someone who laid out my clothes every morning.

Shaking away the sadness, I take the stairs two at a time, follow the narrow hallway and make my way to Rosa's office.

"Merry Christmas." I peek my head around the door.

Axel and Rosa break away at my knock as if I caught them in the act...which I did. Rosa blushes, reaching for her blouse.

"Merry Christmas, boss," Axel says, leaning on the desk.

"Rosa, are you okay?" I grin at her.

"We were just taking a moment."

"I know it's unusual to have me here. I'm not concerned. It's early, and your capable staff is looking after the guests."

If anything, my words cause Rosa to blush more, and I remember her and Claire making dinner together in our kitchen at our Edmonton home.

"I got what you asked for, Noel. I made it to the shop in the nick of time."

"Thank you."

"We're happy to help. You deserve happiness, Noel."

I shrug. "It is a little Christmas fun." I take the gold-wrapped box from Rosa. "See you two out there."

"Later, Noel," Axel says, closing the door. "Now, my beautiful wife, where were we?"

The shriek of laughter from Rosa makes me smile as I stride down the hall to the door that leads to Vixen's Paradise and almost collide with a man wearing a Santa hat running past the desk, being chased by a tall woman wearing a red latex suit.

"Come back here, you brat!"

"Got to catch me first!" the man yells. The notes of "Jingle Bells" float into the room and the buzz of the place is festive, the scent of cooked sugar heavy in the air.

My stomach rumbles, wanting breakfast.

"Noel! Good to see you!" Rick Meaford slaps me on the shoulder.

I shake his hand and grin. "I didn't know you guys were here already."

"Wouldn't miss the Fire and Ice party! Axel's parties are the bomb. Isn't that right, Cat?" Rick squeezes his submissive's shoulder.

She laughs and flicks her short hair. "Vixen's Paradise's play parties are awesome. We had to come to the last one of the year." Cat kisses my cheek. "Merry Christmas, Noel."

"Merry Christmas. It's been too long." I genuinely mean it. Rick and Cat were two of my friends from my old life. When I opened Vixen's Paradise, they were my first phone call.

"We've got to work off that breakfast. See you later!" Rick swings Cat up in his arms, and she laughs as he leads her away down the hall.

My pulse gallops as I see Holly at the top of the stairs. I start over to her when Pauline steps in front of me. The Domme takes my hand in hers.

"Noel! Merry Christmas."

"Merry Christmas, Pauline. It's good to see you. Thanks for coming."

"We wouldn't miss it for the world! Kai is around here somewhere." She puts two fingers in her mouth, emitting the shrillest whistle I've ever heard.

I startle and cover my ears.

"Practice, darling," Pauline grins knowingly at me.

From across the room, Kai darts over and kneels at her feet.

"Here he is. Kai! Look!" Pauline grabs a fistful of his hair, forcing Kai to meet my eyes. He gives me a huge smile.

"Hi, Noel. Great place you have here."

Pauline rests a hand on Kai's head. I catch sight of Holly halfway down the stairs and I want to rush to her, but I don't want to be rude.

"I just saw Rick and Cat. Did you come with them?"

"We did! You know this place is fab, Noel." Pauline launches into a story about their drive down, but my gaze is glued to Holly.

She's chatting with a woman on the stairs; her hair is tied back, falling down one shoulder, and her short skirt clings to her body. She's wearing a lacy red top, showing off her beautiful breasts, and I remember how her nipple tastes.

"You'll come for dinner soon?" Pauline says.

I blink, knowing I had tuned out the conversation. "Yes, I'd love that, thanks."

"Run along, Kai. We must not keep our friends waiting any longer," Pauline demands. She flips her long blonde hair as Kai scrambles along the hall on all fours.

I meet Holly on the stairs before anyone else could grab my attention. She turns to me and a slight blush colours her cheeks.

My heart tugs weirdly, and I know I have the biggest grin splashed on my face, and I don't care. I'll smile every time I see this woman walk into a room.

"I'll talk to you later. Nice meeting you," the woman says and goes upstairs.

"Good morning, Miss Burkholder."

"Merry Christmas, Mr. Brennon," Holly says.

I move closer, close enough to see the glitter in her dark-pink lip gloss. She tilts her head at me and smiles.

Leaving her last night was so hard. Part of the reason I gave her the choice to continue or to pick up our game today was because I thought maybe I needed a push...a push to spend a night in the bed of a woman who isn't my wife.

Another part of me is relieved that she sent me away, even if all I wanted to do was bury my cock in her pussy and make love to her until the morning.

I take her arm, guiding her down the last four steps.

"This is for later." I hold up the gold-wrapped gift. It's heavy and boxy, and I set it behind the reception desk.

"How did you sleep?"

"Great." But a shadow crosses her face, and I want to know why.

"Are you sure?"

"My family hasn't celebrated Christmas together for a long time. Being here with all the holiday decorations..."

She touches a piece of evergreen on the doorframe of the dining room. "Made me miss some stuff. I called my cousin last night. She and her kids read *The Night Before Christmas* to me on the phone."

"Christmas does bring out the sentimentality," I say.

I take her arm and guide her to the dining room.

"Or new traditions," Holly laughs, pointing to the table on the raised platform where we had dinner last night.

A man has his head buried in a woman's pussy, and her legs are over his shoulders.

"I know it's optional, but in the dining room?" Holly's expression is half-amused, and her tone is one of fascination, not judgement.

"It is Christmas. If you tell me what you like, I'll bring you a plate."

Her eyebrows shoot up. "Really?"

"You can enjoy your coffee, and I'll bring the food. There's a table free by the window."

"Lots of bacon, those waffles smell amazing, and something with fruit to balance it out."

"You've got it."

"Thank you, Noel." Her voice is soft and wistful.

I smile, grab another plate from the line, and wait my turn, watching as she makes her way to the table, exchanging polite chitchat with guests.

I go through the line, taking waffles with whipped cream because I can't help myself, a fruit bowl, lots of bacon, eggs, and toast for me. At the end of the line, I balance our plates across my arm, remembering my days as a waiter while in university and praying that I don't spill any of this food. Holly helps me unload the plates, and then I slide into the seat across from her.

"I don't think anyone's gotten me a plate before," she mumbles into her coffee.

Her cheeks are bright pink as if my gentlemanly act has embarrassed her, but I can't believe this gorgeous woman didn't have men falling at her feet, offering to carry all her things or to get her a plate of food.

"It's no big deal, Miss Burkholder. Merry Christmas."

We dig into our food.

"You're a popular guy this morning. I saw you talking to a woman as I was coming down."

"Merry Christmas, Mr. Brennon." Madison, one of our servers, interrupts us. "Coffee?" She holds up a carafe, and I pick up the coffee cup from the table.

"Thank you."

"I noticed your hands were full." Madison winks at me and goes to the next table.

"See? Totally popular." Holly smiles.

"I'm lucky to have good friends."

"Well, if I had a friend who owned a private hotel with a dungeon, I might be here all the time." She nudges my foot under the table with hers and I laugh.

I sip my coffee, my hands sweating. "I've known Pauline and her husband, Kai, for years. Same with Rick and Cat. I met them at a club I used to attend with my wife. I wasn't a great friend after she passed. But when I called them to tell them what I was doing here, they were my first guests and have come back to all the play parties since."

"I'm sure they understand, Noel."

The warmth in her voice melts a frozen section of my heart. I know grief is a living, breathing, and often controlling force, but I was awful to the people in my life. Buying the properties on this road gave me purpose when I realized I wasn't returning to work for the firm.

"They are kind, and I'm lucky."

Holly takes a forkful of whipped cream and holds it to my lips. "My turn to feed you?"

"Just a little," I say and give in to her request by parting my lips slightly. As she slides the forkful in my mouth, the heat between us rises, and I shift in my seat. I close my lips around the fork, and she wipes a tiny spot by my cheek, her touch igniting a fresh wave of desire, making my balls tight.

"There, now I feel like I've given you something."

She smiles; her eyes glow. The background noise floats away. I suppress the wild need to laugh.

I'm eating breakfast with a beautiful woman. All I want to do is taste her skin again. I want to give her another earth-shattering orgasm that severs the ties to the self-control she tightly holds on to.

"You are my present, and I have plans for the first day of Kinkmas."

"Any hints?" A smile curves her mouth as she peers at me from her long eyelashes.

"Nope. But I want you to open your present."

She sets her fork on her plate. "Noel, you don't have to give me anything."

Not this again. One way or another, I'm going to make this woman accept good things. "I like to."

"Is that part of bringing you pleasure?"

"Oh yes, it's a start, Holly."

She fumbles with her coffee mug and squirms on the chair, and I want to ease her discomfort. "Christmas means presents, so does Kinkmas." I brush my thumb over her knuckles, and her blush deepens. "I'm done," Holly says, setting down her mug. My pulse jumps as I stand and gaze down at her, brushing my lips across hers. She reaches up to cup my face. The kiss floods my bloodstream with pulsating need. I want this woman so badly, and I kiss her, tracing her bottom lip, then plunging my tongue into her mouth. She lets out a soft whimper as her tongue meets mine, and an electric tingle slides down my spine. Before I *do* rip her clothes off, I break off the kiss. "Happy Kinkmas. Come on." I take her arm, guiding her out of the dining room. Behind the reception desk, I grab the gold-wrapped present and hand it to her.

"Noel, this is too much." She shakes her head, sending her waves flying.

"You haven't opened it yet."

"Kiss her!" Rick strides past me and points to the ceiling. Above our heads, the mistletoe hangs.

"It's tradition," Holly says, smiling, and sets the gift on Rosa's desk, laying her palm on my chest.

Her hand is warm through my shirt, and I wonder if she can feel the thudding of my heart going double time.

I clasp her hand and lean forward, slanting my lips over hers, in a tender, soft kiss. I kiss her with all the passion and gratitude I have for this woman I met on a plane.

Holly might not believe in coincidences, but surely this was meant to be?

She lets out a soft whimper as I twine her tongue with mine. My hand snakes up her back, pressing her close to me.

"Sorry to interrupt, Mr. Brennon."

I reluctantly break off the kiss, glaring at Rosa.

"Important phone call from Theo."

"Theo?" The surprise in my voice is almost comical. "I'm sorry, I've got to take this." I brush Holly's soft cheek with the back of my knuckles.

"I understand," she smiles.

"Open the gift once you're inside your room, and if you can't follow the instructions, text me."

I had planned to keep her busy until this afternoon and joke about having to be done at three, but this works out, too.

"Okay. See you later." Holly grabs the gift, touches my arm, and strides past me, going upstairs to her room.

"This better be really important," I growl at Rosa.

But Theo never calls for anything small.

"He tried to get you but couldn't."

I take my cell out of my pocket, and sure enough, three missed calls from my little brother.

Hoping it will be quick, I disappear into my office.

9

The present is heavy, and I want to rip it open right in the hallway, but I force myself to not run down the hall and get to my room as fast as I can.

Inside, I tear off the paper, and a card falls to the floor.

I pick it up.

Holly, I would be delighted if you joined me for a sleigh ride this Christmas. Please meet me at the front at 3:00 p.m. Yours, Noel.

The note makes me smile. There is something so gentlemanly about it, so considerate, and it reflects the man I've started to get to know.

Gently lifting the lid of the black cardboard box, I take off a layer of tissue paper.

"Oh, wow."

Reaching into the box, I pull out a velvety soft fabric bundle and lay it on the bed. My heart races. This is so unreal. It's like I'm on the set of a Hallmark movie.

Delicately, I touch the soft faux fur. I hold it up against me, and it glimmers in the light. The dark-green fabric makes my eyes pop. I undo the clasp and slide my arms inside the soft cloak. Inside, the cloak is lined with fleece.

It has pockets! I shove my hands in the deep pockets.

Strolling to the window, I look at the fields toward my Gran's house. Those childhood Christmases brought the peace I hadn't had at home, and I realize I am carrying a little bit of that threat with me into my day-to-day life, where I always feel like I am fighting to keep the peace I've found.

When I am dealing with my egocentric clients, I fight with them to get them to listen to me; when dealing with studios and production companies, I fight to be taken seriously.

But with Noel...I don't have to fight.

Coming here to Vixen's Paradise was the remedy I didn't know I needed. My fingers snag on something in the pocket, something metal and cool. Taking the object out of my pocket, I laugh. It's a gold bullet vibrator; the remote control for this device is curiously missing.

My cell chimes, and I answer the call. "Merry Christmas, Mom."

"Holly! Merry Christmas! It's raining cats and dogs here, can you believe that? I bet you and Phil are having a great time on the beach!"

A lump forms in my throat, hearing my Mom's voice. I understand why we stopped getting together at Christmas after Gran passed, but I think we can create a new tradition and spend the day with each other. When I talked to Stella last night, she said the same thing.

"I'm not on the beach. Phil and I broke up."

"Oh, Holly! I'm so sorry! Do you want to come for some Florida sun?"

"I'm actually —" How do I even tell Mom about this? I blush, wondering what she'd think of this adults-only place.

"It's okay, I'm meeting friends."

"Okay, honey. Did you tell Stella?"

"Yeah," I can't help but laugh.

"And what did she say?"

My cousin is always quick with the one-liners. "Good, because, and I quote, 'Phil is as interesting as a toaster.'"

My mom howls, and I laugh with her because it's true.

"I miss you both."

"I miss you too. I'm going to come and visit soon." I mean it and vow to look up my calendar and flights when I'm off the phone.

"Here's Max."

"Hey, kiddo, how's your Christmas?"

"It's snowy," I tell my stepdad. "Not the beach I was expecting."

"I overheard. You holding up okay?"

"Yeah," I pace across the room. "Getting ready for your golf game?"

"Yep, I'm all set. Did you know I almost had a hole-in-one the other night?"

Tears gather at the corners of my eyes as I listen to Max tell the story. I couldn't ever bring myself to call him "Dad." The dad I knew drank too much and screamed at my mother. I was twelve when my mom finally decided she'd had enough. I was fifteen when Max came along and swept Mom off her feet.

He's stable and steady, and he's always been there for me. When I broke up with my former Dom and was going to quit being a lawyer, he flew out to Toronto, took me to dinner, and told me to only give up if it was on my terms.

With a start, I realize I had spent so much time trying to avoid a relationship that was like my mom and father's that I didn't clue into the one who I was trying to model my own after. Max brings my mom flowers out of the blue. He gets her favourite concert tickets and surprises her with trips. They dance in the kitchen as if it's Carnegie Hall, and he looks at my mother as if the sun rises and sets on her.

I don't need someone steady, stable, and boring. I need someone who can love me.

I don't want a man who wants me to be weak, even if I am submissive in the bedroom. Noel said he'd been in the lifestyle for fifteen years and was a Dom to his wife. If I continue with him, will I lose myself? But so far, Noel has shown me he is a good man.

"Holly? I got to get to my game."

"Okay. Love you, Max."

"Love you, kiddo."

The phone is silent, and I end the call. *We agreed to five days, only five days,* I remind myself.

* * *

"I knew that colour would suit you," Noel leans by the front door. "Are you wearing everything I gave you?"

"Yes." I feel the weight of the vibrator as I move. "Thank you very much for the cloak. I'm at the mercy of what I found in the airport gift shop."

His dark eyes light with mirth. "I saw you stuff belongings into your bag."

"You did not!"

"Yes, and it was adorable." Noel throws on a wool coat and a plaid scarf. He passes me a red knit toque and a fuzzy pair of gloves.

"Thanks."

"Right this way." He opens the door.

The cold air catches my breath, and my feet crunch on the packed snow. The red bows and the hanging star ornaments on the garlands are dusted with snow, making the property look like a Christmas card.

From here, I can almost see Gran's treeline.

"Holly, meet our resident members of Vixen's Paradise," Noel says, gently taking my arm and angling me the opposite the way.

"Oh, horses!" I rush forward, eager to give the two great speckled grey Percherons pats. One snorts at my touch. The horses are harnessed to a shiny red sleigh.

A driver in the front of the sleigh tips his hat to me.

"How many horses does Vixen's Paradise have?" The horses make breathy sounds as they snort, blowing out hot breath.

"These two workhorses and six more. We have a maintenance ground crew and stable staff who live on the property full-time." The pride threads through Noel's voice as he smiles.

"You must rent this out for photo shoots." The sleigh is gleaming, the horses gorgeous, and I'm in the middle of a Christmas fairy tale.

"We don't, actually. Come on."

Noel gives me a hand, and I step up on the back of the sleigh.

"Merry Christmas, Aaron," Noel says, clapping the driver's hand before stepping up beside me.

"Good day for a ride, Noel. Where are we going today?"

"A tour of the property."

"You got it. I'm happy to let these guys stretch their legs. Here, let me pass you that blanket." Aaron unfurls a thick blanket and settles it across my lap.

Noel climbs up beside me, tucking his hand into mine.

"Ready?" he asks.

My heart skips a beat, my palms sweat.

Stop being silly, I scold myself, but I'm literally in a Christmas special with kinky flair, so I can be okay with silly.

"Ready."

The red scarf brings out the gold in his eyes, and he gives me that dimpled smile while he slides his hand over my thigh under the blanket.

The horses start at a trot, and the sleigh slides along the snow. The vast property stretches before us.

"Why no photo ops?"

"Because that would be risking too much exposure. We don't want to hide what we do at Vixen's Paradise, but we do want to be careful with how we market it."

"Have you ever had someone make an arrangement and not know what it was?"

"Occasionally, we have someone knock on the door. In that case, our staff asks them what kind of experience they are looking for or if they want to book one of our theme weeks, and depending on how they answer, they're told we don't have room."

My mind starts to wander, thinking of how you'd market Vixen's Paradise.

"That's a clever way to handle it."

Noel squeezes my thigh under the blanket. "How did you sleep last night?"

"Honestly, I slept the best I've had in months."

"Then I guess I didn't leave you frustrated enough. While we are on this ride, I want you to let go," he holds up the remote that belongs to the vibrator. "Any objections?"

He studies my face as I catch on to his plans, and I squirm in my seat, a mingled wave of arousal and embarrassment making my stomach coil. "Nobody except for Aaron can hear us, and he knows what goes on at this place. What do you say, Holly, a little bit of public play to warm up on Kinkmas?"

And isn't that why I said yes to five days of play? This seems like a good opening act.

"No objections, Noel."

His grin is huge, and he brushes a kiss against my cheek, then his hand slides up against my cheek, and I feel the curve of the remote control. "We're going to have fun." The sleigh turns and jostles me in the seat. Noel wraps his arm around me, and as the horses trot up the hill, small vibrations break out, the vibrator coming to life.

"Noel!" I clutch his arm, even as I'm tightening my muscles against the low hum in my pussy.

"Yes, Holly?"

"I don't know if I should thank you or jump out of this sleigh!"

Noel laughs, his gaze hotly skims across my face. "Both?"

Just as I think the orgasm is going to burst open, taking me under right on this sleigh, the vibrations stop.

I slump against him, slightly wrung out.

"How is your first day at Vixen's Paradise?"

"Aside from the Kinkmas, this feels good. Like I am in my own Christmas card."

The ride is smooth, and the horses are familiar with this path.

"Good," Noel says. "I needed this, too. I'm glad you were on that plane."

Snow starts to fall. I stick my tongue out, catching the flakes. It strikes me that I should be on the beach right now.

"I'm happy that I'm not in Mexico right now."

"Even with the snow?" Noel brushes a few flurries off my shoulder.

"This is a pretty place to see the snow."

"If we still like each other at the end of Kinkmas, maybe I'll take you somewhere warm next year."

"Does the Brennon Consortium have properties in Cozumel?"

Noel tilts his head, steadying me. "How do you know it's a consortium?"

My mind races. I blush, wondering if somehow he's going to find out that I'm one of the people he wants to buy land from, and I don't want that because I don't want to ruin this moment.

"I think I saw it on the website."

"Maybe Theo updated it." Noel says, frowning. "Though we only use that name for legal purposes."

"Do all your brothers have properties?" My voice wavers with nerves as I ask the question. I don't want Noel to find out who I am.

"No, only Evan with Sinful Bites. Hunter and Theo help out. What does your family do?"

"Does not own kink-friendly establishments." I smile and squeeze his thigh, wanting him to relax. "My mom is an X-ray technician and has done that for years, though I keep telling her to retire. My stepfather is a music producer, and my cousin is a stay-at-home mom."

"You are close to them?"

"Yeah. My cousin and I are like sisters."

The sleigh turns, and I can't help but gasp. I wasn't expecting to come upon Gran's property so suddenly, but here is the start of the long driveway and the old house with boarded-up windows. It looks sad and forlorn.

I almost say something, but the vibrations rock me, pulsing hard against my clit. I let out a little shriek and grip Noel's arm.

He grins wolfishly, holding the remote. "Give it to me, Holly."

I draw in a cold breath of air as Noel lightly pulls my thighs apart underneath the blanket, and the heat in his gaze is hot enough to melt the snow that's falling around us. The vibrations are low in my core, spreading hot waves through me, and I lean against his shoulder, biting my lip, not wanting to make a sound. But the pulsating pressure increases, and I squeeze his hand, the pressure building to a force, waves of ecstasy crash through me, and I can't hold back, I bite my lips hard to hold in the scream as the orgasm rolls through me.

"That's a good girl, Holly. Give in," Noel's breath is warm in my ear and the pulsating changes to a quicker, hammering tempo and I can't hold it in, tears leak from my eyes as my core tightens as the wave breaks, the orgasm crashing over me and I let out a low moan, my cheeks burning, knowing the driver of the sleigh can hear us.

"Noel! Oh God." I pant.

"That's the first of many, lovely Holly. I'm going to have fun on this Christmas day."

"And what's my fun, Noel?"

"This is fun for you."

Damn, he's a handsome man, grinning like he won a prize.

Handsome and confident and sexy as hell. The driver laughs, telling the horses to crack on, and they break into a trot over the gentle slope of the hill. Just as they were on the other side of the hill, vibrations ping through me, so hard and fast, I gasp, squeezing my eyes shut against the pressure.

"Noel!" I grab his arm, rightly.

"Be a good girl and give me your orgasm, Holly."

"I...can't," I grit out.

Noel cups the back of my head. His dark-chocolate eyes meet mine. "Yes, you can. Now, Holly."

This is too much, but the vibrations roll through me, even though the aftershocks haven't finished from the last orgasm.

"Noel!" I muffle my shriek into his jacket which smells like cold and the cedar scent of his aftershave.

The pleasure rips through me so fast it feels like it's separating me from my body as I soar higher and higher.

"Noel! This feels so...good...God!" I can't catch my breath. My head is floaty and my body is completely boneless.

He kisses my brow. "That's a good girl. Now, I'll let you enjoy the ride."

A second later, I feel a low hum roll through my body. The man hadn't put away the remote control. He just switched it to the lowest setting to torture me this way.

"Evil!" I protest.

"I have to keep playing with my present."

I lean against him, jostling at the low murmur of sensations rolling through my centre. They are more annoying than anything, leaving me wanting more and not wanting it at all. Like an insect buzzing around my face, it's a constant buzz of annoyance.

I lean against Noel, trying to ignore it.

By the time we are back at the driveway of Vixen's Paradise, the snow is thick, and I'm ready to be out of the cold.

"Are you hungry, or would you like wine in my room?"

"Not hungry. As long as your room has a fireplace, I'm good with it."

"I have a fireplace."

"Deal."

Noel laughs. "You're an easy woman to please."

Aaron stops the sleigh, and Noel gives me a hand to help me down. I blush as Noel waves at Aaron and the horses disappear from view, setting off on the path that takes them around the building. Lights glow from the windows of Vixen's Paradise, the Christmas card coming to life.

"It's pretty."

"You're pretty," Noel says.

I shake my head at him but grin, and he holds the door open for me.

We stomp the snow off our boots and leave them by the door. I notice a rack holding slippers and help myself to a fuzzy green pair.

"Nice touch."

"We try," Noel says.

Laughter floats from the Parlour, where a man with a white beard plays carols on the piano.

A large man runs down the hall, chasing a woman who has tinsel in her hair.

"It's festive here," I say.

Noel laughs. "As it should be. Right this way."

He guides me to a door behind the reception desk. It opens to a narrow staircase.

"It's claustrophobic but worth it."

"Is this a bad time to tell you I'm afraid of dark spaces and caves?"

"I'm always afraid of the dark. I'll hold your hand if you hold mine." Noel reaches for my hand, and I return his firm squeeze.

"Deal."

Following behind him, I hold his hand and the banister with the other, step after step. Three more steps, and there is a column of light from the window, and I can't help but gasp.

The attic has been converted so it covers the entire floor. There is a massive bed under the eaves, windows that let in the light all around the perimeter, and the calm grey tone of the walls, perfect to let the features shine, like the fireplace across from the bed, with a stone surround.

A pair of French doors is across from the bed, and I wonder what's behind them.

"Welcome to my private getaway. You're my very first guest." Noel spreads his arms wide.

"Really?"

"Yes, this was completed in the spring." Noel takes my hand again and guides me to a small sitting area.

"Take off your cloak. I'll get us wine."

I remove the borrowed hat and cloak as he disappears behind the French doors, returning a second later with a bar cart.

"Here we are." He takes out a bottle of red, sets it on the cart, and grabs two glasses.

He opens the wine and pours us generous amounts.

"Noel?"

"Yes, Holly?"

"Are you going to take off your jacket?"

"Of course. I wanted to get you warmed first." He strides over to the fireplace and turns it on.

That's it. I'm a puddle of need and lust. He hands me the glass of wine and raises his glass. "To Kinkmas."

"Merry Kinkmas." I laugh.

The wine is cherry and woodsy on my tongue.

Noel takes a sip, sets down the glass, and removes his jacket, hanging it on a coat tree near the door.

He strides towards me, a look of pure determination on his face. "I'm going to kiss you now."

"Yes, please."

My heart beats so fast I can't hear anything; electricity snaps through the air between us. Noel's hands are warm on my shoulders. He tips my face to his and slants his lips over mine.

"Noel," I say into his mouth.

My body is turning into liquid with every stroke of his tongue and he deepens the kiss even more, making me squirm.

I break off the kiss, my belly a tight knot of nerves.

And maybe because I want to take control, I slide off the chair onto the floor.

Noel's hands rest on my shoulders. I hook my hands around his muscular calves.

"Holly..." He runs his hand through my hair.

"Let me give you a gift now," I say the words lightly, but I'm worried he's going to reject me.

"I think I would like your gift very much." The heat in his eyes sizzles through me.

"Let me help." I reach to unzip his fly.

With a groan, he rolls his pants down, revealing a pair of black silk boxers.

Noel rips them down his legs, clutching my face. "Do you like it hard and deep or should I keep it civil?"

My pulse races. His cock is standing up. It's thick, and I can't help but touch it. It's smooth under my palm.

"Damn, Holly," Noel hisses through his teeth.

"Hard and deep, please."

I'm learning his length, sliding my hand from tip to root. His cock is long and his girth thick enough that I have to stretch my fingers to circle it. "Holly," Noel hisses as I run my hand up and down his length. I cup his balls, squeezing gently. "Yes, Noel?"

"Holly, your touch is going to make me come apart." He tangles his fingers through my hair, massaging my scalp, bringing me closer.

I grip his cock lightly and take it into my mouth, just the tip. I roll my tongue along its underside. Above me, Noel hisses, his grip tightening on my shoulder.

"That's very nice, Holly. Good girl."

And then I am lost in how he tastes, in the sensations of his warm cock in my mouth. I suck, taking in more length and licking it like a snow cone.

It's a tasty treat of male musk and hard steel.

"Damn, Holly, what a gift." Noel rocks on his heels as I massage his balls, lapping his length. I swirl my tongue along his underside, loving how it makes him twitch.

"Holly! You're going to make me explode."

I nod, with his cock in my mouth, because that's exactly what I want. I want him to fuck my mouth, and I want to get lost in this man who has made my Christmas bright.

I suck, hollowing my cheeks and wrapping my hands around his thighs.

"Fuck, Holly!" That's all the warning I get before he takes control, holding my head in place. He thrusts hard into me.

I swallow on his length, keeping my jaw slack.

"Good girl," he grits out, and I will myself to stay still as he plunges his cock in and out of my mouth.

"Those tears are so pretty," he coons.

I feel them wet on my cheeks, but I'm only concentrating on how his thick cock feels in my throat following his thrusts.

He thrusts once, slowing down the pace, and I take the clue and swallow. He tips forward into my waiting mouth, and I sputter, trying to hold my lips around his cock.

"Now, Holly!" But he slides in and out of my mouth, and I do my best to keep contact with his cock.

He pulls my hair, bringing me closer, and I close my eyes as he releases his hot seed down my throat.

I swallow, tasting his saltiness on my lips, and wipe tears away from my eyes. Noel slowly withdraws his cock from my mouth.

"Good girl," Noel exhales, cupping my nape. "You're extraordinary."

I'm liquid at his praise and sit back to look at him. His hair is disheveled, but his expression is one of awe, making me proud.

"I'll be right back." Noel disappears behind a door I didn't notice before, near the window by the bed. I hear water running, and then he's back, holding a face cloth out to me.

He leans down and wipes my mouth with the warm cloth. I take it from his fingers and shyly use it to clean up his cock.

"I haven't had a chance to do that in a long time," I say.

Noel hands me my wine glass, and staying on my knees, I drink it. I'm relishing in how...submissive I feel, and I like it.

"Your ex didn't like you giving him head?" The exclamation in his tone is comical, but yeah, it's true. Phil's idea of sex was two minutes of missionary with the lights off.

"No...my sex life has faltered between non-existent and vanilla for the past two years."

"What an idiot," Noel murmurs.

I laugh. "This is fun. It feels good to laugh."

"You haven't done much of that either?"

I take another sip of wine, my mind wandering to work. At the beginning of the month, a client got trashed on his ex-girlfriend's wedding night, showing up to set the next day smelling like a bar, and nearly got fired. It took a lot of massaging of that producer's ego to keep him.

Another client had a crisis and wanted to quit before the series wrapped up, violating the terms of their contract.

I went with them to set every day for a week and acted as their personal cheerleader.

"Work's been chaotic."

"Is the screen protector business that stressful?" Noel's lips twitch.

"You could say that."

"I needed this Christmas break, too. Thanks for spending it with me."

I take his outstretched hand, and he helps me to my feet.

He hugs me, and I lean against his wall of muscles, breathing in his delicious scent. A part of me could stay in his arms forever. A part of me wants to.

Noel leads me to the bed, and my breath catches in my throat. From here, I can see my Gran's property.

"Everything okay?"

"Yes, fine."

"Holly, I think you are a beautiful, capable woman. If there is anything you want to share, I promise to treat it with the utmost respect." The confidence mixed with gentleness in his tone wraps around my heart.

All of the times that men who were interested in me gave me a similar promise flash through my mind, and I glance at him. He's standing off to the side, his gaze somewhere above my ear. Would he think I'm a liar if I told him who I was? Or that I was trying to influence him somehow when it came to selling Gran's farm?

But more than that, I want the rest of Kinkmas, and I don't want to risk that.

"I know you would," I say. I smile and sit at the end of the bed. "I'm starving. What are our dinner options?"

Noel grins. "I'm so glad you asked." His hand slips into his pocket.

Vibrations shoot through my core, awakening the vibe once more.

"Noel! I forgot you had that!"

And amazingly, I had forgotten it was still in me.

"I thought you might." He grins wickedly, approaching me.

His lips crash into mine, and he kisses me as the vibrations increase. I clutch his arms as the orgasm winds from my centre and crashes over me in a burst of pleasure. It hits me so vigorously that I grab him, resting my head against his shoulder.

"Now dinner." Noel kisses me again, and my head is floaty with all the aftershocks of pleasure.

He kisses me passionately and insistently, making my lips bruise, and I know this man is going to undo me and all my secrets.

10

NOEL

DECEMBER 26TH, SECOND DAY OF KINKMAS

The morning light slants across Holly's face, her wavy hair spilling over the pillow, a small smile on her face.

I carefully set the tray of coffee on a side table and let my eyes roam over the delicate curve of her bare shoulders to the slope of her ass. My cock twitches, the need to have her pulsing through my bloodstream.

Last night, we had dinner with Cat and Rick, and something in my chest loosened as my friends welcomed her warmly, finding common ground because she and Cat went to the same university.

We moved into the dungeon, and we watched them play, the intensity of their scene mixing with the thrill of being there with Holly.

Rick ate dessert off Cat's breasts, the intimate display sending a rush of heat through me. My pulse quickened, but my focus stayed on Holly.

I noted her dilated eyes, the way she worked her bottom lip, and how her hips swayed against me, filing it away for later.

As I watched their scene, I couldn't help but focus on Holly, watching her watch them. It made me want to play with her in exactly the same way.

My present likes sensation play with a little bite, and I'm determined to deliver her experiences that she remembers beyond these five days of Kinkmas.

Now she stretches in her sleep before her eyes flutter open and she sits up, clutching the blanket to her chest. "Good morning, Noel."

"Morning, Holly." She glances at the unwrinkled bedsheets beside her. "Do I snore?" she asks, her voice soft with sleep.

"If you do, it's a gorgeous snore," I say, brushing my thumb along her thumb.

I had slept in my office, still near her but not beside her because as much as I enjoy spending time with this woman, I couldn't bring myself to share the bed.

"Work kept me from coming to bed."

"Okay," she says lightly and glances away as if she knows I'm not being honest.

I break away from the intensity of the moment, reaching for a mug. "Coffee?"

"Noel, you are spoiling me."

"Good. I enjoy spoiling you."

She laughs and drops the sheets, revealing her bountiful creamy breasts, and she crosses her legs, totally unconcerned with being naked.

The sight is so erotic, my throat goes dry as I hand her coffee and then join her on the bed, sliding my hand along her leg, stopping before I touch the juncture of her thighs, but her breathing hitches.

"What's your plan for the second day of Kinkmas?"

I join her on the bed, balancing my coffee cup. "I booked you for a full spa treatment today, including a massage."

"Oh?" She arches her brows, and her face glows with her smile.

"Yes, I need you relaxed in time for the Fire and Ice party," I say, leaning in until my shoulder brushes hers. The contrast of her bare skin against my sleeve makes my voice come out low and gravely. I brush a piece of hair from her shoulder, and lean in, skimming my lips against her jaw.

"We talked about pet play, but we didn't talk about anal." The question hangs in the air, and she pulls a piece of hair back behind her ear. "How comfortable are you with a butt plug?"

She blushes, and the pulse at her throat throbs. But her green eyes meet mine and she lifts her chin, as if she's taking a dare.

"It's been a while, but I enjoy anal play."

Heat rushes through my body. A good portion of my blood flows to my cock. "Good."

I take her coffee cup and set it on the nightstand next to mine because I want to kiss her.

"Merry Kinkmas, day two." My mouth finds her lips, and she yields with a soft moan. I kiss her, my tongue sliding around hers, and I skim my palm along her breast.

She pushes into my hand, wanting more, letting out another soft moan, but I want to keep the anticipation growing.

I pull back, my lips still tingling from the kiss. I reach for the fruit bowl, my gaze never leaving hers. "Open." I offer her a strawberry, watching the way her lips part to take it. "I love watching your mouth."

She blushes most deliciously and, as if she needs to claim control, she grips my biceps, her fingertips digging in, making me laugh.

"It's not funny! I can buy my food, and you can bill me for the spa treatments."

Her independence is something I admire, but right now, for these five days, she's mine. And I'll spoil her however I see fit. It's not about control.

It's about giving her something she can't find anywhere else.

"It's cute that you want to take care of everything. But for these five days, I'm taking care of you."

"Noel…"

"This is what it means to be mine. It's part of the Kinkmas experience." My lips hover a breath away from hers, and her eyes are shiny with heat.

"I like Kinkmas."

"Good." I press another strawberry to her lips, and she opens at the invitation.

"Good girl."

She blushes at the praise.

This is so simple, this peaceful pleasure, and I want to heap her with orgasms and goodness because she's brought so much joy to my Christmas.

"I can take care of you, Holly. Let me."

"Noel…"

I kiss her, cutting her off. She sighs but kisses me back, her lips slightly swollen and sweet.

"I know you are a capable woman who can pay her way. But this is my Christmas present, don't forget."

"Okay!" She giggles as I duck my head and skim along the soft skin of her throat, working my way up to her lips, which I take in a hard, wet kiss that sends ripples of ravenous need through me.

Letting out a moan that echoes around us, she arches toward me, and my chest pounds with pride that I've made her make that sound, and I greedily want more.

I roll on top of her, careful to keep my weight off her slender frame, and kiss the hollow of her throat, my lips brushing her skin from her collarbone down to the valley between her breasts.

Her little breathy sounds are pure music and encourage me onto the plane of her stomach, the dip in her hips. I skirt my lips over every inch of her skin, and when I reach her legs, I spread them, kneeling between her.

"Show me your breasts, Holly."

She cups them and arches forward, offering me her lovely globes.

I slide a small satin pouch from my pocket and pull out a pair of alligator clamps. I hold them up. "How do you feel about nipple clamps?"

Her breath stutters. "Yes," she breathes, and I press the cool metal to the tip of her breast before gently clipping it on.

"Good. Yes, please." She reaches for me again, and I skim my lips against hers, burying myself against her smooth skin.

With my free hand, I massage her breast.

"Oh, Noel!"

Smiling, I take her nipple into my mouth, sucking the hardened tip. She mewls under me, her legs clasping around my waist. I lick every bit of her luscious nipple, her moans of pleasure urging me on.

"Gorgeous, Holly," I say as I come off and find her lips again, kissing her with all the angst I feel.

Taking her bottom lip gently into my mouth, I tug on it, then kiss my way back down to the other breast and suck on that nipple while caressing the other one between my fingers.

"Noel! You're making me all hot."

I laugh with her nipple in my mouth, give it a long pull and break off. Taking the clamps, I settle one nipple between the teeth, and she squeezes her eyes shut.

"Do you like this?" I plump up the other and settle the clamp around the beaded nipple.

"Yes!"

"Good girl. Your nipples look so sexy like that."

And my cock is so damn hard.

"Are you wet for me?"

"Yes."

"Show me."

She spreads her legs open, her hand sliding down and stopping just before her mound.

The tangy smell of her arousal is thick in the air, and her fingers tremble.

"Your pussy is glistening. Is that for me, Holly?"

"Yes, Noel."

I drag my thumb through her wetness and circle her engorged clit. It's so damn pretty it makes my mouth dry.

She lets out the sexiest mewl, her whole body bows back, her hips rising off the bed.

It's been so long since I let myself enjoy a female body, so long since I indulged.

Leaning down, I drop a trail of light kisses on her inner thigh while keeping my thumb on her clit.

"Noel! That's so good," Holly grits out between closed lips. She tosses her head back, and she is so beautiful. I can't believe this woman is with me right now.

I press my lips against her sensitive skin. Holly writhes, and I laugh, loving how she responds to every brush of my lips and every touch of my fingertips.

Her arousal is a tangy perfume that coats the back of my throat, and I want to taste her. Leaning down, I press my lips to her sensitive skin, sucking a breath away from her pussy.

"Noel!" She screams my name, and her cry shoots all the blood to my cock wanting to drive her pleasure even higher. I suck her inner thigh so hard I know I am going to leave a mark.

My cock is rock hard, but I am a patient man with a plan in mind.

Removing my thumb, I press it against her mouth.

Immediately, her tongue comes out, and she laps up my digit, cleaning it and letting out a soft hum of pleasure.

"Remember, your orgasms are mine for Kinkmas," I murmur, low and pleased. "And it's only day two." Her eyes widen, and the smile she gives me says she both fears and craves it.

"Anyone tell you that you're a mean Grinch?"

I laugh and drop a kiss on her mouth. "Who me? Never."

She grabs my arm. "I'm so wet. I want to come so badly."

"Perfect, that's exactly how I want you. Enjoy your spa treatments. I have work to do."

She closes her eyes with a huge grin, then scoots up against the pillows. "Like what?"

Her hair brushes my lips as she settles back, giving me a cheeky grin.

"Ever since we've opened, we've tried to acquire the neighbouring property. They're impossible to get on the phone, but I'm determined to reach the owner today." I trace her jawline, not wanting to leave her.

"That's commitment." Holly pulls a sheet over her body and reaches for her coffee. I notice her fingers tremble and chalk it up to the aftershocks.

"We want to make this whole stretch a retreat. We bought the farm across from us and the next two to the left of us, but this neighbour is the holdout."

"What are your plans for the property?" Her sharp tone takes me back, and I wonder if this makes her uncomfortable.

"I want to move the stable over there. There are more trails on that property, and my brother, Theo, suggested it could be an intimate bed-and-breakfast."

"What do you want to do with it?" She tilts her head, her eyes bright.

"I would love to bring it back to a farm, and then Vixen's Paradise and the adjoining properties could be self-sustained. We could use the space to run classes to give our guests more experiences."

"It's very idyllic to turn this whole stretch into a resort."

"Yes, it is, but we've done extensive projects like this before. We have our restaurant experience at one of the most luxurious hotels in the country. Anything is possible."

"If you have money," Holly mumbles.

"Yes, I'm not going to insult your intelligence by denying that is a factor."

Holly puts her coffee down and leans so close to me that her hair brushes my lips.

"Good, I don't like being insulted." Her mouth meets mine, and she kisses me, grabbing my shirt. Her touch ignites a smouldering fire that rolls through me.

Grabbing her hands lightly, I rock my hips against hers, kissing her mouth hard.

"Noel!" Her fingers thread through my hair.

"Just making sure you're still wet." I smile and roll off her.

"I am so soaked." She flutters her eyelashes in an exaggerated come-hither move, and it's adorable, but I'm not giving in.

"Good girl, I want to keep you that way." I brush my lips against her forehead.

"Yes, Noel." Holly sighs.

"But these should come off." I flick the nipple clamps.

"Please," Holly says.

Reaching down, I remove the clamp.

She cries out as the blood rushes back to her nipple and presses into me.

"Shush." I cover her nipple with my mouth and suck slowly, and she moans, her fingers threading in my hair.

"I can almost come!"

I pull away and breathe in the scent of her skin and love how glassy her eyes are with need. Her desperation is like a tangible thing as she squirms.

"Not yet." I squeeze her nipple between my fingers gently and remove the other clip, soothing and sucking this nipple with my mouth.

"Oh, Noel! I think I'm going to..." Her cry is breathy and needy and slams into my chest, igniting wild desire and making my cock ache with wanting release of its own.

I slam my lips against hers, swallowing her moans. Wild desire makes my cock throb and ache with desperation, wanting a release of my own.

"No, you're not," I rip my mouth off her nipple so fast I feel dizzy. "I'll reward you later. No coming, remember."

"What if I do?" she asks teasingly, smirks at me.

"Then I'll topple you over my lap for that hand spanking."

"Not into pain, but yes, I think I'm going to enjoy that." She grins, and my heart thumps hard against my chest. I want to stay with her and lavish all the sweet erotic things on her, but I need to get on with work and stick to the plan I have for Kinkmas.

"I'll make sure you do, my pretty present."

My mouth grows dry as a shudder racks through her body. I have things to do, like tracking the owner and checking on Theo. My mild-mannered brother wants to buy a bakery/art shop, and he was so distressed yesterday that I didn't get the full story out of him.

She bites her lip, and I pull it out, pressing my thumb across it.

"Noel! I want more!" She bites her lip and flutters her eyelashes at me.

"The wait is worth it, I promise," I say, grinning and dropping a kiss against her cheek.

"Don't leave me waiting too long, Noel."

"I won't, my present." I brush her lips with a soft kiss and hope she doesn't decide to end Kinkmas because of the distance I'm putting up between us.

"I can't wait for later, Noel," she says, clutching the sheets against her.

"Me neither." I swipe her hair out of her eyes, giving her one more quick kiss before turning and leaving the room.

As good as my reasons are, I haven't allowed myself to give over entirely, and I'm sure she can sense it.

11

HOLLY

This spa is five stars, and after a day of facial treatments and full-body scrubs, my skin is glowing.

Because all the tension has been soaked out of me, now is the perfect time to call Stella.

I step out of the women's changing room in a robe, lime water in one hand, and sit down in one of the horseshoe chairs in the warm seating room.

"What's up, Holly?" Stella's voice pounds through the line, rushed as usual.

"I just finished a spa treatment. Thought I'd call you."

"Lucky you! We're on our way to the in-laws." The noise of the kids in the background leaks through the phone. "Okay...I know you don't like talking about it, but did you get a call today from the guys who want to buy Gran's farm?"

My stomach twists with guilt. I should come clean and tell Stella I'm right beside the property, but what good would that do?

"Holly, I asked you to deal with this. I don't have time to take their latest offer to a lawyer. And your mom is always going on about how you're drowning in contracts and good at what you do."

I'm thankful my mom is supportive, even if she gets the details mixed up. She thinks I'm an entertainment lawyer. I did finish law school, but never went through with licensing because I landed an internship at a talent agency and knew what I wanted to do.

Now I spend my days wrangling actors and contracts, which means, yes, I can deal with this offer...and guilt swirls in my stomach for dumping it all on Stella.

"I'm not a lawyer, but I can read a contract. Email it, and I'll go over it, okay? Stella, what do you guys want to do?"

A child screams in the background, and there is the thump of a door.

"Holly, we need a new roof," Stella says, the exasperation clear in her tone. "I want my mortgage paid off and to start saving for all these kids. I want to sell."

I know that's how she's felt, but until now, Stella has tiptoed around the issue, and I've left her hanging. She's right. It's time for us to move on.

"Yeah, I'm ready to sell."

"Really?" Stella squeals.

I'm hit with another wave of guilt. Though Stella and her husband do okay, they are nowhere near my yearly salary. I bought my condo on a deal, with Max and my mom helping me with the down payment.

"Amazing that you don't hate me," I tell her.

"Holly, how could I hate you? I get that your emotions are tied up in it, but I'm in the weeds here, trying to keep tiny humans alive. I loved Gran's farm, but it's time to let it go. She's gone, and it's not the same."

"I know. I'll let you know what I think of the offer."

"Thanks, Holly. Love you."

"Love you, too."

As I hang up, guilt curls in my chest, but I push it aside, determined to keep enjoying this spa day.

A tall man with corded muscles enters the room. He smiles, and his face transforms—warm and open.

"Holly? It's time for your massage. My name is Vince."

"Nice to meet you."

"Right this way."

I follow Vince to a stunning room where a soft waterfall cascades along the back wall. Orange and white candles flicker on every available shelf, filling the air with the scent of bergamot and vanilla.

"I'll give you a moment to get settled," Vince says, his voice smooth and calming.

When Vince leaves, I drop my robe and slide under the soft sheet on the table. This is the comfiest massage table I've ever laid on, and I lay there, my thoughts tumbling as I think of Gran's house and letting it go.

"All ready?" Vince asks.

"Yes," I stretch out and try to find a comfortable spot to rest my chin.

"Excellent, I'll begin."

Vince takes me to heaven. His strong, firm hands work out the knots in my neck—knots I've earned from endless days of talking to clients at my desk. His hands glide down my back, and I can't help but let out a soft *oomph.*

If I close my eyes, I could be in a spa in the Great Alps or a resort in Bali, like the one I went to the year before I met Phil. A girl could get used to this kind of treatment.

Vince is an expert. The tension begins to melt away under his practiced hands as he works over my glutes with professional precision.

Who needs Cozumel when you have this kind of luxury? I never thought I'd find it in the middle of nowhere, Ontario. That's what makes this place special. Even stripped of all its catering to kinks, it could stand on its own.

My eyes close as I let out another sigh. Something warm and soft drapes over my body, and then firm, quick pressure is applied from head to toe. The room is warm. My body feels languid, utterly relaxed, and my eyelids feel heavy as I start to drift off to sleep.

A layer of sheet is lifted off me, and a new set of hands sweeps across my back to my bottom, sending hot tingles through me.

"Did you enjoy your spa day?" His voice makes my pulse quicken, and my pussy flutters in response.

"Yes, it's been lovely," I murmur, the words barely escaping my lips.

"Good." He lifts the sheet that covers my back. The cool air makes me shudder, not unpleasantly, but with an ache for his warmth.

Noel nibbles my ear, then kisses his way down my neck to the base of my collarbone. He kisses the base of my spine now, and his hands circle my hips, sending another wave of desire through me.

"You're gorgeous," he murmurs, his lips brushing against my neck, his words deepening the warmth pooling inside me.

As his hands trail gently down my sides, my thoughts race. Noel is everything I've been afraid to have. The kind of man I told myself didn't exist. The kind who wouldn't be intimidated by my success, who wouldn't pull away because of my independence. But somewhere deep inside, I'm still afraid I'll lose myself again, like I did with my ex.

Noel's firm touch on my hip brings me back to the present, grounding me, and his hands push my swirling thoughts aside. He's here. Right now. And that's all that matters.

"I could have you right on this table."

My skin pebbles with goosebumps. A thrill of excitement causes my pulse to roar in my ears.

"No objections."

I lift my head, wanting to kiss him, and his lips meet mine. He kisses me deeply, with a possessiveness that heats my blood.

I grab for him, wanting him closer, and he breaks off the kiss, firmly nudging me back onto the table.

"I can't wait to feel your pussy around my cock, Holly. I want to see how this looks on you."

Something cool and smooth is laid against my chin. I did tell the man I wanted to try pet play.

A long silicone butt plug is in Noel's hand. It's curved, just like a tail.

"Rainbow coloured?" My voice is thick.

Noel's lips twitch. "I thought it was fun."

"Yeah...it's big..." A shiver rolls down my spine at the thought of that thing entering me—but also excitement that Noel listened to me and something on my list is about to happen.

"It'll fit, gorgeous. Let me show you." Noel disappears out of my sight, then comes back with a bottle of lube.

"Nothing is going to happen that you don't want. Trust me?"

A thrill of excitement heats my skin, wetness pooling between my legs.

"Yes."

"That's a girl. Let's get you ready for your tail." He drops a kiss on my forehead, runs a hand down my back to my ass, and moves behind me.

He kneads my cheeks, and I exhale a shuddering breath. His touch feels good, searing me, making me so wet. I moan, a deep, tremulous sound that echoes in the room, but I don't care.

I want more of his touch, so I arch my hips, lifting off the table to encourage him.

He chuckles, but his palm smacks me lightly on the ass. "Patience, Holly."

I sigh dramatically, but get back into position.

"Let's spread these cheeks." His hands spread my bottom cheeks wide.

I squeal, my face heating with embarrassment.

"So pretty. This little asshole is perfect. I can't wait to slide the plug in and see you with a tail."

His words make me shiver. The idea of being stripped down and laid bare—enough to take on a role, a character—has always appealed to me. I've never found someone who would give me that experience.

Never allowed myself to trust someone to be that vulnerable with.

His fingers trail down over the curve of my ass, and I let out a cry.

"You're so pretty." The timbre of his tone raises pinpricks across my skin.

And I gasp as he slides his fingers into my gushing wet pussy with a touch of heat that is searing me open, wanting more.

"Reach back here and spread your ass cheeks for me." His tone is all lightness but steel command.

Pure, hot desire rolls through my body, arrowing right to my clit, as I reach back and comply.

"Good girl." His praise makes my belly drop to the floor, and I whimper as Noel slowly massages the underside of my ass and lays the butt plug against my cheeks. He holds it there, letting it warm against my body.

"Arch toward me, Holly. Yes, exactly like that. Good girl."

My body tenses as the silicone is worked in, a little at a time.

"Breathe, Holly. You can take this for me." He slides the plug in and out, and I feel muscles clasp around it. I will myself to relax, bearing down.

"There, a little more," Noel encourages.

The stretch of my most private flesh is almost painful.

"I can't."

"Yes, you can. Be a good girl for me and take this plug."

I exhale slowly as Noel works the plug inside me, and a soft, throaty whimper of pure desire escapes my lips, my hips arching off the table.

My body adjusts instinctively, relaxing into the snug fit, the pressure building in ways that make my breath hitch.

"So pretty," Noel murmurs, his voice thick with satisfaction, giving the plug a gentle tug. I feel it shift inside, the sensation both grounding and electric.

"Are you wagging my tail?" I tease, my tone playful but my pulse quickening.

"Yes, I am," he answers, his smile evident in his tone.

I laugh softly, the sound catching in the air. It's a heady mix of amusement and arousal, a reminder of how easy it is to feel safe with him—how much I want this.

"You please me, Holly," Noel praises, wiggling the plug slowly, deliberately.

The sensation of fullness intensifies, and I close my eyes for a moment, letting the waves of pleasure unfurl through me like molten heat, my body responding instinctively.

"Oh, you look so pretty with a tail in." He pulls the tail, and my nipples harden.

Each pull of the plug is taut and aching in all the right places. He dances his fingers along the base, and the vibration only deepens the pressure.

"Oh, Noel!" I cry as he tugs on the plug.

Hot, engulfing, all-consuming pleasure races through my veins. The plug stretches me, feeling both overwhelming and addictive and so full. I want more.

"Such a pretty tail. You're going to be a good pup for me, aren't you?" His voice is thick with desire, low and seductive.

The word *pup* makes my cheeks burn, but the thrill is undeniable.

I want this. I want him.

"Yes!" I cry out, clutching the sheet beneath me.

"I can't wait. That's for later. I'm going to take the tail out of you." He gives it another twist before pulling it out, and my ass gapes, wanting it back.

Noel slides his palm over my ass, along my spine, between my shoulders, and then cups my neck. Leaning down, he kisses me—a slow, tender kiss that makes me want more.

"Beautiful, Holly. You taste so sweet. Every time I kiss you, it feels like I'm falling into a vat of goodness." He strokes my hair, and I mewl.

He moves around the table so he's in front of me, sliding his hand into his pocket and pulling out the little gold bullet vibe.

"You didn't think I had forgotten this, did you?" he smirks.

"I thought I left that on your dresser."

"Oh, you did."

"Is this what happens when the owner of the place seduces you?" I can't help a smile spreading across my face.

"Yep. He helps himself to things left on dressers." His dimples show as his eyes darken with desire.

Whatever we are doing this Kinkmas, it's easy and sweet, and I want to stay here.

"Turn over, please, Holly."

He steadies me with a firm touch on my elbow, and I roll to face the ceiling and the painted cloudy sky I hadn't noticed before.

"Gorgeous." Noel tugs the sheet off me, and his mouth claims my nipple, covering it completely.

He sucks it like a tasty treat, his hot mouth sending a roll of fire through me as he massages the other breast, scraping the nipple with his nail.

"Noel! That's so good."

My hips buck off the table as need ignites in my center, spreading outward to my throbbing clit. He sucks and nuzzles, and mewling sounds escape my lips as wetness leaks from my pussy.

"And you are such a pretty present," he says as he breaks off and shifts to my other breast, nuzzling his cheek against it, and I tangle my fingers in his silky hair. A soft laugh escapes him before his mouth claims my nipple, sucking gently. The throbbing need between my legs intensifies, demanding release.

I lift my hips off the table, aching for more. His hand grips my inner thigh, pressing me back down, and I release a frustrated sigh, my body craving the release he holds just out of reach.

His sucking and lapping become almost torturous as hot pins of desire ignite my body.

Noel lifts his head and kisses me, tugging my bottom lip while sliding the little vibe against my clit, nestling it in place.

Slanting his mouth over mine, he kisses me long and slow, covering every inch of my swollen lips.

"Noel!" I cry as vibrations zip through me, my pussy wet and pulsating.

"Yes, Holly. Give me your orgasm." He presses the vibe in just the right spot, and I cry out, unable to hold back. Pleasure coils low in my belly, and I reach for him, wanting more of his touch.

"I've got you," he mutters, spreading my legs wider.

He devours my mouth as the vibe speeds up, sending my head spinning. It's the way his hand cups my jaw that makes my whole body arch into him. My toes curl as the vibe thrums harder, sending shivers spiraling through me.

"I'm going to come!"

"Yes, give it to me, Holly."

"Oh, God..." I gasp, clinging to his kiss, unraveling completely as he holds me there, grounding me while I come undone.

"Good girl, Holly," Noel smooths a piece of hair that fell across my eyes as my whole body convulses, my pussy clamping around the vibe as I soar again and again, panting and shivering.

His warm, brown eyes blaze with desire, making me feel so wanted, so sexy.

"Please."

"Please, what, Holly? I will give you whatever is in my power."

"I want you."

His eyebrows lift to his hairline. "Right here? I had thought to make you wait." His mouth quirks up in a smile, but I shake my head, the aftershocks rolling through me.

"Now." I want him in me, right here, pleasure-drunk and heavy-limbed.

"I like a woman who knows what she wants." He steps back, removes his loafers, and unbuckles his pants, letting them fall.

No boxers.

His long, thick cock springs free, pulsating in his hand, veins pronounced with a drop of pre-cum at the head.

My pulse gallops as he slowly unbuttons his shirt. The look in his eyes is confident—the man fully aware of his sex appeal.

With one hand, he strokes himself, the other finishing the last button on his shirt. He whips away the remaining sheets, covering me with his body on the massage table.

"Noel—" Only his name escapes me.

He kisses me slowly, savoring me, but I want to be ravished. I kiss him hard against his perfectly symmetrical lips.

"Don't let it be said I don't give my present what she wants," he murmurs against my lips.

He trails kisses down my neck to my shoulder, hands sliding down my hips, his cock pressing against my pussy, hard as steel.

"I can't wait to sink into you, Holly."

I cry out as he removes the vibe, pressing his mouth to mine, a deep, consuming kiss. My head spins, caught in a crest of pleasure that leaves me trembling.

"You feel so good," I murmur into his neck, voice thick with need. "I love how you're...taking control." I whimper as his tongue traces the side of my neck, hands kneading my breasts, leaving fiery kisses across every inch of me.

"Good," he murmurs, voice low and possessive.

Our moans entwine, urgent and hungry, filling the room. My hands glide over his broad back, sliding down to his trim waist, clutching him as if I could fuse to him.

"I'm going to enter you now, Holly. Is that pussy still wet for me?" His words are a low, commanding growl, eyes locking with mine as he braces against the table.

I shiver, heat pooling between my thighs. "Yes...still wet for you," I whisper, breath catching, body aching.

"Perfect." He kisses me, a wet, hungry kiss that makes my lips buzz.

The blunt head of his cock presses against me. For a heartbeat, he waits, breath hot against my mouth, making me ache. Then, with exquisite slowness, he pushes inside. Inch by inch, my body stretches around him, clutching him tight, until I'm filled to the core.

He claims my mouth again as he thrusts. I moan in a long, shuddering exhale. He drives his hips deeper, slow and devastatingly smooth, making me ache for more.

The table squeaks under us as he slides in and out, holding me in place. My body burns, demanding the release only he can give.

"Holly," he whispers against my neck, thrusting even deeper. "Your pussy feels incredible. Hot. Tight. Mine."

I cry out as he moves against me, hips rising to meet his thrusts.

He kisses me, I suck his lips, nuzzling the crook of his neck as his thick cock pushes into my folds.

"Holly!" he calls, and it echoes around the room. I've never felt more wanted, his eyes burning into mine as he rocks one long, deep thrust.

"Now, gorgeous girl, come with me!"

Out of my control, the orgasm bursts from my center, a crashing wall of bliss, as I feel Noel's release fill me.

"That felt…amazing," I gasp, catching my breath.

He leaves a trail of kisses across my damp skin, capturing my mouth in a rough, consuming kiss. "You're amazing."

My hair clings in damp strands, his brow glistens with sweat, and he gathers me close, lifting me from the table as if I'm precious.

"Set me down, please."

He lets me go gently. The floor is cool beneath my bare feet, slippers forgotten, but all I can feel is the steady strength of Noel's arms.

"Have you seen my slippers?"

"No, but I'm sure I can return a pair to you by midnight."

"Would you like your present to be a pumpkin?" I smirk.

"No. I want my present to be a Holly," Noel grins at me as if he's scored a point—and he totally has. I laugh.

And we're giggling, tears streaming down my cheeks.

"You're a little goofy."

"I know. Want to see my shower?" He exaggeratedly waggles his eyebrows.

To my horror, I snort. I cover my face, and Noel lifts my hand.

"You're adorable and gorgeous and all mine. Time to shower."

"You're kind of adorable too," I say, kissing his cheek. "And kind of gorgeous."

He flashes a grin, eyes sparkling, and guides me to the bathroom. The decor matches the craggy stone theme of the spa. There's a walk-in shower big enough for two.

"Sit down, Holly."

I sit on the bench. The tile is cool, but the warm, glowing lights above make it feel surreal.

Suddenly, water rushes down, and Noel walks through the spray. I watch the water cascade over his muscled back, mesmerized. He turns, and rivulets flow down his chest.

"Seriously...kind of gorgeous."

"Are you just going to watch? Come here."

I grin and join him under the spray.

"You're perfect."

The look he sends makes me feel precious, and I could stand in his gaze forever.

"Turn."

I place a hand on his chest, enveloped by his heat.

Noel grabs a sponge, lathers it with sweet-smelling soap, and begins washing me. Unexpected tears slide down my cheeks.

"Shush, it's okay, my present. I got you." He kisses them away, gently washing my neck and pussy.

"Spread those legs wider." I swallow.

The water softens, gliding the sponge over my body, cleaning me slowly, sensually.

"Good girl. You look so pretty like this. We'll have to come here again."

My head is floaty. Pleasure infuses my veins. I feel like I've stepped off a balcony without a parachute—falling.

"Holly, come back to me," Noel says.

Slowly, I rise from the bench to face him.

"I want to finish washing you." He adds more soap to the puff.

Standing under the spray, his molten gaze locked on me, I tell myself I deserve this, the attention of a caring partner, something I've been missing.

Noel circles each breast, and I sigh, lost in the sensation of being cared for.

"That feels nice."

"Good."

I close my eyes as he soaps my belly, gliding the sponge down my stomach and up my back.

"There. You're all washed." He tilts my chin and kisses me long and slow.

Nothing feels better than his tongue against mine, heat pressed against my body.

I take the sponge. "My turn."

"Oh really?" he smirks.

"Yes." I squirt more soap on the sponge, starting at his trim waist, washing up his back to shoulders.

"Hmm, I could get used to this," Noel says.

I circle to his front, washing his steel chest, taking my time.

"Thank you." His hands press my shoulders, kissing me softly.

"I want to do this again."

"Me too."

Noel turns off the shower, takes me by the elbow, and we step out.

He wraps a fluffy towel around me and slowly dries my hair, taking care to wring it out.

"Thank you."

"For what?"

"For giving me another day of Kinkmas."

His gaze sends heat flaring across my skin, and he drinks me in like a treasured Christmas present, and my heart bursts.

Three more days. A small part of me wants this man beyond the agreed-upon time frame.

"You're welcome." I squeeze his hand, throat tight with emotions I'm too afraid to voice.

"Dinner. I worked up an appetite."

I laugh, standing on tiptoes to kiss him.

"And I'm going to have you for dessert."

"What do I get again?" I tease.

"To knock off an item on your try list." His blazing stare makes me immediately eager and wanting.

"I can't wait."

"Come on, I'm very hungry."

I blush as he takes my hand, leaving the spa behind. He may be hungry, but this experience showed me how starved I am for the things I didn't allow myself to have.

12

NOEL

DECEMBER 27TH, THIRD DAY OF KINKMAS

The clink of silverware and low hum of conversation fade into background noise, the chatter of guests goes over my head. All I'm focused on is how Holly feels pressed next to me as we eat our breakfast.

This morning, I hurried through my usual routine, racing downstairs to see her. I met her at her door and guided her down to the dining room. After I made a detour to the dungeon.

Sleep did not come easily to me and it wasn't grief keeping me up, it was Holly.

The memory of our scene on the massage table — the glorious feel of her pussy around my cock, how she yielded to me and gave me her submission — all of that etched its way into my psyche, awakening my Dominant side and left me wanting more.

I wanted to go to sleep with her and see how she looked in the morning, but I couldn't cross that threshold yet.

"What is on today's schedule?" She tilts her head at me, her eyes bright, lips quirking.

"You like schedules?" I tease, arching a brow, my tone deliberately light.

"If I don't have one, I go a little squirrely, it's true." She lifts one shoulder in a small shrug, her fingers trace the rim of her coffee cup.

"Noted." I intertwine my fingers through hers, letting my thumb drag over her knuckles before I tighten the grip. "I'm set up for our pup play scene."

She blushes, her lashes lowering as she glances away, and I squeeze her hand.

"Today?" Holly sets her coffee cup down, her lips curves in a smile.

"On the third day of Kinkmas, yes." I slide my hand higher on her thigh, my thumb stroking her skin in lazy circles. Her breath catches, her body angling ever so slightly toward me, seeking more.

"This seems to be a jump from asking me if I slept well and giving me orgasms." A faint blush makes her cheeks go pink.

"Did you sleep well, Holly?" I take her hand in mine, twinning my fingers through hers. I don't let go, watching how her lips curve as she answers.

"I might have to take that bathtub home."

"That could be arranged. So, pup play. Are you up for it today?"

"Oh yes." She leans against my shoulder, her hair brushes my jaw.

"Good. I want to go over some pet play specifics. I know you said calling you *pet* is okay. Is there any other name you want to use?"

Her fingers trail down my thigh. A sly, teasing touch. My cock jerks against my fly. Negotiation is such a damn turn-on.

"Pet is fine, Noel."

"Good." I brush my fingers through her hair, work my hand behind her head and hold her there for a moment. Her lips part, her breathing shallow, as though the weight of my palm alone has shifted her headspace.

"Do you have a certain pup age in mind that you want to mimic?" I brush my thumb along the underside of her chin, coaxing her to hold my gaze.

"Not ancient, but I don't want to run around on my knees all day." Her voice is shaky but her eyes meet mine and my pulse races.

"Okay. I have knee pads if you are comfortable taking on crawling and walking as a pup?" My cock throbs at the thought, but I keep my tone even, not wanting to pressure her.

Holly licks her lips. Her hesitation makes my fingers tighten on hers, a small pang twisting in my gut as I watch her wrestle with the moment.

But she grabs my arm. Her fingers dig in, anchoring herself on me, as if she's choosing me as much as the scene.

"Yes, knee pads are perfect."

"Do you want to play knowing basic commands or being taught?"

"Like what?"

"Sit. Stay. Shake. Speak. Roll over," I whisper the words into her ear, loving how her pupils dilate.

"Ohhh...those are good questions." Holly rolls her shoulders. Her eyes become glassy, and her lips form the cutest pout. "I want to spend the time in pup play...not being me. I don't want to be forced into being a pup. I want the room to take on the headspace. Does that make sense?"

"Perfect sense. So my pet knows basic commands."

"But I don't mind being taught a trick or two," Holly raises her eyebrows. "And maybe a slight correction here and there."

"We'll have fun, my pet," I draw out the word, slow and deliberate watching a shiver ripple through her as her lips part.

"Yes..." Her green eyes are glassy and filled with want.

"I have some treats for you. I have set up a spot in the dungeon for some of our play. Are you comfortable being on a leash in public?"

"Yes, I'm excited about this, Noel. Thank you for making it happen."

"It's my pleasure."

The way her whole body relaxes with an exhale gives me pleasure. It sets my head buzzing with need, and I am so happy to make this woman's fantasy come true.

"What about speech? Do you want to be fully restricted with a muzzle?"

Her eyes flutter shut as if the weight of the moment presses too heavily, and she lowers her forehead to the table.

I suspect she's overwhelmed between wanting this and fearing it.

I signal the waiter for water, keeping my gaze fixed on her. "Holly, we don't have to do this now." Her small body folds in on itself, and it makes me ache to pull her into my lap, but I force myself to stay still, to give her the space she needs.

She raises her index finger. "Need a moment."

I sit back, giving her space. Lori refreshes the water, I nod my thanks and keep watching Holly, waiting.

"No gags or muzzles. I'm not...ready for that." Her voice is shaky but she lifts her head.

"Can I rub your back?"

She nods her head. I wait until she peers up at me. "Please."

Her skin is warm through the thin fabric, and I let my touch linger.

Slowly, I rub between her shoulder blades, wondering if I've taken her here too quickly.

"I'm good, Noel. I just forgot that gags are often a part of pet play. I can't do that yet." She lifts her head and arches an eyebrow. "But I want this scene."

"It's understandable that you were caught off guard. No gags of any kind." I keep rubbing a gentle circle on her back, until she leans back against the seat, her shoulder touching mine again.

"But speech restrictions, yes. Like maybe I can only answer with whimpers and barks?"

"I like that, Holly. What about bondage?"

She raises her head and crosses her arms in front of her chest.

"I like my hands being restricted and being on a leash, but I can't go further than that."

"Good. We need a stop signal. What would make you comfortable?"

She reaches for the water glass, her fingers trembling a little. "Can I say 'red?'"

"It works. Did you find the butt plug tail to be comfortable?"

"Yes...I like it." She blushes, tucking a piece of hair behind her ear.

I thread my fingers through her hair and cup the back of her head, stroking gently.

"Good girl."

Her lashes lower, and she leans into my hand, rubbing her cheek against my palm.

The soft nuzzle of her cheek against my palm is so intimate, so trusting, it feels more erotic than anything we did yesterday.

My chest tightens. She's slipping, deliciously, into the space we're creating together and I can't wait to give her this experience that's been on her kinky bucket list.

"You said a leash is fine, so a collar?"

"Yes, Noel." She touches her throat.

"I have one all set, ready to go."

"How do you manage to be prepared for every scene?"

"I own an adults-only resort with a private dungeon," The smile spreads across my lips and I kiss her cheek.

Holly laughs, her eyes crinkling at the corners.

While that's true, I also had some help, and I'm thankful for my friends and staff who aided me in all the preparations for this scene.

"Clothes or no clothes?"

"Some clothes? I have a lot of lingerie."

I move my hand to her thigh and give it a slight squeeze. "Perfect. If you could forget wearing panties, I'd enjoy that."

"I can definitely do that." Her head drops to my shoulder.

"Corrections will be given with a spanking. Anything else you're okay with?"

"I don't think so."

"Okay, we'll keep the corporal corrections to a minimum. I have some pup toys to play with, but I'm okay with you rejecting them if we get that far into the scene. Do you want to see them or be surprised?"

"Ah, we're at the point of maybe over-negotiation. Surprise."

"I knew you'd say that." I kiss her, grinning. "I may have a pup bed set up. Is that okay?"

"Yeah," her voice is thick with arousal.

"What about eating and drinking? Break scene, or would you like to try out puppy bowls?"

The subtle roll of her hips against the chair sends a rush of blood straight to my cock. I can almost taste her arousal in the air.

"Bowls."

My pulse picks up because I can't wait to see her eat out of the bowls I've prepared for her.

"One more question we need to address before going into the scene. How are we going to meet your human bathroom needs? Break scene to pee or use a pee pad?"

She swallows and squeezes her hands. She looks at me and away. This is an intense moment where she is considering all the options. I will go whatever way she wants, whatever makes her feel safe, so I wait.

"This time, the first time we play like this? I want to break the scene to use the bathroom."

She bites her lip, her voice fragile, like she's worried this will disappoint me.

"Holly, honesty is exactly what I want from you. You feeling safe is what is most important," I stroke the side of her cheek with my knuckles, wanting to reassure her. "I am grateful for your trust. We don't have to take the scene any further than you and I are comfortable with. We did say we'd remain friends on the fifth day if we still like each other and see what happens?"

"It just feels so easy." Her cheeks flush, and she ducks her chin.

"What does?"

"Being with you," she whispers. Her words make me pause mid-breath, my chest tightening as warmth spreads through me. I pull her closer, cupping her in my lap, needing the contact as much as I needed to hear her say it.

She settles onto me with a soft sigh, her curves pressing heat into my chest and thighs. My cock stirs, but what overwhelms me more is the fierce urge to protect her.

"I feel the same way, Holly," I breathe in her fresh scent, brush my lips against her neck, and hold her. The faint trace of her shampoo mixes with the sweeter, muskier note of arousal, and I want to drown in it.

Holding a woman on my lap feels very good. I don't feel guilt or regret. Instead, I feel protective and eager to give Holly what she needs today.

"Can we get started, Noel?"

"Yes, my pet." I let my voice drop lower, steady and commanding, savoring the way her pupils flare. "In twenty minutes, I will go up to your room. I expect the door to be open and you to be waiting for me like the good puppy you are. You'll find mitts, knee pads, a collar, and a leash on your bed. Please place the collar and mitts on, along with the knee pads. Wait for me, kneeling. Any questions?"

"No, Noel."

"Good girl. I'll see you soon, my pet." I make a shooing gesture with my hands but smile to keep it playful.

She laughs, stands, and leans down so I can spot a peak of her cleavage through her shirt.

The tease is deliberate, and my cock jerks in response. She knows exactly the effect she has on me.

"Can't wait, Noel."

She scampers out of the dining room, stops by the door, and wiggles her bum. The playful sway of her hips has me gripping the table's edge, imagining her on all fours in just a collar and tail. Twenty minutes feels like too damn long.

13

HOLLY

Nervous energy makes my palms tingle as I climb the stairs to my room.

Pet play has been a secret wish of mine for a long time, something on the kinky bucket list, and I haven't had a chance to try it out...until now.

Two women brush by me in the hall, laughing with each other, and I blush as if they know my secret. My tummy hits the floor as I realize I'm going to be doing all of this in public. But if I called "red," I know Noel would heed my safeword. All play would stop, and I would have the choice to end the session.

Right now, I could choose to walk out of here. If I wanted to, I could run myself a bath in the gorgeous deep tub and lock my door, leaving Noel to wonder what had happened or to assume I changed my mind.

But I want to do this scene, and the idea of pleasing him makes me so damn wet.

Playing out these hypothetical scenes gives me a sense of control and maybe that's what I need before I surrender to Noel in a way I haven't to any other Dom before.

I open the door to my room, and there on the bed, exactly as Noel said, is a collar, a leash, and a pair of leather padded mittens.

From the dresser, I pull out a nightie and set it back.

I've never done this before. I've dreamed about it, but it's real now. I'm nervous, but I also feel...thrilled.

Could I go further? I contemplate what it'd be like to be naked on Noel's leash, and shivers rack my spine. Goosebumps prickle my arms, heat pools between my legs.

I want to be played with and fondled. I want his hands on my body.

Naked is the way to go.

I snap the wide leather collar around my neck. Again, this gives me a measure of control. I am choosing to do this. It's not being done to me. I fasten the knee pads, adjusting them so they're tight enough.

Next, the mitts.

I manage to get my hand in one, but getting the second mitt on is impossible. They are too padded for any flexibility.

I set that mitt on the bed.

With a shuddering breath, I kneel to wait for Noel and see right across from me is a stand holding two metal puppy bowls.

One is filled with water, and the other has something in it.

Deciding now or never, I crawl over to the bowl.

It's dried cereal.

Seeing it there reassures me and makes me feel giddy.

Leaving it, I crawl back to the end of the bed, the plush carpet soft on my shins.

The padded mitt is clunky but deliciously restrictive. Kneeling there, waiting, my mind drifts into a different headspace where I only have to obey.

Anticipation hums low in my belly

I welcome the break from my always-on brain, from planning for and anticipating what comes next.

Waiting like this, I get myself into an almost meditative state when I hear the soft click of the door and see Noel's shiny black shoes as he enters.

"Hello, my pet."

His footsteps echo in the room, and a shiver runs down my spine and the edges of my thoughts start to blur. I want to please him.

He lays a hand on my head, then softly pets it.

"You're a gorgeous pet, do you know that?"

I want to nuzzle closer, but I can't, not until he tells me. He opens his palm, presses it against my cheek, and I take that as my cue. I nuzzle his hand, and soft murmurs escape my lips. My heart beats so fast that I'm sure he can hear it.

"Stand up, Holly. I need to break the scene for a moment." He extends his hand to me and I swallow nerves, wondering if something's wrong.

"Nothing is wrong. Forgive me for being rusty, too."

I take his warm palm with my un-mitted one. "It's okay."

He leans against the bed. His eyes are glowing.

"Does that work too? If I say your name instead of 'Pet,' does it break the scene for you?"

My heart leaps into my throat. I've never played with a Dom who is so considerate and aware of boundaries as Noel continues to be.

"Yes, that's perfect. I can't get the other mitt on."

"That does seem challenging," Noel picks up the mitt from the floor and slips it onto my hand. His eyes roam over my breasts, down my belly and I blush.

He tightens the mitt gently on my hand. "There. How does that feel?"

"Good." I flex my fingers. It's tight but soft inside and feels good restrictive, not scary restrictive.

"That collar looks good on you. You decided to go without clothes?" The warm note of approval in his tone sends shivers up my spine. I want to please him.

I go to touch the band at my neck, but can't feel it through the mitt.

"I like how it feels. I want to be your pet...completely."

"Good, that makes me very pleased, Holly. I want to ask you something, and I want you to answer honestly. I don't care either way. This is about how comfortable you are."

My pulse picks up at his serious tone. "What is it, Noel?"

"How do you feel about being touched by someone else? Like, if someone asks to pet my puppy?" He caresses my cheek, and I close my eyes.

My mouth is dry at the suggestion.

But I'm also wet because the idea of others interacting with me, treating me like a pet turns me on.

"Yes."

"Yes?" By his tone, he is surprised, but he smiles. "Okay. Any limits?"

"Touching is fine...anywhere," because honestly, I'm in this far, why not go for it?

"You're stunning, Holly, do you know that?" His mouth crashes over mine, and he kisses me, sliding his hand to my nape, deepening the kiss until my lips tingle. He breaks off the kiss and his dark eyes search mine. "Good girl. Let me put your tail on. And when I give you the first command, the scene starts. Any questions?"

The room sways for a moment because I want this so much I almost vibrate.

"No, I'm good to go."

"Excellent. Turn around, Pet and let me spread you." His sharp command makes my nipples bead.

I let out a whimper as the warmth of his fingers slide against my crack and he spreads me wide open.

Swallowing past a knot of nerves, I force myself to exhale. I hear him squirt lube into his hands, and his warm fingers massage my anal opening.

He holds the butt plug to my skin, waiting for it to warm.

Then I feel it against my opening.

"Bear down for me, Pet."

Gasping, I do as I'm told, and the plug is in, its weight familiar as it slides in easily and my muscles close around it. The weight of the plug feels full and good.

"Good Pet," he presses a kiss against my shoulder blades. "I want to take you through commands now before we go on our walk. On all fours, Pet."

I drop to my knees. The mitts on my hands feel odd. I can't feel the ground through the padding, but the knee pads support my weight. Words slip away. There's no Holly now, only Pet. My world shrinks to the sound of his voice and the tug on the leash

"You're magnificent, Pet. I'm proud to own such an obedient, good girl."

My brain leaves me at his honeyed praise. Suddenly, I am hyper-aware of his musky scent, of his footsteps on the carpet in front of me.

"Walk to the window and back, Pet."

Channelling a pup the best I can, I move one hand at a time, followed by my knee, deliberately moving each limb. The carpet is soft under my knees, but my mitts make it feel awkward, like my body isn't quite mine. It feels...good. I keep my head straight on where I am going. It feels like it takes forever, and wetness pours between my legs, trailing down my inner thighs.

I reach the window and turn back with the slow, exaggerated pup walk.

"Good girl, Pet." Noel steps towards me, reaches into his pocket, and takes out a bag.

He pulls something from the bag and cups his palm before my lips.

The whimper escapes my mouth, the sound unfamiliar to me, something primal and keening.

I lick the gummy candy off his palm, shuddering with a wave of bliss as my tongue licks the warm skin of his palm. I've never felt so small, so controlled. I want to be his. I want to please him like this.

"Perfect, Pet."

Noel ruffles my hair and chucks me under the chin. I close my eyes, swimming in his touch, highly aware of my arousal.

"Speak."

I blink at him, swallowing hard. Nerves and shame commingle through my system, freezing me.

He grabs a fistful of my hair and pulls it so hard I yip. "I said, speak, Pet."

"Arr-rf!" I choke out.

"Louder."

His grip is firm, but his other hand is on my shoulder, half reassuring and half admonishing. "Arf!" My pup bark is louder this time, and the smile that spreads across Noel's face is reward enough.

"Good girl. That one's hard for you, eh?" He rubs behind my ear, his touch calming my nerves, letting me rest in this pup headspace.

He takes three steps in front of me. "Stay."

I laser-focus on him as he picks up the leash and walks to the door. Once he's at the door, he nods. "Roll over, pup."

I drop to my belly, the carpet soft against my breasts, and roll over.

"Spread."

I do, and this makes me aware of those pup mitts.

"Pretty pup. Come here, Pet."

Crawling in that pup-walk, I do, and when his shoes come into my vision, I keep my head down.

"Good girl." He pets me. The pride in his voice makes me want to shake my tail, and I realize that's exactly what I should do.

I turn so that my bum is in front of him, and I move my hips, shaking my bum.

Noel laughs appreciatively. "Very good girl. Time to go for a walk." Patting my bare ass, he tugs my tail and clips the leash to my collar. "You be a good girl and walk right beside me."

I whimper. He ruffles my hair and opens the door. We're out in the hallway, where anyone can see us, and I'm so wet and hot with the high of being in this headspace.

We start down the hall, and I keep pace with Noel, crawling beside him.

"Sit, Pet."

I sat back on my knees, holding my breath.

"Good girl, Pet. Relax. You seem to be waiting for someone to leave their room and see us. Remember, the only thing you have to do right now is follow directions."

As Noel stands with his back to the hallway, a short man with his arms wrapped around a blonde woman comes out of their room, laughing.

They glance at us and continue on their way.

I close my eyes, in relief or wistfulness, I'm not sure.

Noel pats my head. "Okay?"

"Arf!"

"Good girl. Let's continue."

The air between us is tense with lust, and I'm hyper-aware of Noel's every step as I crawl. The carpet fibers press against my nipples with each move. His gentle tug pulls me through the leash, connecting me to his wants, down the stairs.

Rosa glances up at us as we pass the reception desk.

"Noel, can you take a quick look at this for me?" Rosa passes him an iPad.

"Sure. Sit, Pet, wait for me."

I'm ignored as Noel leans against the desk, reading whatever is on the screen. Guests pass me by on their way out for the evening. Piano music floats from the Parlour, and my head grows thick with a stillness I haven't experienced before.

I'm invisible, or at least blended in or accepted as being nothing more than Noel's pet, and I like it so much. Desire heats my blood with want.

After several long moments, Noel reaches down and twirls his fingers through my hair.

"Good, Pet. I'm almost done."

His praise blooms in my chest, almost making me cry. My mind is swimming with pleasure high when he pulls on my leash.

"Come, Pet, to the dungeon."

The hardwood floor is tough on my shins, and I'm super grateful for the knee pads and mitts giving me protection.

The doors to the dungeon are open, and people are playing. I glance up to see a man tied to the cross, a woman with long purple braids working him over with a flogger.

In the next play area, a woman sits on a queening chair being serviced by a man, and the roll of voices surrounds me. It's all very lively and upbeat.

My tummy tightens in nerves and eagerness.

Noel walks me through the space, and I keep my head straight so I'm not catching all of it from this viewpoint, but the space hums with an electric energy.

Leading us to the back, Noel stops. Reaching down, he unclips my leash from my collar and pats my head.

"Good girl, Pet. Hop up here." He points to the step.

I do, and it's an ample empty space —maybe they use it as a stage —on a raised platform.

"Ready to play?"

"Arf! Arf!" I let out a high pitch bark and shake my ass, deciding to go for it because I want to play.

Noel grins. His smile makes me melt.

"Stay."

He walks across the stage to the back, rummaging in a fabric box. He holds up a bone-shaped squeaker toy and throws it in the air.

"Fetch, pet."

As fast as I can crawl, I chase after the toy, grabbing it with my paw mitts. My lips touch the silicone, setting off a new blaze of desire. My pussy is soaked. I return the toy to Noel, rubbing against his legs with my body.

"Good girl. Drop the toy, Pet."

I drop it right at his feet. He throws it again. "Perfect, Pet. Good girl. Fetch."

This heady glow of pure pleasure and adoration suffuses my limbs as I get lost in this game. Nothing matters other than Noel's cool command of "Fetch," of me crawling across the springy floor, finding the toy and dropping it back to him.

I feel the gaze of the people watching us, and it heightens the pleasure.

On my next turn, Noel pats my head. "Stay."

He walks back to the fabric box and drops the toy in. I whimper.

"You liked that game, didn't you, Pet?"

"Arf!"

Taking a collapsible bowl from the box, he sets it down and then grabs a water bottle on the railing. He pours water into the bowl.

"Drink, Pet."

I do, lapping water up with my tongue, not realizing how parched I am until the cool liquid soothes my throat.

"Good girl." He pets my head and my cheek.

"May I pet your pup?" A woman with short blonde hair and crystal-blue eyes asks.

Noel's gaze lingers on me, a smile hovering at the corner of his mouth. "You may, Pauline."

My nipples tighten to a painful point. Pauline gives me a wide smile and pats my head.

I nuzzle into her touch, wanting more. She pets my shoulders, trailing her fingers along my spine and down my ass.

When she grabs my tail and pulls, I whimper.

Pauline laughs, "What a good pet!"

"Good girl, Pet. That's my pup behaving perfectly." Noel's praise encourages me to lean into her touches, to soak it all up.

"Arf!" It comes out more as a whispered moan. Her warm palm moves to my breast. She squeezes one, then the other. I press into this touch, and it is taking me further into that floaty headspace. Her touch is soft but firm, and it sets my whole body on fire. I feel both shame and desire and it makes my nipples bead.

Her touch sweeps down between my thighs, her fingers slip into my wet pussy, and I rock on her fingers, moaning.

Ah! The mix of humiliation and pleasure is so sweet and thick I can taste it on my tongue and in the pores of my skin. I'm floating in pure bliss.

"Bad Pet," Noel yanks me back from Pauline's touch by grabbing my collar. It takes me a moment to realize the connection with Pauline's glorious touch has been interrupted. His grip is firm, a reminder of my place. He decides when it's okay for me to be touched. And I like that.

I whimper, staring up at him. I put a paw up and sit on my heels in a complete begging pose.

His lips twitch. "Did you forget who your orgasms belong to?"

"Arf! Arf!" Oh, so not fair.

Noel's eyes have darkened with desire. Grabbing me by my collar, he stops at the step, sits down, and pulls me over his lap.

I'm just a pile of cells, trying to take in this rapid fire pleasure.

I'm so wet, so gone in this cocoon of pup-space and throbbing with need. I hump him, wanting him to put pressure on my clit, wanting him to give me relief from the needy ache.

His palm comes down on my ass, hard, peppering my bottom with quick slaps. The pain spreads through my centre, almost sending me into an orgasm.

The next spank lands right above my thigh, and I let out a soft whimper.

"I think my Pet likes this."

And his fingers are on my clit. He touches it so softly it barely registers.

"But Pet must not orgasm for strangers!" He smacks my ass twice more.

I am breathing hard, the sensations reducing me only to need and lust. He brings his palm down again, right across my thighs and I let out a yip at the pain, but my body sinks into it, and my hips arch into his palm wanting more.

His palm comes down again, the spanks heavy and thuddy and I moan at the pleasure breaking out across my skin,

"Good, Pet. Good girl."

Noel brings me on his lap and wraps his arms around me and I'm almost sad that the spanking ended.

My head falls back on his shoulder, my eyes closed.

"Pet, it's time for some lunch."

I nod, opening my eyes. The adoration I see in his gaze makes my pulse race.

He clips my leash to my collar. "Walk, Pet."

The sound of his footsteps is the only thing I hear, keeping me grounded. My body hums with need.

14

"You're doing great, good girl. That's it, keep it slow. Yes, good."

It takes a lot of self-control not to tell Holly that she can break scene and walk downstairs, but she's so into pup play, I don't want to take her out of it.

Holly makes her way down the stairs slowly, knees pressing into the pads with a soft thump on each step. The mitts force her weight onto her forearms, making her crawl clumsily but deliberate.

It's fucking gorgeous..

Each shift of her hips pronounces the tail sticking out from her ass. She's struggling just to descend the stairs because she wants to please me.

And I know with absolute certainty there is nothing I won't do for this woman. I want her.

I want her beyond these days of kinkmas, I want her to be *mine.*

The reflection nearly takes me out of the scene, it's so unexpected and it hums in my chest like a physical thing. The lights overhead appear brighter, the chatter louder as Holly finally gets down the stairs, and I guide her to the reception desk.

On hands and feet, Holly curls her body around my legs. I wait until Rosa is done with a phone call.

"Can you have food sent to Holly's room?" I keep my voice low; I don't want to distract my submissive.

"Of course," Rosa gives me a huge smile.

I lay my hand on Holly's hand pausing to take all of this in. I never thought that I would enjoy Vixen's Paradise with a guest of mine.

"Excuse me, may I pet your pup?" a tall man with a beard asks.

I haven't met this man before, but he's standing back respectfully. Thinking of how Holly responded to Pauline's treatment in the dungeon, I can't help but give permission.

"You may."

He gently leans down and pats Holly on the shoulder.

Her eyes are glassy, her skin is all goosebumps, and little shudders rake through her. Goosebumps rise along her skin, and small shivers ripple down her arms. She leans into me, her body trembling with every step.

We spent longer in the dungeon than I expected, and my cock is half-hard.

"Have a good night." The man gives a wave and continues on his way.

"Come, Pet. We're going into the Parlour. Walk."

Holly keeps step beside me, and in the Parlour, two women are playing cards, a man is reading while feeding his submissive something from a tray. The room is cosy, with the fireplace lit and Kai is playing something softly on the piano.

"Hi Noel." Rick is sitting on the couch, with Cat on his lap.

I own Vixen's Paradise. I don't have shame when it comes to kink or sex but for half a second, when I meet my old friend's eyes, I freeze, as if I shouldn't be here, holding the leash of a submissive who isn't my wife.

"Did you find a pet?" Rick smiles at me and Cat grins, putting her hand out to Holly.

"Yes, and she's a very pretty, obedient pup."

"Arf!" Holly lets out the cutest bark and I pat her on the ass.

"Say hello to Cat, Pet." I unclip the leash from her collar and Holly crawls over to Cat.

"Arf! Arf!" She shakes her butt and I laugh, and so do the guests in the room.

Holly sniffs Cat's hand and I sit down next to them.

"Pet, I want you to sit pretty. Show us that chest with those paws clasped together."

Holly sucks in a breath but she elegantly follows my command, thrusting her breasts out, with her mitted hands together.

"Good girl." Reaching into my pocket, I take out the bag of treats I brought and give her a gummy bear.

She licks it from my palm and I pet her head.

"What did you two do today?" I settle back on the couch, my hand resting on Holly's head.

"We wandered around the village. Cat bought way too many kitchen things."

"I did not!" Cat protests with a smirk. "If you gave me another hour I would have bought more!"

"Good thing it's Christmas, my love." Rick kisses Cat, twining his hands in her hair and I'm happy for my friends, though I feel that pang of grief.

Holly nudges my hand, as if she wants more attention and I'm grateful for the distraction of my cloudy feelings.

Reaching into my pocket, I pull out a tennis ball.

"Fetch, Pet." I toss it to the other side of the room.

Playing the happy puppy, Holly races after that ball with a yelp, tries to pick it up in her mouth, but it rolls away from her and she slaps her mitted hand down on the floor.

"Here puppy," one of the women from the table behind the couch says. "I have your ball. Can I throw it to you?"

"Let's see if she catches it," I say, leaning back on the couch.

The woman grins and throws it, sailing the ball over the couch. It lands on the floor and Holly chases it again, but it rolls out of her reach.

"It's here!" Kai says holding it up for everyone to see it.

"Try again, Pet." I nod at Kai and he laughs, throwing it over the couch.

The ball bounces, but somehow Holly paws it and gets it in her mouth and crawls over to me.

"Good girl, very good girl. It's definitely time for a reward."

She cries into my hand as I stroke her face, and I see goosebumps along her skin. Her eyes are still glassy and her whole body appears soft and languid.

My submissive is deep into subspace.

"Time for a reward, Pet. Let's go." I snap her leash back on her collar. "Thanks for playing with us." I wave at the guests.

"It's good to see you happy, Noel," Rick says softly.

"Thanks," I tell my friend, and then lead my Pet to the stairs.

"Pet, we are going upstairs. If you want to climb the stairs on your feet, bark once. If not, show me your belly."

She ducks her head, her eyes clouding before she lets out the sweetest little, "Arf!"

"That's a good pet. On your feet and climb the stairs."

I tug on her leash as she climbs each step and when we are at the top, she immediately drops to her fours and crawls.

"Good girl."

At her door, I let us in, drop her leash and walk ahead of her. I take off my shoes and sit in the plush armchair.

"Come, girl!"

Holly crawls into the room, over to me and shakes her bum so her butt plug wags.

"Good girl. Stay." I rub a small circle on the nape of her neck, get up and close the door.

Her eyes are laser-focused on me, and my cock twitches.

Having someone follow my commands, to give themselves over to me is a healing balm to my wounds that I didn't know I needed until now.

Reaching for my belt buckle, I undo it, drawing the leather out slowly. I unzip my fly and roll down my slacks.

I went commando today. I slide my palm up and down my cock, tracking how Holly's gaze is on my hand. She's licking her lips, and soft mewling sounds escape her glossy lips. Her eyes are so wide, they're beautiful pools of desire.

"Come and lick me, Pet."

She scrambles over to me and reaches for my cock before realizing the paw mitts are going to make touch a little tricky.

I laugh and cup her face. "Lick me, and if you make me cum like a good pet; I'll reward you."

"Arf! Arf."

Her yippy barks are adorable.

Her nose touches my dick, then she takes the head of my cock into her mouth, and I stop myself from clutching her head and helping her out.

Her pink tongue darts out, starts to lick the tip of my cock, oh so slowly. She licks the underside, up and down from root to tip.

I groan. My balls are so heavy, so close to exploding, but I force myself to stay still.

She rises up on her knees, and her lips close around my cock. She sucks it deep in her mouth.

Fuck.

Because as much as I want that, it's not what I asked for. I'm a soft Dom, but I need her to know who is in charge.

I grab a fistful of her hair and jerk her off my hard cock.

"Naughty Pet. I said, *'Lick me and make me come.'* Did you hear me?"

She leans back on her heels, her breasts bouncing. Her nipples are hardened points and the sight makes my mouth water.

I reach out and flick her nipple. "Pet, did you hear me?" I twist her nipple, needing her attention.

"Arf!" Looking up at me, she licks her lip. I keep tugging on her nipple, not harshly, but with a little bit of pain to steady her.

She ducks her head, lets out a soft whimper and I'm satisfied I got her focus back. I hold my cock to her lips.

Her pink tongue darts out from between her lips. Slowly, she licks a circle around my cocks' head.

"Good girl, yes, that's it," I gather her hair in my hands, tugging gently as she licks, and moans around my dick, setting off vibrations that I feel in my balls.

Her tongue is pure fire, heating my skin wherever it makes contact.

I'm holding myself back because I want her to succeed in the task I laid out, but I'm battling for self-control.

As if she feels my frustration, Holly picks up her speed, licking me by the root, her tongue darting out. Her nose touches my balls.

"Good girl," I hiss through clenched teeth.

She licks each heavy sac furiously.

My hand cups her nape, and I keep her right there, her tongue pressed against my balls.

"This feels amazing. You have a very talented tongue."

She lets out the the sexiest little snort and I press her head to my sac and she licks, letting out a half giggle.

Damn.

The way her naked body is gyrating, her body covered in a sheen of sweat, makes me so hungry for my pet.

I want to sink my cock in her pussy and never come out, and this task I've set her is pure torture as she keeps licking with that sexy tongue.

"Enough!"

Gripping her hair in one hand, I pull so her head comes up. She takes the hint and licks the head of my cock.

I breathe deeply.

"Come on, Pet, give me this orgasm, and I'll put you out of your heat."

A tremor rocks through her whole body. Reaching between her legs, I swipe my finger along her slit.

She's fucking drenched.

"You want me to make you come, don't you, Pet?"

Her tongue wraps around the tip of my cock, enveloping it in luscious heat, and I grit my teeth.

This is sublime, and I don't know who is being more tortured, me or her, but I'm soaking up every second.

"Your breasts are so beautiful, swaying like that as you lick my cock. You're such a good pet."

Her cheeks grow red at the praise, and I brush my hand through her hair.

"I'm so close, Pet. Your tongue is fucking fire."

She cries out and licks the underside of my dick with fervour, her determination renewed to do as I asked.

I groan. I'm almost there, and I'm going to explode.

"More, girl, more!"

Her tongue darts out, stabbing my cock right at the root, and that does it. My vision blurs, white-hot fire licking up my spine.

My release comes out in long, thick ropes of cum.

"Lick it all up for me, Pet."

My seed spills onto her tongue, and she furiously works to catch every drop, mewling in a high-pitched yip.

The look of adoration she gives me sears right into my soul, and I need to touch her. I pat my lap. "Up, Pet."

She scrambles up in my lap, and I hold her, nuzzling her neck.

"Good girl, very good girl."

I trace her lips with my finger, and then I kiss her, tilting her head so she opens more and gives me more access.

Her sweet taste soaks into my synapses, and I know I haven't had enough of her. She squirms on my lap, and I laugh.

"Yes, you'll get your reward, Pet. Stand up."

She does, and I turn her so her back is to me. Sliding a palm to her ass, I give the tail one good wag. She bucks against me.

I give it another little twist, delighted by how she shivers, and then I take it out.

"Arf!" she yelps.

I set the anal plug in an empty ice bucket that's by the nightstand and lift her on my lap again.

"Now I get to play."

My hands sweep down to her breasts, and finding her nipples, I tug them at the same time.

"Ow!"

But she arches into my touch, pressing her back against me, seeking more. I pinch both her nipples in my fingers, applying a good amount of pressure.

She licks my neck and turns into me, showing me she wants more. I let go of her right nipple; my fingers trail down her taut belly to between her legs and dip in her heat.

She's still drenched, slick and warm under my touch.

"Nice and wet for me, Pet."

"Arf!"

I circle her clit. She's so soaked that my finger is completely coated in her juices. My cock is starting to harden because this woman makes me feel as horny as a teenager. I plunge two fingers into her depths.

She closes her eyes and rocks on my lap, her breaths quickening, and I want her orgasm.

I want to rip it from her, drown her in pleasure. My fingers slide into her channel and curl to find that spot.

"Please!" she whispers against me.

"Naughty Pet, speaking like a human," I whisper into her ear.

She whimpers as my thumb presses on her clit. I feel her tense, every shiver reverberating through my body, and I know she's so close.

"Come for me, Pet."

I keep my thumb on her clit until she's grabbing at my arm, closing her legs, overwhelmed by the sensations and her whole body shudders.

She closes her eyes as the orgasm rips through her and I keep fingering her, wanting to wrench every drop of pleasure from her.

She turns her face to find my lips and kisses me hotly, fingers threading through my hair.

"I am coming!"

"I know you are. Good Pet."

She exhales, a long shuddering breath, and lays her head against my chest.

I want more of her, and a part of my brain wonders if I'm pushing her too much, but she smiles at me, her body glowing with submission and need.

"Get on the floor. I want to fuck your ass."

"Arf! Arf!" She scrambles down off the chair and gets on all fours.

I laugh, feeling her eagerness pulse under my gaze, and I stand, taking my cock in my hand, palming it.

It's already half hard. Her anticipation is all the reassurance I need.

"Tonight...you're amazing, girl. Lie on your back for me, Pet."

Grabbing the lube from the nightstand, I squirt some in my palm, the cool slickness making my cock twitch as I coat every inch of my length. Taking it with me, I walk around her slowly, savoring the way she waits for me, spread out and obedient.

"You've been the best pet today. Grab your ankles."

Her toned stomach muscles ripple as I help by pushing her ankles until they are right by her ears, her shoulders staying pressed to the floor laid open for me, perfect. My chest tightens at the sight.

"Comfortable?"

"Woof!"

I squat above her, slowly balancing until I am straddling her. I drizzle the lube between her ass cheeks, watching the shine spread as I swirl it around her anal whorl with a finger. The slickness glistens against her skin, and she shifts, presenting herself more fully.

"If you are uncomfortable, say 'red.' Good?"

"Arf!" She lifts her butt even more off the floor, resting on her hands.

I slide a finger into her anus, and her muscles close tightly around my digit, the snug grip stealing a hiss from my throat.

"Noel!"

I work another finger in, moving them back and forth, watching as she twists to the side, eyes fluttering closed.

"Ahh gorgeous pet but naughty," I bring my palm down on her ass and her eyes widen in shock.

"What are you supposed to say?"

Her brows further then she smiles that sexy grin that makes her eyes glow.

"Arf, arf!" she cries out.

"Better, girl. I'm going to slide into your ass and fuck you like the pet you are."

Her high-pitched mewl is the green light. Slowly, I press my cock's head against her opening. My palm on her ass cheek rocks her slightly.

Her skin is warm, soft, and pliant under my touch.

Taking my time, I work my cock in, hissing as it's enveloped in her tight lava center.

"Fuck, you're so snug, Pet."

I close my eyes, sinking into her heat. She lifts up even more, and I can't do anything other than pound into her. Thrusting long and deep, I ride her so hard sweat breaks out on my brow.

Holly cries out. She's so tight, fitted to me in all the right ways. I drill into her as she bears down on me even more, crying out in a screeching, "Yes!"

I am so gone.

Lost in her molten heat, she's gorgeous under me, flushed a pretty pink, nipples hardening. I feel her skin pressing into me, driving my pleasure.

Until I burst, my release coming hard.

"Gorgeous Pet!"

The orgasm rips from my body, and I tremble and withdraw, never have i ever felt this spent.

This satisfied.

She crawls over to me and wraps her arms around my waist. I close my eyes against her softness, her submission so pure I could swim in it forever.

"Good Pet."

For a long moment, there is only the sound of our heavy breathing. I sit on the floor and wrap her in my arms. Finding her mouth, I kiss her tenderly.

"What an awesome present."

She laughs, soft and breathy. I cup her face in my hands and kiss her forehead.

"Holly, how are you feeling?"

Hot tears flow down her cheeks.

"Too much! It's too much."

"I got you. I love those tears. Good girl, Holly," I soothe. With her in my arms, still sitting on the floor, I grab the robe at the end of her bed and throw it over her shoulders.

"Come with me." I stand, offer my hand, and lead her into the bathroom. "Let's get you cleaned up."

"I'm cold."

Her skin is all goosebumps, and her teeth are clattering. Quickly, I turn on the shower and ease her into it. The hot spray hits her shoulders, mist rising around us.

Though I want to take my time and relish her body, grabbing a washcloth, I squirt some body wash on it and clean between her legs, the warm scent of soap filling the air.

"Turn, please."

She does, and gently, I swipe the washcloth between her legs, then, taking the shower head down, I wash her ass, and in between her legs.

Water splashes across my hands, slicking her skin.

"You're hosing me down." Holly giggles as I direct the stream right between her gorgeous ass cheeks.

"I got to take care of my pet," I murmur, watching rivulets of water slide down her back.

"Thank you, Noel." Her eyes are shiny with tears.

I turn off the tap, guide her out of the shower, and take a fluffy towel off the back of the door and dry her off slowly.

She reaches for her robe that's on the back of the door.

"You should probably wash off, too."

"Yeah. I'll be quick."

"Can I watch?" Holly smiles, leaning against the sink, still wrapped in the towel.

"Be my guest."

I step into the shower and give myself the quickest wash ever. Steam curls around me; I want to get back to holding her, to the aftercare she so deserves.

"I'm done."

Holly hands me a towel.

"How are you feeling?" I drape my arm around her shoulders as we walk back into the room.

"A little emotional. A little shaky."

"Perfectly normal reactions," I reassure her. I grab a bottle of water and an energy bar from the fridge, pressing the cold drink into her hand.

A knock sounds on the door.

Grabbing my pants, I throw them on and, bare-chested, open the door. Hank, one of our servers, has a cart with dome-covered plates, a bottle of whiskey, and other things.

"Thank you."

"Of course, Mr. Brennon, have a good night," Hank says.

I wheel the cart into the room.

"Sit at the table, Holly."

She does, and I lift the domes off the plates, placing them on the table. The food smells delicious, buttery salmon and roasted vegetables filling the air, and I suddenly realize how ravenous I am.

"Eat," I order her gently.

She's hugging herself with a dazed look on her face.

"Did you like it?"

Her voice is so small, so far from her confident way of speaking.

"What?" I'm not sure I've heard her correctly.

"Did you like it? Was it okay?"

In two steps, I'm kneeling beside her chair, cupping her face in my hands. I kiss her soft lips gently.

"Did I like it? Holly, that scene was amazing. I loved every second of it, and you were glorious."

"Thanks." She glances at the floor.

"I was giving you a few moments before I started to run the scene down, but we can do it now if you need to. Did you like it?"

"Yes." She says it even before the words are out of my mouth.

"But?"

She shakes her head and squeezes her eyes up tight.

"Holly, tell me," I stroke her shiny hair, bringing her close to me.

"Noel, I could have stayed like that for longer. If you hadn't called my name, I would have, and that scares me." But she flashes me that confident, sexy grin. "I knew I had safewords, and you checked in with me, so I wouldn't have lost myself, right?"

"No, Holly. The scene had a beginning, middle, and end." I stroke her hair until she relaxes.

"Okay," she says to herself as if confirming something in her head.

"Thank you for your trust. For your submission." I trace her jaw.

She shudders under my touch.

"Thank you for giving me space to let me indulge in my submission." Her green eyes stare into mine, and the realization hits me. I have fallen so damn hard for this woman, and I'm going to do whatever it takes to make her mine.

15

HOLLY

DECEMBER 28TH, FOURTH DAY OF KINKMAS

With a towel wrapped around my hair, I peek out the viewfinder before opening my room door and push back the wave of disappointment.

"Hi, Rosa."

"Good morning, Holly. Noel asked that breakfast be sent up to your room. He got called into a meeting."

"I understand. Thanks for this." I say the words, but I wrap my arms around myself. This is what I wanted, right? No strings. So why, when I woke up this morning, did I feel so alone, the space next to me so empty?

Noel's scent still clung to the pillowcase because he'd taken care of me after our scene. He ran me a bath, checked me over for bruises, then held me until I felt drowsy in his arms, leaving a dark chocolate bar on the nightstand. But he said good night and left me. I told myself that was good. Safer. Exactly what I'd asked for. So why did I want to beg him to stay?

"Enjoy, Holly. I know Noel is eager to get to you as soon as he can," Rosa says as she wheels the cart into the room.

"I'm just as eager to see him."

After she leaves, I pour myself coffee from the carafe and tuck into the breakfast, definitely feeling better with some calories in me. When the coffee does its job, I get my laptop and bring up the Brennon Consortium offer. It's a solid offer, but I think they can go higher because I feel that Gran's property is worth more, especially given why they want to buy it. It's a fair price, but if they really want that neighboring property, they can go higher.

I sip my coffee, trying to focus on numbers, but every word makes my chest tighten with longing. My brain gets lost in the numbers and legalese, but underneath it all, I can't shake the ache of missing Noel. That's exactly what I don't want.

It took me years to get where I am in my career and a lot of hard work. The hours I work are awful; the demands of my job can be all-consuming, but I'm not going to give it up, no matter how much I want a relationship that meets all my needs.

An hour later, I'm getting ready to head out, thinking I'll go tour the village when a text lights up my phone.

Want to go skating?

My heart skips a beat. The idea of cold air and doing something where I'm going to make a fool of myself sounds perfect to shake off the last of the sub drop.

The rink glitters with white lights strung overhead, and Noel loops his arm through mine as we skate along the outside of the oval. His cheeks are flushed red, the gold in his eyes gleaming, and I feel carefree as he keeps pace with me.

"You're pretty good at this."

"We all played hockey growing up, though I'm not the athlete."

"My aunt taught me to skate," I say, swallowing over the unexpected emotion because keeping the fact that I own the farm he wants to buy is getting harder every moment I spend with him. I never expected to like him, to want to share all my secrets with him.

"My brother Hunter is the hockey player."

"Yeah? Did he play pro?"

"Hunter's a superstar but never wanted to turn pro. He did one year in the league, though, before an injury sidelined him."

"That must have been hard."

"Yeah. He's kind of the lone wolf of us and keeps to himself. My brother Theo hated skating but still did it, and Evan's happy to give anything a try for fun."

"You sound close to them."

"We are definitely a close-knit family," Noel says, flashing me that grin and squeezing my arm. "I can't wait for you to meet them."

His words freeze me because I don't know what to say. We agreed to five days, nothing that would involve meeting the family. But my heart skips a beat when he gives the invite and I don't know what to say.

"Help me up!" Cat calls from the middle of the rink. She's landed on her bottom, and Rick is skating figure eights around her.

"Not till you say please!" Rick teases.

Kai skates up beside Noel, clapping him on the back.

"Want to race, old man?"

"Old? You're a year older than me?"

"Then catch me!"

Kai takes off, and I skate back to where Pauline is, and we watch the guys racing each other, while Rick is still skating in a circle around his submissive. The warm group of friends and laughter is exactly what I needed, and I feel lighter by the time the guys come back to us, panting.

"This guy cheats," Kai says to me with a wink.

"You're the cheater, Kai!" Rick says, skating over to us, his hand linked with Cat's.

"I needed this, guys, thanks," Noel says to his friends. He takes my hand and squeezes it.

"Now I need to get out of this frozen cold! Let's go get a hot toddy!" Pauline says.

"We'll race you back!" Rick says.

"You're okay?" Noel asks, wrapping his arms around me and holding us back as his friends go ahead to change out of their skates. Aaron is waiting to drive them back to Vixen's Paradise.

"This was fun."

"I wanted to come and see you right away this morning, but one of our safety monitors had to pull out of the Fire and Ice party, and I had to find someone else."

"The party is tomorrow; I understand."

He leans in closer, grabs my chin with his gloved hand, and slants his lips across mine. It's a scorching kiss, warming me from the inside, making me moan against his mouth. I could stay here all day in the freezing cold, as long as Noel kissed me like this.

"Let's go get warmed up," he says, his eyes darkening with desire, and my belly flutters with anticipation.

"Can't wait."

His palm on the centre of my back guides me upstairs, and my thoughts spin, wondering what he has planned for the second to last night of Kinkmas. His palm is firm but warm through my sweater, making me melt.

He stands back as I unlock the door, but as soon as we're inside, he spins me so my back is pressed against the door and he captures my lips in a fierce kiss that sets my lips vibrating, hungry for more. My fingers clutch the doorknob for balance.

He lets out a soft grunt as he cups my nape and his thumb rubs the fine hairs at my neck, making me shiver.

"Finally, you're all mine, my present." He waggles his eyebrows, and it makes me laugh but the heat in his eyes thrills me. I reach up to trace the dimple in his cheek.

"Can I ask what your plan is for tonight?"

"That I need to taste you and make you come so many times you are begging me to stop."

A shudder rolls through me as heat creeps up my neck, and he presses his body against mine, his muscles rippling under his shirt, the hard plane of his chest against my breasts.

"Yeah, that sounds acceptable."

"Good." He traces a line down my jaw, and I cry out as my nipples bead and my pussy throbs. I want him so much. But it isn't supposed to matter...this is only five days, that's what we agreed to.

"Good."

Noel pulls me from the door, walking me backwards towards the bed, kissing me, his palms kneading my ass, making me giggle until I fall on the mattress, clutching his arms.

"All day, I've wanted to taste you."

His hands go to the hem of my sweater, my fingers fumble the fabric, desperate to be bare for him. Finally I get the sweater and my T-shirt off. Noel's lips drag across the hollow of my throat to my collarbone, setting a trail of sparks on all my nerve endings.

I let out a soft moan, his mouth slanting over mine. For a moment, I pretend that this man is mine. Even though I told myself I wouldn't fall for him. My fingers trail through his silky hair, and I arch my hips in invitation as he hovers over me, his warm brown eyes bearing into me.

Noel unbuttons the lace clasp of my bra, tossing it to the floor. He thumbs my nipple back and forth as if it's a guitar string, and I cry out at the electric touch, wanting more pressure, needing him to take me. He leans his head close to my breasts, and he takes my nipple into his mouth, my back bows off the mattress, needing him.

Oh God. I'm lost in the sensations he's awakening with every hard, long pull of my nipple. He's tasting me as if I am a dessert to savour. Heat spreads through my body, quivering sensations swirl through at every lap of his tongue.

I reach for him because I want to touch him. I want to be as close to him as I can now. I want him to stop because the heat and the sensations are making me wild. Why does he make me feel safe even when I'm coming undone?

"Noel!"

I feel like I'm going to shatter. He lifts my breast, holding it in his hand as he switches sides and fuses his mouth over my other nipple. Desire courses through my veins and I try to get my pants off.

Noel laughs, and with his nipple in my mouth, the sound vibrates through my body.

"Impatient, are we?"

"Yes!"

"But I want to take my time with you, Holly."

Noel stands and smiles at me. I clutch the sheets in my palms and his gaze drags over my body, as a soft guttural groan escapes his lips.

He opens the nightstand drawer and pulls out two long lengths of silky rope and a new vibrator in a package.

"You really do have elves that help you."

Noel laughs. "I pay those elves very well. Tell me that you want me to tie you up."

My mouth grows dry in anticipation. "I want you to tie me up, Noel. Please."

"Good girl."

He takes my arm, stretching it out across the bed, then makes a loop in the rope, forming a bracelet. He slips this over my hand and ties it off to one of the hooks on the side of the headboard. The rope is soft against my skin and feels perfect. I flex my fingers, testing it out. If I had to, I could get out of the bracelet.

"How does that feel?" His eyes darken as he watches me test the bond.

"Good. You could make it tighter."

"Excellent."

Noel adjusts the slack on the rope. It's tight as I pull on it, and I won't get out of it easily. He ties my foot to the hard point at the bottom of the bed and repeats the tying on the other side.

"Very pretty."

He stands between my spread and bound legs, staring right between my thighs. My belly tightens, and my body tenses, craving his touch, a tremor ripples through my thighs.

And he gives it to me — his firm fingers press on my inner thighs. Flashing me a grin, his mouth is on my pussy, his tongue flicking my clit. The wall of need breaks open so fast that I am gasping for breath and my toes curl into the sheets. Intense bliss heats every single one of my nerve endings and I can't hold back the wave; it crashes over me, blazing through me in a hot rapid heat that makes me tremble and soar higher.

"Noel!" I scream his name.

"That's one." His voice drips with rich satisfaction.

But his fingers don't let up, right through the aftershocks. My head is swimming. I feel flung from my body in a whirlwind of pleasure. I never let anyone push me this far but with him, it feels right. His thumb presses down roughly on my clit.

"You look so pretty when you come, Holly. Give me one more, you can do it."

His fingers slide in and out and, as if his voice is a leash to my pussy, it contracts in a pleasure so intense it's almost painful. Gibberish falls from my lips as my head spins, the orgasm crashing over me, slamming into me.

"Noel, Noel," I chant in a gravelly whisper.

"I want more. I'm feeling very greedy tonight," he kisses my sweaty brow and I whimper against him, chills blazing through my skin at the overload of sensations.

He swipes his fingers on my leg, crawling up the bed, and trails his lips over my waist, across my stomach, his stubble scraping my skin, leaving a hot path. With the barest pressure, he skims my breasts, dragging his lips to caress up to my neck until they meet mine.

I kiss him, wanting more, even though I'm a wreck and in pieces in this post-orgasmic high.

"Be a good girl and beg for another orgasm," his hot breath shivers against my ear and I mewl, the pet play scene flashing through my mind. And maybe it's because I trust that he'll stop me from going too far, that I know I'm going to beg.

"Please, Noel. Please make me come again. Please."

He kisses my brow. "Of course, Holly. I love how your eyes get dark, and your toes curl before your body bows to the orgasm. I want three more."

His tone drops, all steel and command and I whimper — three! I think I'll explode.

"Yes, Noel," but the words are out of my mouth in breathy gasps because I want to give him what he's asked for. I'm making those mewling sounds as he shows me the vibrator and shiver as the plastic slides against my skin. He turns it on and sets it against my breast. The vibrations are fluttery and pulsing and I'm arching against my cotton bonds.

"Please."

"Please, what?"

He turns off the vibe, skims it along the underside of my breast, and grasps my nipple between his fingers.

Ah! The tug of pain is refreshing and narrows my desire to a point. My thighs press together, trembling, needing more.

"Please use the vibe on my pussy."

"Good girl, Holly, for asking so sweetly."

I close my eyes, basking in his praise. And then the vibrator is in me, the weight sure and comforting as he turns it on. My clit is so sensitive from the previous orgasms that it doesn't take much. Noel grins at me. As I stretch my neck, the vibrations shoot through my core. Exploding in a mess of heat and need and ache, I grab at his arm, tugging on him.

"Too much! Oh too much!"

"Good girl for coming, Holly. You can give me two more."

I don't know if I can. "I can't!"

I reach for him.

"Yes, you can, Holly. Be a good girl, and give me your orgasm."

Noel's fingers plunge into my core. The pain-pleasure rolls through me, but my back arches, as if I can't stop myself from taking more. I'm panting with need and the ache of the intensity. I close my eyes against the tide pulling me back into the pleasure, and I open them. Noel has moved the vibrator so it's right against my clit. His hand presses against my thigh.

"Look at me, Holly."

I meet his stare, and my heart leaps out of my chest. I've never felt this completely exposed, this vulnerable, and yet so safe. Because at this moment, I want to be wholly his. I can't deny or ignore that commanding tone, the way he looks at me with the expectation that I am going to do exactly what he says.

"Yes, Noel?" I squeak the words out as the vibe drums against my clit.

"Come, now."

He touches my shoulder, but the heat in his eyes scalds me, cementing me to him. His fingertips trail tiny sparks across my breasts and down across my stomach, stopping above my mound. My entire body tightens and then launches like a rocket into hot surrender. The orgasm crashes through me, and I scream, wanting it to stop because the intensity is so damn much I think it's going to swallow me whole. I want to curl in a ball, but the rope bondage doesn't make that possible.

"See? That wasn't so hard."

"Yeah, it was."

I pant, stretching my arms, the rope smooth against my wrists but tight.

"You're a good girl for giving me what I want, Holly."

He presses his lips against mine, leaving me breathless. I exhale as the vibe stops. And then I scream as his mouth is on my pussy again.

"Noel!"

I reach to touch him and can't, but with the slightest bit of nip, his teeth are on my clit. Shivers roll through me, and I'm lost in not quite pain, not quite pleasure, as he sucks my clit and a delicious painful sting shoots through me.

I want to run away from the intense sensation, but I groan as a sizzling, rolling fire starts at my core, blooms upwards, and blurs my vision. I am ripped from my body, thrown against a wall of razor-sharp ecstasy so intense that tears leak down my face.

"Noel, Noel," I sob, reaching for him.

He keeps going, his tongue swirling over my clit, then his mouth is on my inner thigh. I close my eyes, lost in the overdose of pleasure, my body aching. My tears are hot, and I want to move, to wipe my nose. I want to hug this man and lay beside him and never move. I want him.

His dark-brown eyes meet mine, and a slow, sultry smile spreads across his face. It wasn't supposed to be anything more than a fling. A sob catches in my throat because I want to push down these feelings of desire and attraction, of how much I want this man beyond tomorrow. The thought terrifies me.

"Good girl, Holly."

Noel is working my wrist free. The right one, then the left. He rubs my leg until he gently removes the ties that bound my ankle.

"You did very well."

Lifting my leg, he kisses my knee so tenderly it makes me sob more. "It's okay to let it out."

He moves to my left leg, quickly setting me free.

"I hate crying," I whisper.

I'm overwhelmed by the sensations, the forced orgasms taking me under, this scene more intense in ways I didn't expect. How my body responds to this man is different than any other man I have been with, and that scares me because it has to mean something. But what if it doesn't mean anything? What if I never see him again?

My hands tremble, and I curl into myself slightly.

"Come here."

Noel slides up to me and wraps his arms around me. He pulls the sheet over my body and nuzzles my neck. He holds me like that for long moments, where my heartbeat finally returns to normal, and I stop crying.

"I've never come so many times or so hard."

"You are splendid," he kisses my brow. "What do you need now?"

"We never got to the hot toddy."

"I will remedy that now." He brushes my hair off my face.

"And I want a shower. But myself."

He cocks an eyebrow at me but extends me a hand. I clasp it, grateful for it because I'm shaky.

In the bathroom, he opens the shower door for me and guides me to the bench.

"Take your time, pretty girl," he gives me a soft kiss.

"Okay."

I turn on the taps as hot as I can stand, letting the hot water add to the languidness I feel. For a long moment, I stay on the bench as the water pours over me. I needed this so much. This release, the kinky fun time, yes, but more than all that, I needed to be looked at like how Noel looks at me. I needed to be appreciated and understood and it's a need I thought I had repressed.

My career is challenging and stimulating and for a long time I told myself that's all I need. But it isn't. The thought of not having Noel makes me feel hollow and empty and I try to push it away as I comb conditioner through my hair, before stepping out of the shower.

I throw on the silky robe and still shaky, I enter the bedroom, where Noel is arranging the table.

"I ordered cake."

"I never say no to cake."

I brush my hand along his shoulder as I take my seat and pick up the glass. The amber liquid is warm and lemony on my tongue, soothing.

"How are you feeling, Holly?" Noel reaches for my hand.

"That scene was more intense than I thought. Not as intense as the pet play, intense in a different way."

"You gave me everything I asked for."

I blush at his glare, the praise in his tone. He cuts into the chocolate cake with his fork. I close my eyes against the thought, but before I lose my nerve, I open them to meet his curious stare.

"Will you feed me the cake?" My voice is barely more than a whisper, and I tense, afraid of a moment of rejection.

But he lifts the fork to my mouth. "It's my pleasure."

The cake is delicious, dark chocolate and smooth. It dances on my tongue as he feeds me bite after bite in silence. I remember the first time he fed me. The pleasure he takes from this is a burst of electricity. I can feel how much pride he is taking in it as he feeds me the cake.

"Is there anything else I can give you?" Noel asks.

I take another sip of the hot toddy. His head is turned slightly, a small smile on his face. I shift on my chair, and nerves form a tight ball in my stomach.

"Will you spend the night with me?"

I want him to say yes more than anything in the world.

16

NOEL

I pause with my fork halfway to her lips. The stare she levels at me is blazing with tension as she leans back in her chair.

The robe dips open, revealing her creamy breasts.

I place the fork down and stand, wanting to touch her.

Her hair is still wet from the shower, faintly scented with lilac. I place my hands on her shoulders, and staring into her gorgeous green eyes, I drop a sweet kiss on her lips, tasting the chocolate cake.

I can either stay where I am or jump—breaking off the kiss, I kneel beside her chair, clasping her hands in mine.

"Holly…I…" I don't want her to see me as weak, but the words stick in my throat. "Yes." The word doesn't get stuck this time. I say it as if it's an exclamation mark because I mean it.

Her perfectly arched eyebrows rise to her hairline.

"Yes?"

"Yes, I will spend the night with you."

The smile that spreads across her face lights up the whole room. I return to my seat, picking up the fork again, and lift it to her lips. Her lips part around the fork, her tongue flicking it, and the thought of her mouth on me makes my cock twitch.

"I would love to spend the night with you. I wonder how many times I can make you come," I say teasingly, wanting to diffuse the tension.

She closes her eyes as a delicious shudder rocks through her body.

"Wasn't it five?"

"Oh, you're right. Maybe it's time to see how long you last without coming."

"Haven't we done that before?"

"We have." I nod. "But I like repeating good things. Don't you?"

The small smile she gives me makes me hum in appreciation.

"Yes, I do. And what happens if I do unravel?"

My mind whirs with possibilities. My foot slides along her calf, claiming her skin.

"Deal, Noel. If I come, you get to spank me at the party."

Heat surges low, my cock strains so hard it aches.

"Good." "Why are we waiting?" She pushes her chair back.

I stumble out of my chair, like an oversized ogre to her cool ice princess. I own the damn building, and yet this woman's offer is so heady, so enthralling, I am knocked off balance.

She grabs my arm, tugging me toward the bed.

"You're always impatient," I laugh.

"Yes, when it's something I want." She keeps tugging my hand, and I go with her, allowing her to push me down.

Her robe slides off her body, and I lean close, sweeping my hands down to fill my palms with her soft, heavy breasts. Her nipples pebble under my touch as I tease and roll them.

She closes her eyes, tilts her head back, offering me her neck, and I kiss it, right where her pulse is hammering.

She gasps as I keep the pressure up, and I want more of her sounds. I pinch and tug harder until her gasp turns sharp, making my cock throb.

One night? A huge part of me wants to give this woman more than one night. I want to hear every noise she makes, to take in how the pleasure softens her features. I want more of her sweet surrender, how her whole body bows under my tongue and hands.

Holly reaches for the hem of my shirt. I grab it and press a kiss to the pulse point on her wrist. I get my shirt off.

"You're beautiful." Her nails skim my chest, circle my nipples, and my balls are boiling. A groan tears from me as her wet tongue flicks across my nipple.

I want to cement this moment in my memory bank, and I want to give her every ounce of pleasure she'll accept.

Our lips meet in hot, devouring kisses. Our noises mingle in the room, her sharp cries making me so damn hungry that I barely register my pants sliding down my legs. I kick them aside.

She kisses my lips teasingly, darting to my chin and cheek.

Having enough of that, I growl. I tease her bottom lip, tilting her head to get more access to her mouth.

I ravage the kisses with all the hunger I feel.

Her body softens against mine, and those delicious exhales drive me on.

But then she pushes at my chest.

I laugh. "It's like that, is it?"

"Maybe," Holly smirks, her dimples pressing into my chest as her fingertips graze my ass, making me cry out.

My cock is so damn hard, I want to pull her under me, but the torture of her kisses—across my collarbone, over my abs—makes me burn for her even more.

"Holly," I hiss as she wraps her hand around me, palming my cock with a slow stroke.

"Yes, Noel?" she says, as if she doesn't know her long pulls are driving me wild.

"I want to feel your mouth on me."

"Yes, Noel," she whispers, gracefully sinking to her knees. I fist her hair as she takes my cock in her hands and teases the tip with her tongue.

Her mouth is molten, divine, sucking me deep, then easing up, and I groan as her tongue strokes the sensitive underside until I'm trembling on the edge. She rocks back and forth, taking me even deeper.

Last time she was restricted to only using her tongue, and as if she's intent on reminding me, she's working me with so much force I'm sure I'll explode before I can have her. I've had enough. I want her under me. Right now.

Tugging her hair, I guide her off my cock.

"Noel?"

"Need you now, sweetheart." I lift her up, bring her to the bed, and twine her hair through my fingers.

I'm on top of her, bracing over her, staring into those gorgeous emerald eyes.

"I've got you, and I'm going to make you unravel."

"You can try," she squirms against me, her eyes lit with amusement. I take her hands in mine and stretch them above her head.

My lips merge with hers, heat arcing between us as I kiss her like she's mine.

Never have I had an experience like this. This woman reminds me there is more to life than the next project. I want to stand on the edge of a mountain cliff and look down with her by my side. I want to travel to far-off places and see ancient artifacts.

My heart rate spikes as I swallow her moans with my kiss, her breath hot and desperate against my tongue.

Sliding down her body, I swirl my tongue around her nipple, teasing it until it hardens, and she presses me closer, demanding. But I'm quick about it because I want to make her shatter. I take my mouth off her nipple and drape her thighs over my shoulders.

Her legs naturally fall, wide and pliant.

"Noel!" Her hips arch off the bed. "I need you."

Her swollen clit gleams, slick and pulsing, begging for my mouth.

"You have me, gorgeous girl. I need to taste this."

I swipe my tongue over her clit, her spicy taste so familiar that I know I need this woman. I'm not going to let her go.

Her taste floods my tongue, sharp and intoxicating, and I groan against her heat. Somehow, I must show her that she belongs with me after tomorrow.

"Noel!" she cries, legs trembling against me.

With my pulse hammering, I move her in line with my cock.

"I need you right now," I growl.

I dive into her in one fierce thrust, burying myself in her wet pussy, and we both groan as her sheath tightens around me.

I thrust, capturing her lips; my teeth graze her bottom lip.

Her nails rake me, a hiss spilling from her lips as her hips lift, urging me deeper.

"Never… I'm never coming out of you." She giggles, her breasts bouncing as her hips rise.

I thrust harder, the bed shaking beneath us. My balls are heavy, and I'm going to come undone. But I want her to come first because I want to spank her tomorrow.

Leaning forward, I find her lips. I dive into her mouth as I rock into her core, kissing her. My tongue dominates hers, stroking deep as I pound into her at a relentless pace, both of us gasping and sweating, craving more.

I hook her leg over my arm, opening her wider, plunging deeper. The wet slap of our bodies echoes in the room.

"Noel! Yes! I need more! You're making me burn!"

She closes her eyes, the pulse at her throat visible and lovely. Her little mewls of pleasure are exactly what I want to hear as I rock.

I'm infused with her, not sure where I begin and she ends.

"Holly!" I yell her name, only to hear the syllables.

I plunge even deeper.

She holds on as I slam into her with all the greedy want that's propelling me into her. I'm so far inside her I don't think I could ever untangle. And I don't want to.

"Hang on, baby," I whisper near her ear.

We are both panting; moans of pleasure dance around us.

She mewls, I groan. I groan, she yips.

It's a back-and-forth dance, but what it isn't is subtle. I grind my hips against her, taking her even further.

"Noel! I can't!"

Thrusting even deeper, my lips fuse to hers. I grab her ass, pressing her closer.

"Give it to me, Holly. Come for me, baby. Right now."

Her eyes open, glossy with pleasure, sparkling emeralds behind a glass.

"Noel!"

She clenches around my cock; the second her body tenses, she convulses, tight and pulsing. Her cry tears through me as she gives in.

"Gorgeous, Holly," I whisper against her neck.

My balls are heavy; I can't hold back. I roar her name, hips jerking as I spill deep inside her, vision blurring white.

I release deep in her core and lay for a moment, bracing above her, panting.

"I owe you a spanking," I rasp.

"Yeah." Holly smiles, swiping her hand through my hair. "But it was worth it."

I withdraw from her, kissing her belly. I swing my legs to the floor. I need to clean up, but her hand on my arm stops me.

"Stay here with me for a moment."

"Okay." I spoon around her, holding her against my chest as my heart settles but pulses with a different beat, the one of wanting her. I fall into a kind of half sleep until something wakes me. Now, it's ten after two in the morning, and I've just stepped out of the shower. I don't know if I've slept a whole night since my wife died. Even though I have this gorgeous woman in my bed now and I want her to be mine, my heart pangs, reminding me of my loss.

"Hey." Holly is lying against the pillows, her hair mussed, her cheeks pink. The glow of her phone screen lights her face.

"Did I wake you?" I slide under the covers, wanting to hold her in my arms.

"No. I'm doped up on pleasure." She sets her phone aside and stretches beside me.

"Good." I trace her lips with my finger, and she parts them.

"Can I ask you something?"

"Anything. Ask me lots of things." I find her hand, slipping my fingers between hers.

"Where do you live?"

Sliding my arm under her, I draw her to me and laugh.

"Is that too personal?" she whispers, as if worried she asked the wrong thing.

"Nope. It's just a little complicated. I haven't really settled anywhere for the last three years since Claire died."

I have a condo in Vancouver that's seldom used, and with my brothers, an apartment in Toronto.

"In March, I moved back to our house in Edmonton. My wife's family is from there, and I realized I wanted to be there. For now."

"Where did you grow up?" She slides her palm over my chest, until it hovers near my slackened cock.

"Vancouver. Any other questions?"

"What kind of law did you practice?"

"Corporate law, until my brothers and I made the consortium."

"What about your family?"

I love how she asks without bluster.

"My dad invented a special cover for a solar panel, so they absorb more power."

"Your dad is an inventor?" She props herself up on her elbow, smiling at me.

"Yeah. It took him years to get any success. My mom worked as a paralegal."

"Is that why you became a lawyer?"

"Kind of. I thought I'd be good at arguing—and I am. My house was chaotic with four boys, my dad's bits and pieces everywhere—but it was good."

She stiffens beside me.

"Holly?"

"My house wasn't. My bio father abused my mother. Not me, for whatever reason."

"I'm sorry." My chest tightens; the words are thin, but I mean them anyway.

"My Gran's house was a safe place. That's where we spent Christmases." She glances away.

"Hey, I'm here," I gently grab her chin with my fingers. "And your mom left your father?"

Her gaze swings back to me.

"Yeah. That was a happy day."

"What did you want to be when you grew up?"

"I wanted peace and quiet. But I just wanted something...more...something brighter than I was living." She tucks her head against my chest, and I wrap my arm around her shoulders.

"Did you find it?"

"Yeah." She grins at me before planting a kiss on my lips. "I'm great at screen protector sales."

I laugh and kiss her brow, burying my face in her hair. "I'm happy you found it."

"Thanks. I'm happy this is how I spent Christmas."

"Think we should do Kinkmas every year?" The question escapes before I can stop it; I hold my breath, heart thudding.

I ask about next year because the far future feels safer than the near one.

"Definitely." She yawns, curling into me.

Her breathing evens, slow and deep, and I lie awake, skin still humming from her touch, certain in a way I've never felt before.

17

HOLLY

DECEMBER 29TH, FIFTH DAY OF KINKMAS

Something prickly glides up and down my foot and I can't help but squirm and twist, giggles bursting from low in my belly.

"Noel! That tickles!"

"Does it, my Pet?" The prickly thing is taken off my foot, replaced by something soft and sweeping it sends a chill down my spine as it's swept from the bottom of my foot to behind my toes, till it's weaved in and out of my toes, giving a light tickling sensations that's making tears roll down my face

Noel presses his thumb to the middle of my foot making it twitch involuntarily, my breath coming out in stutters, and drags it slowly around in an agonizing circle.

His hot breath tickles my shin, as he presses his lips to my leg, trailing kisses up to my thigh, my flesh flaring with goosebumps and trembling.

With the softest of pressure, his tongue scrapes beside my mound and it makes me crazy, hot prickles flare all over my skin.

"What is this?" I cry out as he grazes my inner thigh with his teeth.

"This is making you wet."

"This is driving me mad!" I tease, kicking my legs and feeling them restrained in the rope bonds.

My belly muscles are sore from laughing and I'm so wet, the sheet under me is probably drenched.

After spending all night in his arms, then eating breakfast, Noel tied me to the hardpoints on the bedposts, spread eagle.

When he suggested a tickling scene I had no idea what to expect and I'm happy I said yes because he is waking up nerve endings I didn't know I had, with the sleeping mask covering my eyes wet from tears.

"Good." He moves his mouth way from my pussy, back to the sole of my other foot.

"No! Oh my god!" I cry out as his tongue scrapes the bottom of my foot, the sensation setting off a new wave of pinpricks, my back arches off the bed, trying to get away from them.

It's tickling in the most sensual, extreme way and this isn't what I thought it was going to be when Noel suggested it this morning.

"I told you I was going to find all your ticklish spots."

The pads of his fingertips scale up my leg, around my calves, close to my upper thigh and he tickles me, his hot breath following, heating my skin.

I squirm back and forth, rasping breaths coming from low in my gut, caught between tickling and almost arousal; almost pleasure is a strong sensation that's taking my breath away, literally.

"This is...ahhh! I didn't think it'd be like this!" I cry out as works around my stomach in a circle, making my legs pull against the bonds, wanting to escape but can't.

"New experiences, that's what Kinkmas is all about." The pleasure in his voice is clear and it makes my heart flutter.

"Ahh! So much!"

"You're beautiful when you let go, Holly." His lips skim right along my inner thigh again and it takes me by surprise just as much as his words do.

Let go.

What Noel has given me this week is precious, a gift I could never have found the words to ask for.

"Noel! Yes! Please," I whimper as his mouth closes around my clit. I squirm at the tiny flick of his tongue, my hips arching off the bed, trying to for more friction.

Hot curls of pleasure spark in my low belly and I need his touch, more than what he's given me.

It's so frustrating and at the same time, arousing, my pulse hammering in my ears, the rope on my ankles, rubbing across my skin.

My skin is cool from where he lifts his face and he kisses my belly button, while his fingers make a ticklish circle on my thigh.

"Please!"

"I know you need it, Holly." The amusement in his voice drips, it's rich and sensual and I could listen to him forever.

"Yes!" His mouth is back on my pussy.

Sucking.

Driving the orgasm closer with every lick of his tongue, every swirl around my clit.

Then something soft and feathering sweeps along my inner thighs, over my belly as he lifts his mouth away.

I giggle so hard, I'm crying, frustrated that the orgasm wasn't given to me, it's a painful throbbing ache.

"You're so gorgeous." He captures my mouth in a hot, quick kiss and it sends tingles through my skin.

"But I want you to wait. Till later. We have a party tonight." I hear the grin in his voice and my fingers curl, clawing the bedsheets but at least he removes that feather thing from my body, and wipes the tears from my cheeks.

"Tonight is forever!"

"Not quite." Noel gently unties the sleep mask. "Close your eyes."

I do, squinting behind the mask.

I feel the light on my face as he takes the mask off and shiver as he kisses my arm, up to my wrist before untying my wrist from the hardpoint in the bedpost.

"You should be okay to open them. How do you feel?" He massages my wrist, and I flex my fingers.

My skin is tingling and my pussy is aching.

"Fine," I huff out.

Noel laughs, his brown eyes crinkling and he's so damn handsome I can barely believe he's with me, still.

He unties my other wrist and my legs and I patiently wait for him to undo me, even though I want to move, to get off the bed and...I don't know...throw a snowball at him for him leaving me this frustrated.

"There you are, all free," Noel says.

I lay there for another moment, watching as he coils the rope, my pussy still aching.

I swing my legs to the floor and stretch. "That was fun."

"Yeah, not too frustrating?"

"Frustrating but in a good way."

"That makes me happy to know," Noel moves to put the rope away and then comes back with a gold wrapped box. "Happy Kinkmas."

He puts the box in my hand and I shake my head.

"You can't—"

"Yes, I can, my present, now open it."

Noel spending the night with me was the best gift he'd given me, but I unwrap the present, opening the box to reveal a set of tiny emerald earrings.

"I thought they matched your eyes."

I hold one up to the light, my throat tight with tears. This is too much. He's shared with me and given me everything I've asked for and I haven't reciprocated. My stomach rolls with guilt clashing with the warm, gooey feeling in my chest.

"Thank you, they're beautiful."

"You're welcome. Are you okay?" He squeezes my shoulder, his intense stare searching my eyes.

"Yes, I just have to tell you—" His phone buzzes interrupting me.

"Sorry, I need to take this, I'll be right back." He kisses me quickly before moving over by the window.

I get up and quickly give myself a quick shower, the water soothing but doing nothing to absolve the ache between my legs.

My hand slides down my belly but I stop, letting out a squeal of frustration. I agreed to give him my orgasms.

I throw on a pair of leggings Rosa had given me and my soft sweater from Patricia, my heart in my throat the entire time.

It's time to tell Noel who I am.

"Hey, gorgeous," Noel says as I come back into the room. "I'm sorry I have a meeting with Axel about tonight's final arrangements. Can we talk later?"

I swallow my disappointment. Of course we can talk later but I had worked up the courage in this moment. I don't want to be the kind of woman that wallows while waiting and I don't want to demand more of him, but I'm not sure if I am going to get another dose of courage.

It shouldn't be a secret, what I do for a living.

I'm not a politician or a spy. But I've had so many dates where guys hear talent agent and they either ask me to make them a star or they scoff at me, as if they couldn't imagine that i work with movie producers and actors.

And I should tell this man, who I don't want to say goodbye to, that he's trying to buy my farm.

"Not to be selfish but can we grab a quick coffee in your apartment first?"

His expression goes from all detached focus on his business to softening. He wraps me in his arm and exhales.

"I'm sorry. There isn't a fire anywhere or nothing that can't wait. We just had a scene and I don't want to rush off. I got caught up. All I want to do is spend time with you." His lips crush against mine, and he threads his fingers through my hair, deepening the kiss. It makes me feel like I am precious and cared for, instead of making me want to run out the door.

"I understand if you do have something urgent. I'm not one of those women to call you a million times or whine about you working late. I work late."

That's an understatement. My email says I'm available until five unless it's an emergency, but I usually eat dinner at my desk, and my car is the last in the parking lot most of the time.

"I know that about you," Noel says. "It's only..." He stands, paces in front of the bed and spins. "Do you want to go for a walk? I'll grab to-go cups of coffee."

"Okay."

"Good."

We finish getting dressed and are out the door a moment later. The resort is quiet, kind of like nobody is here.

"There was a special breakfast in town today, a fundraiser for the art gallery. Several guests have gone to that. The place is going to be packed tonight for the party."

A quiver of excitement rolls through me. I can't wait for this play party.

Downstairs, Rosa smiles warmly at us. "Good morning, Mr. Brennon, Miss Burkholder."

"Good morning, Rosa. Is everything well?"

"Yes, we are right on schedule. Can I help you with anything?"

"I was going to grab coffee from the kitchen."

"Let me." Rosa smiles.

I don't know if I can get used to Noel having helpers do whatever he wants, but that's the perk of having money. There's nothing wrong with that. I work with the grossly overpaid every day. So why am I feeling...weird...about it now?

I frown trying to puzzle it out. Noel takes my green cloak from the hook and holds it open for me.

I put my arms through the velvety sleeves. "Thanks."

"You're welcome."

He puts his coat on and plops a hat on my head. I'm sliding my feet into boots when Rosa appears.

"Here. Two coffees to go."

"Thank you, Rosa. You're amazing."

"Have a good time." Rosa waves.

"Ready?" Noel opens the door.

"I think I am." It's the only honest answer I can give him.

He takes my gloved hand in his, leading me outside, fresh snow on the ground

Noel takes my arm and we follow the path. I'm waiting to let him speak because he seems lost in thought. I sip my coffee. Noel guides me around the back of the building, snow crunching under our boots, through a winding path that would take me right to my Gran's back door if I veered off. Frosty air makes my cheeks sting.

"Last March, I started to take a cooking class."

"Okay." I bite back the laughter that wants to escape because Noel looks serious; his tone is grave, but it's not what I expected.

He leans on the snow-dusted fence that leads to a small garden, his shoulders hunch.

"Growing up, my mom was determined that us boys would learn to cook and look after ourselves. She didn't want our partners to be maids."

"Good mom."

"She's the best. But when I married, Clarie did all the cooking and when she passed...I didn't know what to do...with anything but suddenly my cooking skills had disappeared. My brother Evan suggested I take these classes last year."

"I eat takeout more often than I cook," I admit.

"No judgements, that's not where I'm going with this...the classes were a way to get me out and around other people, to remind me that life was still going on. But what I realized, is how much time I missed while my wife was in the kitchen cooking for me or our family and friends, and I was so focused on ironing out the next big contract or chasing the next big acquisition for a firm that didn't care about me, despite how many hours I gave them."

That's the nature of big corporations. I know this, and you kind of have to accept it and be in it for the love or money. In my case, it's a little of both, but the thrill I find in my work is what keeps me there.

"Did your wife mind?" It was a dumb question, but I feel like I have to fill the silence somehow, and not asking something about his wife feels like I'd ignore what he's shared with me.

"That she did the cooking and I worked? No. But she did mind the missed anniversary dinners and how often I'd get interrupted at home. I wasn't always a good husband."

He takes my arm and leads me around the garden, circling back to the resort.

"When you asked if we could talk now, I realized I had a choice. I could be the former me, the one who thought everything was a crisis, or I could be the new me, who knows very few things are actually a crisis. I chose to be the me who spends hours in the kitchen cooking."

"Do you really?" It makes me smile.

"Yeah, I do. What did you want to tell me, Holly?"

I know this is the perfect moment to tell him about what I do and maybe even who I am, but he is so serious, and what he shared was so personal it seems so trivial to bring up what I do for a living.

"After my Gran passed, my family made this pact not to spend Christmas together. At least, I thought it was an agreement, but being here, taking this time away, has made me realize I'm the one who said no to spending Christmas with them. Like, if I couldn't have it how it was, I didn't want it."

This is more vulnerable than telling him how I spend my nine-to-five or nine-to-nine.

"What about being here made you realize that?" Noel brushes my arm.

"Being here, slowing down. It's finding peace because you're relaxing in the Parlour or walking into the dining room and smelling cinnamon or turkey. It reminded me of the good parts of Christmas, which I want to repeat with those I love."

"Happy to be of service." Noel flashes me a grin.

"This has been my favourite coffee date."

"Now, who is the easy one to please?" Noel loops his arm through mine.

I laugh. "I don't consider myself difficult."

"At tonight's party, how do you feel about ice and wax play?"

"I don't have experience with either. I'm open to trying it." The thought of hot wax covering my body is appealing. I'm not sure about the ice part of the equation, but there must be some kind of appeal to it, and it is Kinkmas.

"Good. I can't wait to play with you tonight, Holly."

My cell rings from my pocket, and I fish it out. Stella's number flashes on the screen.

"Why don't I leave you to it, and I'll go see what needs my attention? I'll text you if I'm free for lunch."

"Sounds good."

He holds the door of Vixen's Paradise for me, and I step into cozy warmth, the score of a Broadway musical being played on the piano.

"Good. See you soon." He cups my nape, his lips brush mine, then he's deepening the kiss, and I'm twining my tongue with his. He breaks the kiss, leaving me bereft.

"Be good."

"Yes, Noel." I grin and watch him go behind the reception desk to his private oasis. I hang up my cloak, take off my boots and walk into the Parlour. The room is filled with people lounging and talking.

"Hey, Holly!" Rick calls me over to their small group.

"Hello."

"Are you ready for tonight?" Cat asks.

"Yeah, can't wait."

"I can," Kai grumbles from where he is kneeling beside Pauline's chair.

"Oh, you'll like it," Pauline says, ruffling his hair.

"Sit and hang out with us." Rick pulls out a chair.

I sit, my cousin's phone call forgotten, as I lose myself in good company and anticipate my last night at Vixen's Paradise.

18

"Damn."

"Hell yeah it's amazing," DJ Flexmight calls from where he's setting up on the stage by the dance floor. The big guy is built like a quarterback and is dancing to the beat that fills the room.

"Love me a theme," Rosa says, passing me with a rolling cart filled with candles. She's filling the empty baskets that are waiting on metal stands.

Vixen's Paradise might have started as a flung out there wild idea but standing here in the luxe play space that is transformed into a kinky winter wonderland, I grin stupidly, like a proud ringmaster.

My mouth goes dry, thinking of Holly as my guest and I run my knuckles over the leather spanking bench, picturing her here, her ass bared for me, because my pet has a spanking coming tonight.

Taking out my phone, I fire off pics to my brothers and wander through the Ice side of the room; soft blue lights cascade from above bathing the space in a cool ethereal glow.

Threads of light shimmer within them, twinkling. Buckets sit expectantly, waiting to be filled with ice.

The murmur of voices are by the doors, guests eagerly waiting to be waiting in.

"Not bad, eh?" Axel strolls in from the orange and red side of the room. He moves a stand that brims with candles of different sizes and colours, all body safe, waiting to be lit.

"It's fucking amazing."

"Help me move this table, I don't like how close it is to the kneeling box."

Taking one end of the table that's covered in a red, glittery tablecloth, we move it closer to the wall.

"That's better," Rosa says and grabs UV black light toys from her cart and arranges them on the table, an invitation for guests to create wearable art.

It pays to have a trusted team around you because there isn't anything I can fault in this space and we're ready to let guests in.

But needing to do something with the anticipation coursing through me, I try to lift the medical table.

"Yeah, okay we can move it half an inch." Axel comes to help me, lifting the locks for the brakes even as he shakes his head at me.

I go to move the medical play table because it's slightly in the main area.

"Sorry. The place looks fantastic, Axel, honest."

"I'm looking forward to playing tonight."

"So am I."

"Yeah, you deserve it Noel."

We fix the table and Axel stands next to me, both of us lost in our thoughts of what the other's been through.

"The other Dungeon monitors are chilling in the back room and I'm playing at the last hour."

"Boo," Rosa calls out with a grin.

"More time for me to gather ideas to use on you, sub of mine."

"The crowd sounds like they're getting impatient." But I don't move, drinking in the scene.

"They have fifteen more minutes," Axel says.

"Got to keep them on their toes." My phone buzzes. "See you soon. Thanks you two, for all of this."

They wave me off and I give the DJ a quick handshake, slip through the door to a tiny staff area, waving at our Dungeon monitors for the evening. In the hallway, I take out my phone.

"Evan, what is it? I'm a little busy."

"Winterhaven Farm is asking for half a million more."

The words hit like ice water. Half a million.

"We can afford it," I say, jaw tightening. No point dragging it out—we want that land.

"Brent's drawing up the new offer. You want to see it before it goes over?"

I shake my head even though Evan can't see it. "No. I trust him."

"Good. This is big, Noel. Feel free to crack a smile."

"I'm smiling," I tell him.

"I'm going to go celebrate. Are you going to celebrate with that girl you met?"

"Woman, and yes, I am." I take a seat in the empty dining room.

"Good. See you soon." Evan hangs up.

A project I set out to create has come to fruition and though my brother might celebrate, a wave of emptiness sweeps through me.

I've long since known that I am more energized by the pursuit of something than the actual having of it.

My chest tightens, unbidden, with the thought of Claire.

She loved helping to decorate Sinful Bites when Evan first opened the restaurant but never wanted to play.

"I want to keep that private," she'd say, though occasionally we'd go to a club and play in a private dungeon.

She never wanted to be out in the open as a submissive, but at home our D/s flourished.

I'll always miss her.

But he thought of telling Holly about the sale of the neighbouring farm heats my blood.

I don't know what she does for a living but my instincts tell me that she'll get the relief and excitement that comes when you finally get that person to sign on the dotted line to give you what you want.

Laughter breaks my solitude from the hall, guests have started to make their way to the Dungeon. Pauline's tall frame is clad in a latex suit and she waves at me from her group across the room.

Are you ready? I text Holly.

Coming down now.

My palms are sweaty on the banister as I wait at the bottom of the stairs.

Catching sight of her...

Damn.

Fuck.

The way that corset hugs her breasts and the short, sheer black skirt clings to her hips is divine. She tucks a piece of hair behind her ear and smiles when her eyes meet mine.

"Tonight, I'm the luckiest man in the entire world." I offer her my arm.

Her long hair is in a loose braid, flowing down her back and her pair of black stilettos completes the look and makes me want to throw her over my shoulder, caveman style.

"Good evening, Mr. Brennon."

"Good evening, Holly."

And because I need to touch her, I lift her off the bottom stair and she giggles as I twirl her around and capture her lips in a bruising kiss, groaning into her mouth.

"This is going to be a good fucking night."

"I can't wait!" She runs her palm down my shirt, hovering above my belt and my cock twitches at the lustful grin on her face.

"This way, my Pet."

Her cheeks pinken just a tad and I set her on her feet and guide her to the dungeon.

The cries of guests as they indulge, the sweeping neon lights that cast bright spots on her creamy skin, all of it is a festive kinkish affair and my pulse races.

"Dance?" She pulls me a step towards the stage.

"You got it." Though I can't remember the last time I've danced but Holly grinds against me and I pull her close.

"This place is stunning." Holly brushes her lips against mine, tilting her hips.

My cock throbs against my leathers and I cup her ass, wanting to be even closer to her.

"Thank you. My team is the best."

She drapes her arms around my shoulders and we are lost in the beat, matching each other beat for beat. Her hips sway and I dry thrust into her; she giggles and I press her closer against me.

"So what's the plan?"

"I give you such a good night you agree to go to dinner with me on the second of January."Her smile wavers, she touches her neck as if to feel for the collar that isn't there."Noel, I..."

"I know," I whisper into her ear. "You don't want long-term commitment, but we did agree we'd see where it goes and that's all I'm asking for."

That kind of makes me a liar because I want more than that. I want to claim her for mine and have her forever.

She dances away from me for a beat, then spins back, grabs my waist and grinds against me in step to the music.

I laugh and match her step for step.

I'm committing to memory how free she looks right here, with her head tilted to the lights, her palms cupping my ass cheeks, the feel of her breasts against my chest.

The music shifts to something slower and with my hands on her hips, whisper into her ear.

"That was a great warm up. And I hope you're warmed because it's time to cool you down."

"Is it?" She bites her lip, her eyes are bright with arousal and I'm damn hungry for her.

"Yes." I lead her over to the ice side of the room where a bench is free.

"Do you remember you're owed a spanking?"

"I might." The corners of her mouth lift up in the most adorable way and I can't help but lean in and kiss her.

My mouth slams into hers. I kiss her long and hard, a kiss that takes all my breath and makes my balls feel like they're going to erupt from the heat.

"Oh yes, you came last night and you weren't supposed to. Remove your skirt and hop up on the bench."

Holly grins, wiggles out of her skirt, and sets it on a cart. Her red panties barely cover her ass.

She hops up on the bench. "Now what?"

"Now I get to spank you and you're going to hold ice cubes while I do." From the nearby stand, I grab ice and press two cubes into each of her palms, curling her fingers around them.

"Ow! Cold! So cold!" Her eyes close and a shudder rolls through her body. I slide my palm down her back, dragging a slow circle around her ass. Her skin is hot and a contrast to the cool ice.

"If you drop those while I am spanking you, you don't get to orgasm all night." I spank right in the centre of her ass and she twitches under my hand.

"No!" But it's a fake protest. She squeezes her fists closed around the ice, a rivulet of water runs down her wrist

Picking up her arm, I lick up the trail of water and her eyes blaze into mine as she trembles.

"Yes, Holly. Do you accept this punishment?" I cup her nape, pulling her against my chest and she sighs against me.

"Yes, Noel."

"Good girl. On the bench, please."

Rolling her hips as she strides over, she gets on the bench, propping herself up on her elbows.

She shakes her ass at me, and my cock throbs.

I wish for a moment I could pick up a flogger but we only agreed to hand-spanking.

"Gorgeous." I slap my palm against her ass and she giggles.

I pick up another ice cube from the bucket. I run my fingers along her inner thigh holding the ice cube between my fingers, rubbing it along her skin, her body twitches under my palm as goosebumps raise.

"Noel!" she shrieks.

"Do you like this?"

"It's...cold! But yes, keep going."

I run the ice cube over her panty-clad ass, between her ass cheeks. I nudge her legs open, so I can see the red strip of fabric covering pussy. Leaning down, my nose brushes the damp heat between her thighs.

Her scent hits me—tangy, intoxicating—and I drag my tongue slowly over the fabric, tasting her through the lace

I lick her pussy over the fabric, setting off a whole body tremble.

Fuck.

I can't get enough of her smell of how she tastes, of her submission.

"That'll be later." I roughly glide up to her ass and run the half melted ice cube along her waistband of those lacy panties, the melting drip leaving wet marks across her skin.

She jerks away, a squeal escaping her mouth.

Her brows are furrowed and her expression is so damn adorable.

I chuckle and kiss her forehead as she flings her legs out, trying to kick me.

"Be a good girl and stay still. Or I can cuff you?"

"I'll stay still." Her green eyes flash as she glares at me.

Letting go of her thigh, I draw a circle over her ass with the half melted ice cube, covering every inch of her gorgeous globes.

"Five swats on each cheek. Count for me, Holly."

I bring my hand back and let it land, the heat of her skin burning my palm with a hard, satisfying thud.

"One, Noel."

Her breathy voice sets my pulse racing, I bring my hand down harder across the other cheek.

"Two!" She presses her ass into my hand and that thrills me, sends a shiver of excitement racing down my spine.

I rub the spot I swatted in a tight little circle, until the tension in her shoulders has gone. Then without warning, I lay the next three spanks down, alternating cheeks and she calls out the numbers, as fast as they land.

"Five! Noel!"

"Good girl." I'm so touched by her trust in me that I swallow over a sudden lump in my throat.

Never did I ever think I'd find a submissive who I wanted something more with than casual play.

But I did and she's mine.

Even if she's not ready to admit it yet.

She wiggles on the bench, her hips rising up, offering me her ass.

"Very good girl." My palm comes down hard on her right cheek, twice ."Six. Seven," her voice trembles in a half moan.

"Is this turning you on, Pet?" I pinch her left ass cheek, slide down her waistband and skim my fingers through her slickness, making her shiver.

"You are very, very wet."

"Yes." Her breathless cry rings out as desperation and it makes my cock throb with the need to be buried in her sweet pussy.

"How are those ice cubes?"

"Still holding them," Holly says. Her voice is husky and syrupy with arousal.

I rub small circles between her shoulder blades. She sighs and puts her head down on her arms.

My hand trails back down to her ass.

With a lift of her hips and a long mewl, her ass rises to meet my hand.

My hand covers her ass in a quick three beats rhythm.

"Eight!"

I grin, pausing. "I think you missed some. But I'll give you more."

"Yes, Noel!" Her voice is like honey. I can't wait to ravish her completely.

The sting in my palm deepens as I land more spanks crack across her skin.

"Nine! Ten." She pants, whimpers, and twists on the table, as if she's trying to dislodge the ache in her ass.

I stroke her hair, lifting her up from the table. "Good girl, Holly. You took that very well for me. How's the ice?"

"Cold. And gone?" She wipes her palms on my shirt.

I laugh and kiss her because I have to feel her lips under mine right this hot second.

She kisses me back with fervour like she doesn't want this moment to end either, and I'm encouraged.

My chest tightens thinking of never seeing her again.

I hold her close to me and take control of the kiss, slowing down the pace.

My lips press against hers, and I slowly take in her bottom lip, nibbling it gently.

I could look into her big emerald lake pools forever. "Come."

When she steps down, she grabs a wipe and cleans off the table. I pick up her skirt, and she takes it, throwing it on.

"Good girl," I tell her because I can, because it makes her blush a little under the lights.

My gaze wanders over the scenes that are happening in the room, but I don't linger on them because all I care about is the woman next to me.

"What now?" Holly asks.

"Now it's time to warm you up," I throw my arm around her shoulders and lead her to the hot side of the room.

"You're going to play with fire?" Her fingernails glide along my shirt, driving me wild.

"We're going to play with fire, baby."

19

HOLLY

"I'm already burning, aching for you." My insides are buzzing with the high of pleasure drunk which explains why i said something so ridiculous. I hold my breath, my heart beating, almost fearing his response.

But with the way he spins me to face him, his grip firm, his dark eyes banked with heat, he slants his lips over mine and kisses me.

Scenes are happening all around us, the crack of leather through the air, the buzz of a violent wand, the cries and whimpers and laughter of guests but all of that fades as he kisses me, my pussy throbs with another fresh wave of want.

My skin is ablaze with heat from the spanking. The echo of Noel's palm, the impact, spread out through my whole body.

"That's what I wanted," Noel says breaking off the kiss, his eyes glint with need.

Noel's firm palm on the small of my back increases the blaze. My cheeks are scalding...with embarrassment? No, with the thrill of being with this man.

He grabs a small pail of ice from one of the stations, taking it over to the fire part of the room. The whole Dungeon is gorgeous tonight, I feel like I've stepped into the pages of a fantasy because this place is perfect for wintry kink exploration. The smell of candle wax is thick in the air, reminding me of church and it makes me remember my first impression of this place.

"Can't wait for this," Noel mumbles.

A Dom has just finished his scene, wiping down the medical table. We wait as he does.

He shakes Noel's hand but I don't hear their conversation because a thrill of fear has me frozen to the spot, my stomach in knots.

"Holly, it's our turn now." He pats the medical table, beckons to me, and somehow my feet move. It's like I'm stepping into the abyss, I don't know what is ahead but nervous anticipation has me rubbing my shoulders, though I'm not cold.

Noel takes a step in front of me, and my breath catches as he lifts my chin in his thumb and index finger and his other arm wraps around me, his hand slides down to my sore ass and I yelp as he kneads the tender flush.

Grinding his hips against mine, his rock-hard erection pushes into me; I let out a whimper as my knees buckle.

"Undress for me, Holly." He rubs his thumb across the bottom of my chin.

My nipples bead and I tremble with want.

My tongue forms the words, "Yes, Sir," and I jump back as if I've been burned.

It's been so many years since I uttered that honorific and I swore I wouldn't do that again. But Noel has shown me I can trust him. That he is as much of a gentleman as he is a Dom.

My fingers tremble as I work the fastener off of the corset. I bought this for the trip to Mexico and I'm thrilled it's getting a new purpose; the silky fabric slides off my skin, freeing my breasts.

"Gorgeous." Noel cups my breasts, lifting them and pressing his thumb into my nipple.

I bite my lip.

"Want me to lose the shoes?"

"Yes. Your toes curl before you come and I want to see them." I swallow a lump in my throat. The heat in his gaze sears me. I step out of the stilettos and leave them beside my clothing, the floor cool under my bare feet. Noel takes my hand and helps me onto the table. The sheet is cool against my back.

"Ready?"

"Yes, Noel."

"I want those hands restrained." He raises an eyebrow.

"Yes, please." My belly tightens in a knot of anticipation, a shiver traveling my arms.

Noel takes my right hand, cuffs it to the table, walks around, and does the same to my left. "Comfortable?"

I stretch a little, testing the restraint. The cuff is velvet-lined and soft against my skin.

"Yes."

"You tell me if it's too tight."

"I will."

He turns to the table, picks up a bottle of oil, and squirts some between his hands.

As he starts to massage my shoulders, his hands coming down to cup each breast, I'm taken back to that day in the spa.

My breath snagged when his fingers grazed my stomach, then lower. Every nerve lit up, every ounce of me screaming yes. this is what I've been missing, what I've been aching for in a Dom...but I decided that a relationship wasn't a possibility.

"Oooh!" I exhale as Noel brushes his slickened hands across my stomach, down my legs and I squirm as he tickles the soles of my feet.

"I remember how ticklish you are." His voice is rich with amusement.

"Every inch of you is covered." He pimples his fingers around my belly button and it makes me giggle. "Time for fire. You ready?"

"Yes." My fists clench, a thrill of fear raising all my nerve endings.

"Here we go." Noel hovers a purple candle over my torso, and I turn my head as he lights it.

"Let's test out how hot you find it."

My mouth goes dry and I swallow hard, wondering if it's going to hurt.

"This is a bad time to tell you I'm sensitive to heat."

Noel's lips purse, and his eyes darken. "Exactly the reason for a test. Thank you for telling me. Are you okay for me to proceed?"

"Yes."

Noel holds the candle high above my leg.

I startle as the first droplets of wax fall and drip onto my skin, spreading warmth.

He does it again, his gaze glued to my face. This time, he holds the candle closer to my skin.

I jump at the sudden heat but relax as it quickly lowers in temperature.

"I like it."

"Good." Noel rubs the wax spots on my left breast, rubbing it into my skin.

"Oooh!" I let out the moan because it sends waves of pleasure deep into my bones

"You are so fucking gorgeous. I love how I can see your pussy all shiny and wet." He pushes his hand against my inner thigh and I suck in a breath as he reaches behind him and lights the candle again and this time he brings the candle to right above my mound.

Purple droplets fall, and my hips arch, the fear mixing with pleasure and the way he's gripping my sensitive skin.

He slides his thumb down my mound, to my clit and rubs a slow circle around it as the wax cools further on my skin.

"Oh god."

"Yeah baby, it's fucking good."

Moving to my feet, he grabs a blue candle. He lights it, and I follow the flame as he holds it above me and lets the wax drip.

He moves the candle above my legs, painting me with trails of blue wax.

"That's my girl." He massages the wax into me. "You like this, don't you?"

"Yes," I purr at the warmth-infused touch.

Keeping one hand on my breast, he moves to my stomach with the purple candle. The wax pours onto my belly in a wide circles

But I jerk in the bonds, my hips rising, my belly more sensitive to the heat than my leg.

"Shh. You got this, Holly."

I watch the strings of wax decorating me like icing on a cake and exhale. I feel slightly chilled as the wax coats my torso, goosebumps rise across my skin.

Noel clenches his jaw as he studies me and flicks the candle, spraying my body with more droplets. HIs forearm flexes as he comes close to my cleavage, and raises the candle high above, and lets a single drop fall right between my breasts.

"Oh my god! Noel!" I cry out the words stuck in my throat.

"Yeah, you love this." He teases my mouth with a graze of his teeth as the wax drips in between my breasts.

"Yes! I love this," I cry out in agreement the heat infusing my body making me swoon.

He turns from me and comes back with a red candle.

Holding it above my breasts, Noel lets the wax drip close to my skin. I shiver as a flow of wax crosses my nipple.

"Gorgeous. You like this, Holly?"

"Yes, yes! Yes." The droplets of wax are warm and soothing. My head feels floaty, the room spins.

The wax builds up so slowly around my breasts, droplet by droplet, my breasts are covered.

Noel massages the wax into my breasts, and I am so hot with want and need I feel like I'm going to combust and break out through this shell of wax and my backs arches as if i'm trying to catch every droplet of wax.

He keeps building up a multi-coloured cone shape around my breast, and I can't predict where the droplets are going to hit.

The sensation ebbs a little as he continues, one long wax strand after another.

I feel like a painting in progress, and he's almost detached, as if he has to apply the next brushstroke.

My boobs are covered in blue, purple, and red. The strands are beautiful, and a part of me wants to stay in this wax cocoon forever.

Noel leans down swipes mouth with his tongue. his familiar taste flaring my want even more.

"May I blindfold you?"

My pulse hammers in my throat and I feel sweat break out at my back.

But this is Noel, and I trust him.

"Yes."

The silky blindfold settles over my face. I can't see through, but I can make out the light.

I jump as rivulets of wax splatter, unable to see where the wax will land on my body, heightening the sensation of dulled fire touching my skin.

Quicker than I can follow, ribbons of heat drape across my flesh.

A moan claws its way out of my throat, as my fists clench and another drop falls.

I hiss in surprise, but the next droplet burns sweeter than the last.

The Dungeon fades into a red blur, the throbbing arrowing to my pussy as the wax keeps coating my body, and Noel murmurs soft praise.

I moan, hips shifting restlessly.

"Beautiful." Noel drags his fingers through the cooling wax, as if he's painting my body, and he tugs my nipple, twisting it in his hand and I gasp.

"Now this."

A cool metal teases my cheek, shocking after all the heat.

"Is that..." I whisper, but can't finish the sentence.

"Is that the vibe?" I grin.

"Yes, Holly. I want you to come as I coat every inch of your body in wax."

He rolls the little vibe down my leg, and slips it in my pussy. My body clenches around it; I'm ready wet and ready.

Droplets of wax fall like a warm rain, competing with the hum.

The intense and pleasurable sensations pull my head in different ways.

the wax brush my skin in wider arcs, and the vibe increases its rhythm. A bead of wax lands on an uncovered spot on my nipple. At the same time, the vibrator roars to life at the strongest setting. I am so lost.

"Noel! I can't!" The words rip out of me as the vibrations make me soar, higher as if I'm floating outside of myself. Light flares behind my eyes and tears streak down my temples, the ragged panting is mine.

"Yes, you can, Pet."

Pet.

The honey way he caressed that endearment did it and the orgasm explodes through me, ripping me apart and I know I am screaming trying to get off the table but the hardened wax clings, anchoring me to the table.

"Good girl, shhh." His hot mouth is around my nipple and the vibe is pulled from between my legs, replaced with his fingers.

"You're so soaked. Give me another one, Holly." The gentle command in his voice makes me close my legs against his touch.

My clit is throbbing and super sensitive.

"I can't..." I moan, my voice hoarse.

"Yes you can." His thumb presses down on my clit. It's too much. The press of his thumb, the rock of his fingers, I can't help but give away to what he wants my body to do.

But my body doesn't care as it erupts in another wave of pleasure, enough to make my head spin and my breath pant, tears drip down my cheeks as I come, hard on his fingers.

"That's a girl. Good girl, Holly. That's exactly what I want." The orgasm sails me further over the crest, parting me from my own control.

"Please, oh please, Noel." I don't know what I'm saying; I blubber a spew of syllables flowing from my lips.

His thumb brushes my cheek and my throat closes, a fresh ache swelling.

"Holly, I'm here. I got you."

A sob tears from my chest, the wound that I've worked so hard to push down cracking me open.

The wound of not being wanted.

"Close your eyes." His voice is like a balm and I squint my eyes closed tight and feel the blindfold sliding off my face.

"There's those pretty eyes."

I blink, adjusting to the light.

Noel's face is close to mine, his dark gaze steadying me.

"Are you okay?" Noel traces my eyebrow and the light gentle touch calms my racing pulse.

I swallow. Exhale. Feel like I'm coming back to myself.

"I am because you are here."

"I'm not leaving." Noel kisses me so tenderly I want to cry again.

"Are you okay to continue?"

"Yes!" I want to see this through and push my jumbled emotions aside.

"Now it's time to clean you up." Noel grins, holding a credit card, flicks it like a magician."

"I'll try to be still."

"Do that."

The first scrape of the plastic card in the wax mound on my nipple brings me off the table.

Noel laughs, setting me back in position. "Not easy, is it?"

"I already got my orgasms."

"Yes, you did. Be a good girl and stay still; you might get more." His smile is so endearing I try to tighten my muscles to keep myself still.

The credit card digs into my skin as he scrapes the card along my breasts through the build up of wax

Noel swipes it across, the dull edge not painful but slightly ouchy. Tiny curls of wax lift from my skin.

My back arches, and I let out a half yelp half laugh.

"Noel, please..."

"Holly what is it?" His tone is all concern and his gaze searches my face.

"I don't like the scraping sensation." My throat tightens, I don't want to disappoint him and the emotions that the previous scene brought up are simmering under the surface.

"Hmm, I wonder if you'd like a comb. Want to give it a try," Noel's firm gentle touch along my jawline soothes me.

"Yes."

He turns to the cart, rummaging in his bag and shows me a thin comb.

"Go for it," my voice is thick and husky.

He lays it flat against my breast and scrapes down, a shudder ripples down my spine, this is less tense, the indentation the comb leaves feels pleasant.

"This is better.

"Excellent," he takes the comb across my belly and works it around in tiny circles and i try to stay still.

He continues to work and I hear the murmur of people close by us and wonder if guest have watched our scene.

The digging of the comb, lifts away the wax easily and he works it up to my left nipple, dragging it across my skin.

"That tickles!" I giggle, my shoulders shaking.

"Want me to keep going?

"Yes!"

The merriment in his eyes doesn't dull the heat as he keeps working the wax off my breast, the teeth of the comb sinking into my nipple and it sets me off into a complete giggling fit.

My body is shaking so hard, I snort, can't breath.

"What am I going to do with you?" His voice is teasing and he presses a kiss against my lips.

"The endorphins are doing things to me!" I sit up, thinking we are done.

"Stay right there Holly."

"Why?"

"Because I promised you more." He drops a kiss below my ear, his dark eyes staring into mine.

"And you think I can take it?" I lay back down against the table, but I'm smiling.

This man shows me his dominance in gentle, confident ways. Another dominant might say, "The scene isn't over until I say it is," but Noel has led me to where he wants me. I follow his lead because he's shown me I can.

I exhale, knowing that I can indulge and give him my submission even if it's for this short time.

This man has shown me all week that I can indulge and give my submission to him. He's not going to hold it over me.

He's going to treasure it and care for it and damn, how I want more of this.

Butterflies swarm my belly, thinking about tomorrow.

I want to see him beyond tonight.

Even if the idea of a new relationship is scary, I still want to try it.

"I want these legs spread even more." He's pushing up my thighs, so I am laid open and bare for anyone to see me.

"Gorgeous. Your pussy is coated in juices and i can't wait to taste it."

The flick of his tongue surprises me, his hot mouth covers my pussy and tingles race through my veins.

"Noel!"

He flicks his tongue over my clit, then he's sucking it, his teeth grazing it.

A coil of pleasure spirals itself tightly from my core, my thighs want to close around him but he grabs them, keeping them n place and i pant, my pleasure ramping up until I can't hold it back anymore.

The orgasm breaks through me in a gushing pressure that sends me soaring, leaves me shaking and breathless.

"Yeah, good girl, Holly," Noel praises, then his head is back between my legs and he's lapping through the aftershocks as I let out a low guttural groan.

I swallow a lump in my throat, those emotions are so close to breaking free.

When he comes up, I see his lips shiny with my juices and smell my arousal as he kisses me like he owns me, all deep and forceful in the best way.

"Good girl." He strokes my hair and I relax into his touch.

"Thanks," I whisper.

He rubs my arm, then uncuffs my right hand, checking my fingers for circulation.

"That scene was wonderful. Tonight was more than I ever expected." He unclasps the other cuff.

"Me too." My hands tremble.

He helps me off the table, and as he cleans up the space, I realize I don't want to get into my clothes.

"Here, Holly." Noel holds open a robe. I gratefully slip my arms into the soft, silky material. "Let's get you some food."

My legs are wobbly, but he guides me across the room to where there is food and a little seating area.

Sit." He holds a chair for me, hands me a bottle of water.

"Thank you."

"Are you okay here for a moment? I want to get us food."

The table is less than five feet away.

"I'm okay." I cinch the robe tighter and Noel brushes a kiss on my temple and goes over to the table.

I sip more water and try to get a hold of my racing thoughts.

I drink the water. Across from me, a woman is feeding her submissive ice cubes.

At the table next to me, a man is feeding his submissive on his lap.

"Here we are." Noel puts down a plate of finger foods.

I take a nibble of something, pop it into my mouth as Noel glances at me, his gaze intense. "How are you feeling?"

I chew, and to buy time, I take another pastry-wrapped morsel.

"That scene brought up emotions I didn't expect."

"Yeah?"

I keep eating, staring into nothing, until I exhale and push the plate away.

"Want to talk about it?"

"Maybe."

"Come here," Noel tugs me gently into his lap.

I lean back against his chest, tears pricking my eyes.

"For a long time, I have felt unwanted."

My voice catches on the admission, and I realize it's true.

"My ex din't even try. Not once.

"Oh, Holly." His grip tightens on me. He nuzzles my neck, and I blink back tears because I feel safe in his arms.

"I had an ex who took it too far. And you know about my father."

"Baby, that's a lot. You were so very good for me tonight." His praise eases the ache of my raw emotions and he wraps me in his arms, cuddling me against his chest.

"Thank you for giving me this experience tonight."

"You're welcome."

"Will you stay with me tonight?" I turn my head to see his face and his lips curve into a smile.

"Of course. Let's get out of here."

Slowly, I get to my feet and he leads me out of the party, nodding and smiling to his staff and guests.

It's a blur as we leave the super high colour of the party back to the rest of the place and back to my room, where Noel somehow got us inside.

I don't know how i'm sitting on the bed, but Noel is taking the robe off of me and fusing his lips against mine.

"Let's sleep, Pet." His gentle tone sets tears pricking at my eyes again but I follow his lead as he turns down the bed and I slip into the luxurious sheets.

The bed dips as Noel sits on the edge, taking off his dark-blue dress shirt.

I scoot up to my knees to help him. I trail my hands down his hard pecs.

"So handsome."

He grins and unzips his fly.

Not needing another invitation, I lean down and take his long cock all at once into my mouth. His taste is familiar. My tongue rolls under it as if I know exactly what's going to drive him wild.

And as I press my tongue to his balls, I realize I do.

It makes me giddy, and I put more of myself into it, sucking and rocking on my knees.

"That feels amazing, Holly." Noel holds my head, and he thrusts hard and fast into my mouth.

I open my jaw as wide as I can, and he increases his rhythm, his eyes close and I squeeze his balls, as he tilts into my mouth so hard it's an effort to keep my mouth on his cock.

"Holly!" he grunts out, a low primal cry.

His cum shoots into my mouth, hot and fast and using my tongue, I lap it all up, even as I'm swallowing. His cum is salty and musky, and I could lick him every single night.

I squeeze his muscled ass, not wanting this to end.

"Good girl." Noel twirls his fingers through my hair and I want to purr.

He leans back against the headboard and because I want to, because I absolutely need to show him...to give him my submission, I put my head on his thigh.

"Oh, Holly." He cups my face with so much tenderness my heart explodes. He strokes my hair and I bury my face in his leg, holding him tighter.

It's going to kill me, but I know it's better to leave Noel in Vixen's Paradise.

* * *

The work ringtone of my phone breaks into my cocoon of sleep, and I throw the blankets off me, reaching over Noel to the nightstand to grab it.

"Hello?"

"Holly, have you seen the news?" My assistant's voice is rung with worry, and I curse myself for being off-grid.

"No, Meg, what is it?"

"Xander Durand's kid broke his leg skating, and he's refusing to go back on set until the kid is healed."

"What?" My mind kicks into work mode, spinning with what i have to do to prevent this from becoming a crisis.

"Yeah. He made a social media post about it."

"I'm flying home tomorrow morning. I will call him."

"I tried and couldn't, but the producer said Durand better be there on Monday."

"Got it. Thanks, Meg."

Reality crashes back into me as my mind whirls, wondering how I am going to get Xander Durand to listen to me. He's snobbish and egocentric but also one of the first clients I signed that is making the agency gobs of money.

I scramble up and pull clothes on.

My client's show is currently number one in the rankings and he has to be in L.A. to resume shooting, no matter what.

I Google, "How long does it take to heal a broken leg?" and curse.

"Holly, can I help?" Noel snaps me back to the present.

"I have to...I have work to do. I'm going to leave in the morning."

I say this as much to myself as to him because I'm pretty sure I can't get a flight out tonight.

"I know. Can we spend this night together?"

My heart breaks because I want to, but I don't know what it will cost me if I say yes.

I have to look after my client and get back to the real world.

"I don't know...I have calls to make."

"Okay. You know how to reach me if you're done with your calls and want company."

"Yes, okay," I say.

"Holly."

I turn to look at him. He has his shirt back on.

"I used to be a workaholic, and there's nothing wrong with that. But I think having a balance of work and other things..." He raises an eyebrow. "Is a better way to do it?"

"Maybe," I whisper.

"Good luck with your phone calls."

"Thanks."

There is nothing more to say. I watch as he leaves, gently closing the door, and I stop myself from chasing after him.

Pressing Xander's number, I go to the tea service and put the kettle on, smiling as I remember Noel showing it to me on that first day, correcting me.

"Hello?"

"Xander, it's Holly. I'm sorry about your toddler, but you must show up on set."

"Fuck, Holly, I can't leave him," Xander says.

"Yeah, I know what that's like." I launch into my spiel, even as my heart is breaking.

20

NOEL

DECEMBER 30TH

With my head pounding, I throw on my dress shirt, determined to join Holly for breakfast.

Last night was intense, and she pushed away my attempts at aftercare. Even though I did send Rosa to check on her last night, I need to make sure she's okay this morning.

A flash of anger makes me grit my back molars.

"What?" I growl into the phone.

"Who pissed in your cereal?" Evan says, his tone is all cool amusement.

I pinch the bridge of my nose, trying to clear my head. With my bed empty next to me, I got no sleep.

Despite how many times I told myself that Holly just needs space and not to take her rejection personally, it still feels like cold water being thrown in my face.

In only a few hours, she'll be on a flight home.

"Noel, did you hear me?"

"You were talking about the contract with Winterhaven Farm. If there's a problem, get Brent on it."

"Like I was saying, Brent's on vacation for the next two weeks. The name is incorrect on the contract."

"Stella something, right?" I drudge the name from memory. The woman always sounded harried when I called her with a lot of noise in the background of kids crying. Maybe she misspelt her name in a rush or something.

"Right, that's who I thought owned the property. But that's not the name on Brent's offer sheet."

"So he made a mistake?"

"Yeah, or something weird is going on. Can you please fix it?"

I open the door to my private suite and take the stairs two at a time. "Okay, what's the name on the offer sheet?"

Maybe it's a simple fix, like missing an *l* or something, and I can fix it within an hour.

"Holly Burkholder."

"Say that again?" I stop mid-step. My stomach lurches, my grip tightness on the cool railing.

"Holly Burkholder. She has an Edmonton address."

It could be a different Holly, I tell myself, but my brain doesn't buy it and fury rolls through me but I try to push it away.

Why is her name on the contract?

"An address in Edmonton?"

"Yeah, I think it's a condo. Anyways, if I can email this to you, can you try to contact her? If we get it done today, we can celebrate at the party."

"I'll take care of it." I end the call and run back to the resort, to Rosa's desk and she looks up, flashing me a smile.

"Hi Noel, last night was amazing!"

"Hey, where's Holly?"

"She called for a ride. She's outside now. What's going on?"

"Got our signals crossed," I say to Rosa.

I push through the front doors, and the cold air immediately freezes my cheeks. I slip in my dress shoes as I race down the driveway, pushing away the anger. Holly is standing next to Martin's open trunk.

And she's wearing the cloak I gave her.

Martin catches sight of me and whatever he sees in my expression makes him close the trunk and hurry inside the car.

"Holly." I grit out her name.

Her shoulders hunch but she turns to me, her mouth set in a firm line.

"Noel, hey." She crosses her arms over her chest.

"What's going on?" I shove my hands in my pockets, they're freezing and it stops me from touching her.

"I'm leaving." Her eyes dart everywhere except my face.

"You weren't going to say goodbye?" My jaw tightens, as I say the words.

"We did that last night. Look, Noel, this has been nice, but..."

"But what?" The words are hard to get out.

"I was honest from the beginning. I told you I didn't know if I could have another relationship. What you've given me...we agreed to five days."

"Yes, we did, and they were the five best days I have had in a long time. But are you sure you've been honest from the beginning?"

She shakes her head and grabs the door. "I've got to go."

Despite spending all that time with her and knowing I want her, I don't know the little things about her. I don't know her favourite colour, what music she likes or how she handles conflict and I don't know what she does for a living.

"Are you a journalist?" I take a step closer.

"What?" Her brows furrow. "No!"

"Not out for a story to expose all this?" I gesture at Vixen's Paradise behind me.

"Noel, I wasn't pretending with you." She juts out her chin. It's cute that she's angry.

"I didn't say you were. Only that you weren't honest with me."

"I told you, I don't like telling people what I do for a living."

"How do you know Stella Kent?"

She throws her head back as if I've slapped her and grabs at the car door.

"Or are you trying to pull off some kind of scam?"

"No scam. Stella is my cousin, okay? I gotta go. I can't talk about this." She stares at the ground, still pulling the door.

"Holly, if the scene last night was too intense, we can talk about it."

She toes the snow with her boo and I want to push her up against the car and kiss her, I want her to look at me.

"The scene was fine. This isn't about the scene."

"Holly, I don't want to part like this." My voice is hoarse.

"I have stuff I have to deal with, and I can't..."

"Can't what?" I place a hand on her arm.

"Talk to you any more about this or anything. I got to go, Noel." Her voice breaks and she sharks off my arm.

The emotion in her voice twists my heart, and my anger fizzles away.

"Fine. Holly, call me later, okay?"

"Okay." But I see by the set of her chin that she's made up her mind and isn't going to call.

She slams the door shut.

And I stand there, until the car is out of view.

Even though I'm freezing, I walk along the trail that takes me to the farm next door.

If Stella is her cousin, then the old lady who owned it is probably their grandmother, or a great aunt or some relative. The safe place Holly had to escape her abusive father.

But why did she come to Vixen's Paradise?

I shove my hands in my pockets, hunching my shoulders against the wind, whipping at my back.

How did she know that Vixen's Paradise was next to her grandmother's place? Holly is bright. She must have researched what was happening with properties in the area. If she had done a holdings search on Brennon Consortium, the list of properties we own, Vixen's Paradise, and Sinful Bites would have shown up, and she would have seen the address.

Speaking of which, I call Theo once I'm in the warmth of Vixen's Paradise, sitting at a dining table with a cup of coffee and a shot of whiskey.

"Hi, Noel."

"Hey, Theo. So tell me again about this café you found."

"You sound awful. What's wrong?"

I could never hide anything from Theo. He's the quietest of us but keenly observant.

So much for trying to distract myself from Holly's leaving.

"The woman I played with this week just left. I really like her, Theo."

"Did you tell her that?"

I grin at his practicality. "Yes, but I think she's scared. Her ex-boyfriend just dumped her, and her previous serious relationship ended badly."

"Tell her again, then. Maybe she needs to see that you mean what you say."

"Yeah."

I contemplate showing up at Holly's door, but I don't know if that would be a dramatic gesture or a scary stalker move.

"And you are a widower. You must be scared, too."

The words hit me right in the gut. I throw back what's left in the shot glass.

"I'm scared, but she's worth being scared for. I want to see her again."

"Then go for it. That's what you're always telling me."

I laugh gruffly. Theo had a bad relationship that should have ended before it did and hasn't taken a risk since. s forever to make a decision, but once he does, his mind is made up and unchanging.

"True. The café, run it down for me."

"Technically it's a diner."

"Okay, but it's not a lifestyle café, all right? Just a normal everyday place where clothing isn't optional, it's required."

Theo supports our properties with his tech wizardry and know-how but he's super private.

"Where is this cafe-diner-very-clothes located?"

"It's in a little town called Rising Harbour. I was visiting a friend's winery. My car broke down. I went into this café and met this woman."

"Oh?" I grin.

"It's not like that, Noel." Theo brushes me off.

"I can hear it in your voice," I tease him.

"And she told me the café is for sale."

"And you want to buy it?"

"Yes."

"You want to buy a diner in the middle of nowhere, about four hours from where you live, and it has nothing to do with the very attractive woman who runs it?"

"How do you know she's attractive?"

I laugh. "What do you need me for?"

"Can you handle the sale for me? I don't know how much they are asking, but I want the building it's in, too."

I smile as I drain the last bit of my coffee. "Let me guess, she lives there."

"Noel, look. I have the money, and I can do this good deed."

"What's her name?"

Theo sighs. "If I tell you her name, will you help me buy the place?"

"Yes."

"Callie."

"Are you bringing this, Callie to the New Year's Eve party?"

"No! I mean, I can't. It's not like that, Noel."

"Okay, send me everything you have on the café, and I'll get to work."

"Thanks. You should go get this girl of yours."

"She's not mine."

"But you want her to be."

In a choir of laughter and conversation, guests enter the dining room, and I stand, moving out of the space.

"Yeah, I do."

"See you in a few days."

"Bye."

Turning the corner, I see Axel leaning over Rosa's desk, locking lips with his submissive and my heart tugs in a tiny flash of jealousy which I stamp down, I want my friends to be happy.

I just want what they have.

"Hey." I lean against the wall.

Rosa jumps back, her chair scraping against the floor. "Sorry."

I wave off her apology.

Axel grins. "Great party last night. Everything's been cleaned up, and the Dungeon is back to normal."

"I know. Thanks for all of your effort in making it work."

"Anything for you, Noel." Axel slaps me on the back.

"Rosa, can I have Holly Burkholder's address?"

Rosa smiles and taps on her keyboard. "Sure. Want me to text it to you?"

"Yes."

At the door to my private suite, I pause. "And Rosa? Can you book me the next flight out for Edmonton?"

"I can do that," Rosa says, grinning as she taps on her keyboard.

"Good for you, Noel." Axel reaches over and squeezes my shoulder.

I nod and go through the door, taking the stairs two at a time. I have to pack.

Theo is right. I have to go tell Holly that she is mine.

21

HOLLY

DECEMBER 31ST

"Holly, go home. It's New Year's Eve," Mr. Preston, my boss, says, leaning against my door. His voice softens and he glances to my couch. "You've been here since last night."

My rumpled blankets give it away along with the empty coffee mugs.

Managing the crisis needed my full attention but it also kept my mind off the broken, haunted look on Noel's face when we said goodbye.

If I went home, I knew those emotions I've been pushing down would swallow me whole and I came close after the scene at the Fire and Ice party when Noel cuddled me agains his chest, the warmth of his touch and his soft praises soothing me bringing me back to earth.

The chaotic work has helped me push away those overwhelming emotions because i can't afford to break.

"I won't be much longer," I tell him.

"Good job with Xander Durand. I thought I was going to have a heart attack."

"You and me both."

"That was a great save." Mr. Preston raps his knuckles against my door. "See you next week."

"See you in the New Year."

With him gone, I'm back to my solitary silence but my eyes are glazing over so I close down my system, gather the files on my desk, and lock them in my cabinet.

Getting my client on the plane to L.A. with his leg-in-a-cast-toddler had been a feat. It took hours of me on the phone, cajoling and promising. Yesterday, just off the plane myself, I had to meet him at the airport to make sure his butt was in that first-class seat while Meg and my other assistant, Charlie, worked to find a nanny in L.A. and a doctor that would follow the toddler's recovery and then we came back to the office, making sure everything was set once they landed.

Wincing, I close the blinds on my windows, my body is starting to feel the effects of the play party; I know I can't stay here forever.

I'm proud of the work I do here. I know it doesn't seem like much to be a hand-holder, but this is the career I wanted to pursue.

Helping to make people's dreams come true is something that drives me. It fulfils me, meeting that quest for bigger i had since i was a child.

And yes, sometimes I'd like a break from the pressure and the stress of the job, but nothing is worth losing everything I've worked so hard for.

I pick up my briefcase. Throw on my favourite pair of boots. Since returning from Vixen's Paradise, I have been going nonstop.

If ending things with Noel was the right thing to do, why do I feel so lousy?

I stab at the button for the elevator, biting my lip to keep focused. Inside the car, i close my eyes, but swallow a sob.

Maybe there was another way I could have handled it.

Yeah, i could have told him i was Stella's cousin. But if I had told him that right from the start, would he have seen me as anything other than an opponent? Its' a flimsy excuse considering the Brennon Consortium gave us that half million we asked for without any pushback.

Every day in this office, I want to be seen as fierce and independent, cool and smart, someone you can't push around and someone who doesn't give in easily. You could say that I spend my working days in the role of opponent.

Noel didn't know who I was, and he flirted with me on the plane. He treated me as if I was a sexy woman, someone like-minded who played in the lifestyle. That made me feel good, sexy and wanted.

His attention made me feel attractive in a way I never had before. And how he touched me set my skin on fire.

With him, I was able to be vulnerable enough to allow him to help me explore a fantasy I had never voiced to anyone.

My cheeks flame at the memory of being his Pet, the firm touch of his palm on my head. The way the plug felt in me.

But I could do that with Noel because I took off the armour I wear every day.

So no, if he knew the real me, none of that would have happened.

We would have been two lawyers duking it out over a negotiation that dragged on and on. Maybe we would have found our way to a glass of wine, but it wouldn't have been five days of sizzling play.

I push through the glass doors to the freezing cold air. And maybe it's because he didn't know who I was that when I asked for more, the Brennon Consortium simply accepted the counteroffer.

Like I told Noel, sometimes things can be over-negotiated.

My apartment's tub is nowhere near as luscious as the one at Vixen's Paradise, and I really should have taken that tub home.

But it's not the tub I should have taken home, it's the owner.

The elevator doors open, and I swipe at my watering eyes. It must be the air freshener in the hallway.

At my door, I unlock it, kick off my shoes and hang up my coat. My condo is cozy and my sanctuary, but it feels like I'm standing somewhere cold...and lonely.

On my counter is one of those bottles of wine that I was given at Christmas.

I took this one home because it's from a winery near Niagara Falls, and the picture on the bottle is stylized in gold.

I thought maybe my Mom would like it. Finding a glass in the cupboard, I pour myself a generous helping.

Taking my favourite take-out menu off the fridge, I'm hoping the place that makes the best spring rolls is still open.

I'm confirming my order when there's a knock on my door. It must be a neighbour because all guests are buzzed up.

The wineglass kind of bumps the doorknob as I check the peephole. My hand shakes, spilling wine onto my fingers.

A tremble rolls through my body and my heart throbs against the cage in my chest.

There, standing on my doorstep, hair all dishevelled, his shirt wrinkled is Noel. I open the door.

"Hi." That sexy grin of his lights up his chocolate eyes.

"Okay." That was a dumb thing to say, but my mind is scrambling to figure out why he is standing on my doorstep.

"Can I come in?" Noel goes to touch me, and stops, dropping his hand back to his side.

I move to the side, my throat dry.

"Why are you here?"

"I wanted to come yesterday but couldn't get on a flight. Do you know that the New Year's Eve flight was empty?"

"You're supposed to be at Sinful Bites with your brothers." Noel shrugs. "It's not the first New Year's Eve party I've missed. Can I come in, Holly?"

He strides past me into the middle of my living room, with my flat packed shelves i've never upgraded.

Noel runs his hand along my 1960s low couches. I had them recovered in a deep burgundy as a gift to myself after my first year of being a talent agent.

"It's nice," he says taking in the room.

"Yeah, it's okay."

Noel leans against the buffet table my Mom gave me and suddenlyI see things that make me cringe everywhere, like the Hello Kitty vase Stella gave me, a pair of Mickey Mouse ears from a trip to Disney, my favourite stuffy bunny from when I was a kid.

"It's good to see you."

"You only saw me yesterday." I cross my arms over my chest, but his words make me glow. I know I'm blushing.

"Yes, but I didn't get to have coffee with you this morning. I didn't get to feel your mouth on my cock."

My cheeks flame and my pussy throbs.

Suddenly, he's in front of me, radiating heat and sexy promise and it's too much.

"Noel, I don't...I can't."

"Holly, if you tell me to go, I will leave. The ball is firmly in your court. You can decide to contact me in a week or never. But I need to tell you, I want to be with you. I came here because I want to go into this New Year with you by my side." He cups my face in his palms, brushes his thumbs across my cheeks.

"You don't even know me," my voice cracks on the words.

"I know you are a strong woman who has been hurt in the past, and you're afraid of giving me your heart. I know your submission is like a fine whiskey, something to slowly savour and keep in the right conditions. I know I don't want you to tell me to leave."

"Noel, I'm so scared you'll resent how many hours I work. My clients are very needy, and I might have to drop everything because someone didn't get them the right dinner, and now they're walking off."

"Off of what?" Noel's lips twitch.

"Off set," I mumble. Last year, one of my clients had walked off the set because someone gave her a meat sub instead of the vegan wrap she ordered.

"I told you, I understand being glued to work. That's why I left it. I'm happy working with my brothers. I have enough in my life to keep me busy, Holly. I don't need you to wait on me."

"You say that now."

Hot tears fall down my cheeks. I want this so much. I want to believe that he is going to be there for me and not get frustrated because I keep cancelling dinner on him.

"I don't say things I don't mean. I'm scared, too." Noel runs his hand through his hair."Then why are you here?"

"Because I didn't get to kiss you this morning."

He leans down, and I don't pull away.

I rise and meet his mouth, before his hand snakes up to my neck and he kisses me so hard my lips buzz, sending my pulse galloping.

I clutch at his shirt and slip my hands under his shirt, caressing the skin over his pecks, needing to touch him.

He showed up for me.

That makes my heart dance in a pitter-patter, and I am lost in his kiss, my thoughts growing silent.

"There, that's better." Noel breaks off the kiss, holding me close.

"Is it?"

"Yes." He smiles so huge I can see his molars. Tilting my chin, he slants his mouth across mine.

I hiccup, trying to stop the tears when a knock on my door comes.

"Dinner," I explain. I practically run to the door.

I pay with my credit card, take the bag of food, and place it on the counter.

"Want to stay?" I take out two plates from the cupboard.

"Yes, I do."

"Noel..."

"You invited me to stay, Holly. You could have easily told me to go." He swallows the pace between us and takes a step, causing me to back into the counter.

I don't want him to go.

I want to wake up to this man every morning, even if I can't give him all of my nights.

"I want you to stay," my voice trembles.

Noel takes the plates from my hands and gently sets them on the counter.

"I'm not going anywhere, Holly, unless you tell me to. Not tonight, not tomorrow, not next year. I'm yours for as long as you want me."

He rests his forehead against mine and wraps me in his arms and now the tears flow, freely and I can't stop them.

22

NOEL

"Shush, my pet, I've got you." I kiss her forehead, and she leans into me, her tears soaking my neck.

Her hair is soft and shiny as I run my hands through it, while I rub circles on her back, until she stops crying.

"Hate crying," she says, sniffling.

"Noted. Better?" I lift her chin, searching her face. Her eyes are watery but bright, and her lips part, and I crush my mouth against hers, swallowing her moan.

My chest tightens, my cock aching as I press harder, needing to bury myself inside and make her mine.

Lifting her off the floor, she squalls as I cup her gorgeous ass and carry her down the hall, guessing the correct door.

"Noel," she breathes against my lips, the sound of a desperate plea and surrender as her fingers clutch the back of my neck, clinging to me while I lower her onto the bed.

"I'm here." I brace myself on my forearms, dragging my lips along her neck, to the curve of her ear.

She whimpers, her hips arching against mine.

"I want you inside me."

She yanks at the buttons on my shirt and then slides it off my shoulders, and my mouth never leaves hers. My hips grind against her, the hard press of my cock against my slacks.

I shove the fabric down her shoulders, fumbling in my urgency, but she takes over and gets it off.

"Noel, I need you!"

"You have me." My fingers work the clasp of her bra, and when it gives, her breasts spill free into my hands.

"So fucking gorgeous."

I bow my head and capture her nipple with my mouth, sucking hard, flicking the beaded nipple with my tongue.

She moans and I can't stop—licking, dragging my teeth, shifting to the other peak while she fumbles at my belt, tugging it open, then my fly. I let her strip me, never stopping the greedy worship of her breasts.

"Oh God, more, please!"

My balls tight, our naked flesh already slick, her fingernails trail down my back to my ass, and I yelp.

"You are so sexy," I tell her, breaking off the kiss. I trace her swollen lips as I thrust my hips into her soft body.

"You showed up for me." She lifts her hips, bruising her mound against my cock.

"Always. I will always show up." I kiss her deep, the fire between us threatening to consume me, but I won't give in, not until she's undone beneath me.

She spreads her legs wide with a small smile, and they come around me, grasping my waist. I shift her slightly so I have a better angle, and with a groan, I plunge into her.

She's soaking wet.

I close my eyes, savoring the tight heat of her pussy as she takes me in. Holly gasps when I tilt my hips, sinking deeper. And deeper. Until I'm buried in her, every inch claimed.

A hiss rips out of me, echoing off the walls. "I want to fuck you hard and deep," I growl into her neck.

"Yes," she pants, clutching my shoulders. "Do that."

Her sweat beads along her upper lip, her chest rising fast against mine as I drive into her, my cock sheathed in her pussy.

My vision blurs as I pound harder, faster.

"You're perfect." My lips drag over her throat, needing her taste. "Best damn present I've ever unwrapped."

A giggle explodes from her mouth, high-pitched and fucking adorable as she grinds on me, giggle taking me even deeper.

"That's it," I groan as her pussy pulses around me and gyrates against me, surging heat thorugh my viens.

"Please, Sir, harder," she cries out.

Like my nerves have exploded with the honorific, I swallow her news and pound into her, with long quick strokes that she meets, lifting her hips

I push back her thigh for better access and I piston into her and she wraps one leg around my back, driving harder into her slick pussy.

"Oh, I'm...yes...I'm going to come!"

Her face contorts, and I want to make her come undone because I remember how beautiful she looks as the orgasm hits her, and I can't wait to get her there. Blood roars in my ears, my heartbeat frantic.

"Please, Noel."

Never have I been so sure of anything in my entire life as I am sure that I don't want to live a second without this woman beside me.

Her arousal permeates the air and drives me to quicken my pace. The bed is slamming against the wall, and I don't care.

My balls are going to explode when she lets out a low, piercing mewl that makes me growl.

Mine.

"Holly, come for me now, sweetheart. Give me your orgasm."

She mewls, presses herself against me so we are skin to skin. Nothing is getting between us.

Shifting without breaking my thrust, I reach in between us and find her clit. At the touch of my thumb, it hardens to a swollen bud.

"I love you," I growl the words into her ear, but the way her pussy clamps, I know they hit their mark, and her pussy tightens around me even more.

"I love you, Noel!" Her orgasm rolls through her body, her pussy spasming on my cock.

"Fuck!" My seed releases into her in one hot spurt. We are both gasping for air, my heart beating overtime.

Holly kisses my nose, my mouth, my ear. "I love you," she repeats with confidence.

I suck in a lungful of oxygen, needing more air. Without detangling from her, I wrap her in my arms.

"I love you, Holly. So much."

She curls against me and laces her fingers through mine.

"I can't think of a better way to spend New Year's Eve."

"Me neither."

I know that whatever this year brings, it's going to be phenomenal with her by my side.

23

HOLLY

Noel rolls onto his back. His arm flings across the sheets. His eyes flutter open, and like the empty space next to him woke him up, his eyes flutter open, and he stretches his long frame, with his arms above his head.

He's in my bed.

This man has given me so much that I blink back tears. I never believed I would find someone who accepts me like he does, and seeing him here, in my bed the next morning, overwhelms me with emotion.

"Good morning, pet."

And like he lit off a fuse, wetness instantly pools between my legs when he says that. Noel props himself up and pats the space beside him and like an excited pup, I rush over, barreling into his side, flinging my arms around his neck.

"Morning. Sorry I had to take a phone call." I lick his collarbone. The taste of his skin tingles on my tongue, and I let out a soft moan as he plays with my hair, tugging it gently.

"I understand. All okay in your work world?"

"The usual chaos. But my client is happy, so I'm calling it a win."

"A good way to start the day," he pulls me down beside him and presses his lips against the column of my throat in a hungry caress and flows between my cleavage.

"You being in my bed is a good way to start the day," I tangle my fingers through his hair, and scoot down and turn so I'm facing him.

I trail my hands down his chest, over the ridges of his abs. His muscles ripple, warm under my touch.

"I love being in your bed, though this is on the small side."

"It's a queen!"

"Like I said, on the small side. Want to move into my big house? Or we can find something new." His dark eyes are serious, and his lips are curled up in a little smile.

My mouth feels parched as his stare lasts, and I understand he's serious.

It's not that I doubted his words of desiring me and loving me because I mean them too. I love him.

But I worked so hard to buy this condo, and giving it up doesn't make me happy.

"Holly, you don't have to sell your condo." Noel brushes my shoulders.

"How do you read my mind?"

"Your eyes started to flutter, taking in everything in this room. We can find a place together, or I could move in here."

"I love you." I kiss him greedily, loving how his lips feel under mine, how he growls in the back of his throat and takes control of the kiss, making me whimper.

He drags my bottom lip with his teeth, gently grazing it, and his tongue tangles with mine.

"I love you too." His voice is all husky with want, and I slide the sheet off his lower half, then nudge his legs.

He spreads them open with a huge grin, and I want to make his morning every day.

Noel slants his lips against mine and kisses me deeply, and my pulse pounds, but something in me opens even more to him, deciding to trust his strength, his words.

"Are you serious about not selling my condo?"

"Wherever you are, Holly, I'll be there. I don't need space. I just need you."

His words slam into me like a blast of heat, and waves of lovey-dovey syrup crash over me, and I kiss him frantically as if my next breath depends on it.

Between his legs, with my hands on his thighs, I nip the sensitive skin of his inner thigh and press my mouth right beside his half-hard cock.

"Holly..." He groans above me, and I slide my palm up the full length.

"I'm saying good morning," I tease and, bending down, I lick the crown in a slow circle, tasting him, savoring the heavy musk on my tongue.

"Love you, Pet." The pleasure hums through his tone, and his words make me feel so cherished, I lap and keep sucking him, drawing him deep.

He jerks, a raw groan tearing from his chest. That sound lights me up inside, and I want to hear it again, louder.

I want him to unravel. I wrap my lips around his cockhead, giving it a slow, greedy suck before taking him deeper into my mouth.

His leg hooks around my shoulder. His foot strokes down my back, and I shiver, whimper, my pussy throbs.

I slowly lap the length of his penis before taking the whole thick length of it in my mouth.

"Holly!" He says my name like it's something profound, and I keep going, working my jaw muscles, wanting him to fall apart, needing to give him this on our first morning together.

I swallow him deep. Suck harder. He groans, thighs trembling under my hands.

"I'm going to come in your mouth, Pet," he grits out.

I whimper around his length, that's exactly what I want and reaching up, I squeeze his balls, drawing back on his length, then lapping it again, taking it as far back in my throat as I can, all while playing with his sac.

"Fuck!" His voice breaks.

His hips thrust hard, and I take him deeper. His cry rips through the room as he pulses hot and thick on my tongue. I drink him down, every drop, greedy for more, until he collapses back against the pillows, trembling.

"Come here." It's a command, and I scramble up, lay my head against his chest, his quick heartbeat loud against my ear.

"I want to wake you up like that every morning."

"Accepted." He leans down and kisses me, a rough wet kiss that makes my nipples bead.

"What should we do now?" I curve my lips in a smile and sweep my thumbs over his nipples.

"Enough of that," he growls, making me laugh.

"Breakfast. We're going to need our stamina."

"Is that a promise?"

"You can count on it." With the way his gaze banks with heat, I believe him.

After the bathroom, I throw on his dress shirt from the night before, his scent thick against my skin.

In the kitchen, I cringe at my messy counters and living room.

"I'm a bit of a slob." I twist the hem of the shirt in my hands.

Noel kisses me on the forehead. "You're a gorgeous slob who looks so fucking hot in my shirt."

He's thrown on a pair of my boxers, but I dance my fingertips down his bare chest.

"You could be a hoarder, and I'd still love you."

"Wait until you see how little I have in the fridge."

"Okay, I'm out then," Noel says, giving me a smirk.

"But I have wine and cheese," I point at the two overflowing baskets on my counter.

"In that case, I think you're worth keeping." Noel laughs, kissing me hot and fast.

"I need a shower," I tell him.

"You smell like me. I like it."

I know I'm blushing furiously, and my pulse is racing. If this is how we start each morning, I'll never make it to the office.

Pulling the basket of jams, cheese and crackers, I untied the ribbon.

"From clients?"

"Yeah, and other industry people," I say as I open it.

The other basket is full of specialty chocolates and dessert wine.

"Think this brie is any good?" I hold up the wheel.

Noel takes it from my hands. "It's from Denmark. It looks fancy."

"Is this the kind of thing you eat?"

Noel cocks an eyebrow at me. "Because I'm a rich snob?"

"I have a client who eats smoked salmon for breakfast every day and another who won't work unless there is a box of Kraft Dinner in their dressing room. So you never know."

Noel opens the wheel of brie. "I do not eat this every day. You'll laugh, but I like Pop-Tarts for breakfast."

"Strawberry or raspberry?" I try to hide my smile and can't.

Noel reaches for the raspberry jar of jam. "I like the variety pack. It also comes with blueberry."

"I don't have PopTarts. Coffee?"

"Yes, please."

I spoon coffee into the filter, humming as I do, and I can't help but smile. Noel sets the crackers on the board, opening more jars of jam. This feels so domestic I stop with my finger on the start button of the coffee maker.

"Holly?" Noel's tone is that sugary one that makes me look at him instantly.

"Yeah?"

"What's wrong?"

"I'm just thinking how amazingly normal and lovely this feels."

"And it scares you." Noel takes my finger and presses the button, making my old coffee machine whirl to life.

"And it scares me," I echo.

He steps into my space and wraps me in his arms. "I love you, Holly. We don't have to get married tomorrow. We can have a long engagement."

"How long?" My heart is fluttering wildly.

"Spring?" Noel raises his eyebrows. His expression is so boyish that I laugh.

"Okay, spring."

Did I just agree to marry the stranger I met on the plane? I think I did.

Noel smiles huge, picks me up in his arms and spins me around.

"My mother is going to be thrilled," I say against his neck.

"Good. I can't wait to meet her and Stella, too. When can you take time off work next?"

"I don't know," I mutter.

"We'll figure it out. We can do weekend trips. You have to meet my brothers." He takes my hand and kisses the top of it.

"Am I going to like them?" Nerves swirl around my belly.

"I like them. Evan's birthday is next month. They're probably pissed at me for missing our New Year's Eve bash."

"I don't want to start off like that," I say. I pour the coffee into the mugs. Noel passes me the cream from the fridge, and I take down the sugar.

"They'll be happy for me. You take the coffee. I'll grab the cheeseboard."

I follow him into my living room, and we settle on the couch.

"You know," Noel says, spreading brie on a cracker with a little pear jam. "There's an old wives' tale that says however you spend New Year's Day is what you'll be doing the rest of the year."

"I could get used to it." I open my mouth, and he feeds me the cracker. I chew. It's slightly tangy from the cheese and sweet from the jam.

"Good." Noel slants his mouth across mine. His hand reaches for my thigh, and before I know it, I'm under him, and he's above me on my couch, and it's perfect.

"I love you," I tell him.

"I love you, Holly." His gaze sears into me, making me all hot and flushed.

"About your gran's farm..."

My shoulders tense, but he drags the back of his hand along my cheeks.

"Why didn't you tell me who you were? I get why you didn't tell me what you do, but why didn't you tell me you own the farm next to Vixen's Paradise?"

I shift so I can see his face better. His dark eyes are serious, studying me.

"I don't know. At first I wasn't sure how to. Your dinner invitation took me by surprise."

"Yes, a very good surprise. And then I thought if I brought it up...that it would destroy or change what we had. That you would have thought I was there under some kind of pretense or that I was trying to influence the offer or something."

"I get that. But nothing can change what we have, Holly. What I have with you is the magic of Christmas morning. What I have with you is another chance to love. It's the most unexpected gift, my present."

"I should have told you."

"Don't keep things from me, Holly. Not the non-work things you can share."

That's going to be different from how I usually operate, but looking into his deep pools of chocolate, I answer the only way I can. "I'll try, Noel. I'll do my best to share everything."

"We can work on it." He kisses me, long and slow, setting my nerves buzzing, heat spreading through my body.

"Noel..."

"Yes, Holly?"

"I want you to fuck me."

"Right here?"

"Yes, please."

"You don't need to ask me again." He lifts me up and I squeal, giggling as he turns us, so I'm lying on the couch and he's braced behind me. "

"Then what are you waiting for?"

24

NOEL

The way her arousal perfumes the air drives me wild, and her pulling off my boxers makes me want to ravage her until she's shaking.

I want to claim her as mine right now.

"I love you asked for what you wanted," I grit out through my deep. My blood is rushing in my ears, my cock is throbbing hard, and all I want to do is sink into her sweet heat.

"That's what Kinkmas gave me," she says so softly I barely hear her, but then her face lights up, her green eyes shimmer. "It gave me the space to ask for what I wanted instead of settling."

"You'll never," I brush my lips across hers, then slide over to her ear, nibbling on its delicate shell. "Ever," and drop a fervent kiss on that hollow of her neck. "Settle with me, Holly."

"I know." She squints her eyes closed as if it was too much emotion, but I pulled her bottom lip with my teeth.

"Open those eyes and tell me what you're feeling."

"Noel,I..." She swallows, and I glide over her body, up and down, giving her a bit of space to collect her thoughts.

"Overwhelmed. For years, I hid my desires, what I wanted, and tried to settle, but it was picking away at me. With you...I have everything I need, Noel. I love you."

"And I love you, pet," I slant my lips against her, swallowing her cries, loving how her nails dig into my back.

She's everything I didn't think I'd ever have, and I'm going to do whatever it takes to make her happy.

"I'll do anything to make you feel safe, cherished, but right now, I need to bury my cock in your pussy."

She gasps when the tip of my cock brushes against her slick heat, the pulse of desire sharp enough to make my whole body thrum.

With a low growl, I push her leg up over the back of the sofa, the angle perfect, my fingers sliding into her with ease as I feel her warmth, her slickness. She moans, her body arching against me, desperate for more.

"You're so fucking ready, aren't you, pet?" I whisper in her ear, my fingers moving in slow, teasing circles.

"Yes, please... I need it." Her voice trembles with hunger, the sound of it going straight to my core.

"How can I resist when you beg like that?" I watch her face flush, her body trembling with anticipation.

I slam into her, a slow grind that builds into a pounding rhythm, the couch creaking under the force.

Her nails dig into my back, pulling me closer, and I laugh at the sheer hunger in her eyes, the way she's already becoming undone.

"You're mine," I growl, pulling out just to thrust back in, deep and relentless. My eyes stay locked on her, watching as my cock disappears inside her—so fucking sexy, it drives me wild.

"Yes," she breathes, her voice full of need. "Yours."

Desire ratchets through me, and I tilt my head back, my balls aching, needing to release.

Her pussy clenches around me, urging me to go harder, deeper.

Holly's breathing hitches, she cries out, and I feel her pussy clench around my cock as I thrust, hard and fast, loving how her breasts bounce to the rhythm.

"Going to spend all the New Year's with you, pet."

"Yes! I can't wait!" Her scream echoes around the room as the tingling at my spine increases, and I slide out of her heat, with a roar only to thrust back in, deeper.

"I love you!"

Her pussy spasms on my cock, quivering and slick, milking me with every pulse., and I hold on, desperate for every pulse, every flutter of her surrender, her everything.

"Give it to me, Holly."

She tightens under me and bites the inside of my cheek, holding back. Damn, she's gorgeous, with her green eyes shiny and her hair all messed up, her skin pink.

"Fuck! Come now!" Winching, I hold back until her pussy clamps down on my cock and she draws in a tight breath, then lets it out, crying out.

"I'm coming!"

"Yeah, that's it, pet, good girl!" I thrust through her aftershocks, feeling her pussy flutter around my cock.

Heat races across my skin, and I can't hold back, and I scream her name as I come, in long spurts of cum, deep inside her.

We lay together, panting, her lips bruised from my kisses.

"That was...good."

"Very fucking good," I echo.

I slowly slide out of her, get to my feet, but I wobble and sit down on the couch.

"Noel?" Her palm is on my shoulder, concern in her voice.

"I'm fine. You just made my head spin."

"Good," she kisses the spot on my shoulder where her head was and then she gets up.

"Where are you going?" I grab her by the hips, and see my seed drip down between her legs.

"Thought I'd clean up and get you a glass of water."

"Yeah?" I drag my fingers through the sticky mess and wipe them on her breasts. She bites her lip as a shiver rakes through her.

"We need more sustenance." Her smile lights up her face, and my heart beats wildly in my chest.

"I love you."

"I love you, Noel," she pats my cheek, and I watch her cross the room, pouring me a glass of water, and strut over to me with a roll of her hips.

I sip it and let out a roar that makes her giggle.

"What was that for?"

"For you. For how you make me feel."

"How's that?" Her voice is a breathy whisper.

"Safe. Cherished. Cared for."

I tug her back across my lap and wrap her in my arms. She makes me feel like that and more. With Holly, I feel like I can live again, and that is priceless.

"Love you, Noel."

I slant my lips against hers, kissing her with all the passionate fire I feel, and with a silent promise never to let her go.

25

EPILOGUE

HOLLY

If I had any doubt that Noel is rich, that his family is wealthy, being in the Hugo Hotel has smashed those doubts to pieces.

An outdoor terrace overlooks Coal Harbour and the North Shore Mountains. But as nice as the luxurious high thread count is on the bed, the room's dark tones make me feel a little claustrophobic.

Polished cherry furniture gives the room a decidedly heavy feel, and I miss the unexpected charm of Vixen's Paradise.

"Are you ready?" Noel steps out of the shower with a towel wrapped around his waist.

"I guess." But I'm not. I'm literally sitting on the bed, scrolling through my phone. My stomach is fluttering with nerves.

"Holly, they're going to love you." Noel brushes his lips against my neck. "And if they don't, it doesn't matter. I love you."

But I want them to like me.

Family is essential to Noel, and I want his brothers to think that he's making a good choice in marrying me.

"I love you, too."

He pushes me back against the bed, and I laugh, threading my fingers through his hair. "Noel, if you have your way with me now, we'll be late, and then I'll make a horrible impression on them."

"I'll tell them it was my fault. That I had to have you before I subjected you to them."

I kiss his perfectly symmetrical lips, loving how soft they are, and the heat in his gaze tells me exactly how much he wants me.

But I duck out under his arms.

"You can't get away from me!"

"I just did." I laugh from the end of the bed.

Noel growls and lunges for me. I try to twist out of his reach, but he's faster and pulls me to his front.

"Noel! I need to put on my make-up."

"Okay, I'll let you go. But I have something I want you to wear tonight."

"Your ring on my finger isn't enough?" I hold my hand to the light. An enhanced blue diamond is nestled in a white-gold braided band.

"Nope." Noel drops kisses behind my ear, making me flushed and wet.

"Noel, I don't want this dress to get wrecked," I say as his hands wander down the lace-up back.

"You look stunning in this dress, and I will ruin it later."

I close my eyes at his promise as his hands sweep over my breasts through the silky fabric of my dark blue dress.

With one more kiss, he turns from me and reaches into the closet for his suit and shirt. The deep purple brings out his eyes, and the charcoal suit is a perfect match.

"I love that colour on you."

"I like this colour on you." Noel grins, holding up the golden bullet vibrator he first gave me at Vixen's Paradise.

My cheeks flush as I lick my lips.

"What do you say, Holly? Want to be mine to control throughout this evening?"

In answer, I grab it out of his hand and run into the bathroom. "If you make me orgasm in front of your brothers, I'll never live it down."

Noel chuckles. "Wait until we get to the restaurant. You'll fit right in."

After I slide the vibrator in place, I step out of the bathroom and take his hand.

"Give me five minutes to do my make-up."

"You got it." Noel leans in the bathroom doorway.

"You don't have to watch me." I quickly lay powder foundation on my face, followed by a touch of concealer.

"I love watching you."

My make-up brush falls out of my hand as vibrations pulsate through me, and I gasp. "Noel! Let me put on my make-up before you wreck it."

"Fine." He sighs in an exasperated way and slips the controller into his pocket. "I'll wreck it later."

I smile at him, loving how easy it is to be with him. He can be playful one moment but still give me what I crave.

He makes me feel so treasured. Being with him still feels like a dream.

With a swipe of lip gloss and one quick fluff of my hair, I turn to him.

"Ready."

"Damn, I'm a lucky bastard." Noel steps into the bathroom, wrapping me in his arms. "Why do you love me?"

I laugh but stop at the seriousness in his tone. "Because you're you."

He grins and takes my hand. "I love you because you are you. And you're so hot you'll raise the restaurant's temperature."

I shake my head at him.

Slyly, Noel reaches into his pocket, and I feel the low hum ripple through me.

I slip my feet into low-slung back heels and walk through the door Noel holds for me. The hallway carpet is so plush it feels like walking on a cushion.

Noel presses the elevator button, and the car opens to a dark panel wall. My heart is in my throat as it rises two more floors.

"Holly, no matter what happens tonight, you're mine." Noel fuses his lips to mine, and I clutch his arms as the vibrations increase.

"Be a good girl and give me that orgasm right now."

I can't believe how ready my body is that it bows to his command, but as he leans in to kiss me again, deepening the kiss, the vibrations rise to a crescendo. My orgasm falls so quick and fast, only my body shuddering in the aftermath is the sign that it happened.

"Good girl."

The bell chimes to tell us we have arrived on our chosen floor, and we step out. Two men dressed in tuxedos are in the hall. By the earpieces they're sporting, I guess they are security.

"Good evening, Mr. Brennon. Your brothers are already waiting for you in the back of the dining room."

"Thank you."

Great, we're late. My stomach turns with a little bit of anxiety.

But Noel drapes an arm around my waist and leads me into the gorgeous restaurant. I stop because I've never seen anything as glamorous as this place.

Crystal chandeliers hang from the ceiling. Every table in the place is glass; some are oblong shaped, some are high-top squares, and some are banquets with seating for eight guests.

The chairs are leather, not quite black, a deep blood hue. On one side of the room, there is a throne. There are cages and spanking benches along the wall as if they are art exhibits.

"Wow."

"Oh yes, it gets better," Noel says.

He leads me past the guests, and I avert my eyes from a woman dressed as a kitty, her gorgeous breasts on display. She's kneeling on a cushion at one of the shorter tables, and her breasts are literally on the table.

Her companion, a woman with a French braid, is picking a canape from her naked breasts.

The wait staff is dressed in black and flutters by us. The guests are dressed in varying degrees, and scenes are going on around me, but the setting is intimate; me walking by them feels intrusive.

"Noel, we didn't think you'd ever make it!" A well-built man with hair that is slightly darker than Noel strides towards us. He's not as tall as Noel, but his muscles are evident under his white dress shirt. This guy doesn't skip arm day.

"I've been busy." Noel leans in to hug the guy. "Evan, meet Holly. Holly, this is my younger brother Evan and the brains behind Sinful Bites."

"Nice to meet you."

Evan takes my hand and stares into my eyes. His eyes are so like Noel's, but his features are sharper.

"I hear you are what's keeping Noel busy. Nice ring. The others are in here, come."

Evan leads us through a set of double wooden doors that open to a private dining room.

One man is sitting, facing the doorway. He has a stuffy beard, and his arms are crossed over his chest.

"Finally, big brother." The guy gets up, and he moves a lot more gracefully than he looks like he can.

"Hunter, good to see you." Noel gives him a quick one-armed hug. "Meet Holly."

"Why does he get to meet her first?" A man comes between us, slinging his arm over Noel's shoulders.

"I'm Theo." He extends his hand to me.

"Hi, I'm Holly."

"There, you met her before Hunter. Are you happy?" Noel asks.

Theo flashes a grin. "Thrilled."

"Congrats, Noel. Holly, I'm thrilled you managed to make this guy smile," Hunter says.

"I have the first course coming out in two minutes. Sit down." Evan gestures at the table.

"So Noel, do you notice anything missing?" Theo sits across from us, with Hunter on his right. Evan sits at the head of the table, and Noel guides me to a seat on his right.

"It's a good crowd for a Thursday. Can't say I noticed anything. Holly?"

"I don't know, but this is my first time in a restaurant like this."

"It's the only restaurant like it in North America," Evan says.

"That can't be true." Theo shakes his head, his sandy hair falling into his eyes.

"It is true." Evan glares at his younger brother.

"What does it matter?" Hunter says.

"Are you going to tell us?" Noel glides his hand to my thigh.

Being in the room with the Brennon brothers is a little overwhelming, and I'm trying to take in all their facial gestures, trying to figure out if they are happy I'm here or if I am a fifth wheel when the strongest pressure rolls through my centre.

I gasp and grab Noel's arm.

Noel passes me the filled water glass in front of me, his smile so mischievous I want to lick him.

"There's not a single flower in the place because Evan fired the florist."

"They did horrible work!" Evan protests.

Just then, the doors open, and a whole team rushes in, sitting down plates before us. The most delicious aroma fills my nostrils, and I don't know what's on my plate, but I'm going to eat it all.

"Please enjoy." The waiter bows her head, and the team leaves the room.

"But now he has a photo shoot and needs flowers."

"There must be a million florists in this city. Choose one," Noel says.

He picks up his skewer and pulls off his meatball, smiling at me.

I reach for mine and pull back as my body is on fire with the pulsating rockets of vibration.

"Holly, are you okay?" Theo, a sly smile on his face.

My cheeks are burning.

"Fine. So what florist do you want, and why hasn't she agreed to take the job?" I say it through gritted teeth.

Thankfully, Noel lays off the remote control.

Evan pauses with his skewer at his mouth. He lifts his wine glass to me. "You got all that in five minutes?"

"Holly's a great reader of situations. It comes in handy in her job." Noel is smiling so hugely. I want to climb onto his lap.

"I guessed from Theo's reaction. He looks as if he has a secret. Noel's right. There are lots of florists in the city, so there must be a reason why you cancelled your floral order."

"Yes, the previous company fired her, and now she's started on her own and won't take my calls."

"Sounds like a smart woman," Hunter says.

Theo and Noel laugh, but Evan glares at his youngest brother. Hunter shrugs and pops the skewer in his mouth.

"Why won't she?" Noel asks.

"She doesn't like this place." Evan shrugs.

"It's not to everyone's taste," Theo says.

"No, but she hasn't even tried. She can't judge without giving it a fair chance," Evan says.

"Then why don't you invite her to experience it as a guest?" Noel says. "That's how I got this one."

I giggle as he holds up my hand, my cheeks flaming.

"Maybe. I don't like people telling me no."

"A woman dared to tell you no? I like her too." Noel grins. "What's her name?"

"Mara." Evan stares at us coolly.

"Ooh, Mara," Theo says.

"And Theo, how's it going with Callie?" Noel asks.

I grin as his brothers laugh, and Theo wags a finger at Noel. "I told you, it's not like that."

"That's why he's going to the middle of nowhere again next week." Hunter grins.

"I wish you guys all the luck in your pursuits or non-pursuits," Noel adds, glancing at Theo.

The next course comes in with more wine, and I settle back, holding Noel's hand under the table, listening to the brothers talk.

It's clear they love each other, and I can't wait to meet their parents.

"Mom is going to freak. She's going to want to hold the wedding in the backyard," Evan says.

"This time, I'll let her. If that's okay with you, Holly," Noel raises an eyebrow at me, and I sense the collective held breath around the room.

Noel's wife will always be a part of him and a part of his past. Just like my past, it sometimes comes out into the present moment.

But it doesn't matter.

I love Noel, and I know the next moment we create is more important than anything that's ever come before.

"That sounds amazing," I say and squeeze his hand.

Finally, the desert comes, and Noel stands.

"We'll join you guys tomorrow for breakfast. I need to take my wife-to-be back to our room."

"Noel, she's cute when she blushes," Hunter says.

I am grabbing his hand so hard I'm sure I'm bruising it.

"She's cute all the time," Noel says. The look he sends me leaves my throat dry. My pulse races, and I don't care that his brothers know he's going to have sex with me. I'm a moment away from telling him to ravish me right here.

"Nice meeting you all," I say.

"Good night," Theo says.

Evan gives us a salute, and Noel waves.

The restaurant is quiet. A grey-haired man is dangling a cherry to a petite woman he has on his lap.

She giggles as she tries to catch the cherry in her mouth.

"What a place," I say.

"Yeah, Evan is proud of it."

And why shouldn't he be? It takes the parts of a dungeon and puts them on display over appetizers.

I get the appeal, but I'm not sure I want to be a guest there.

But the memory of Noel feeding me at Vixen's Paradise rushes through my mind, and I shrug.

Maybe I get the appeal after all.

In the elevator, Noel pins me to the corner of the car, slants his mouth over mine and kisses me.

He tastes of the red wine we had with dinner. His hand slips under the skirt of my dress.

"How wet are you for me?"

"I'm so soaked." I close my eyes, arching my body as he pushes my panties to one side.

His touch ignites the storm of desire he'd built all evening long. I shriek as the elevator tumbles to a stop, the doors flying open to a couple.

"Evening," Noel says to them.

He takes my hand, and both of us are running down the hall, like we're teenagers who just escaped being caught.

Noel swipes the keycard at the reader, and we're in the room.

"Now I get to have what I want."

"Yeah? What's that?" I kick off my heels and reach behind me to unsnap my dress.

Noel undoes the clasp, and I get the dress off.

"You. You are all I want, Holly." He takes off my bra. I shudder as his hands slide down to the waistband of my panties.

He reaches between my legs, gently pulling the vibe out.

"It's soaked with your juice. I love your smell." Noel holds the vibrator under his nose as if he's smelling a flower. He gives me a wink and then goes into the bathroom.

My whole body is red with heat and a little embarrassment, but the kind that is making me wet.

When he comes out of the bathroom, he's naked except for his pants.

My heart is in my throat as I turn to kiss him. He's serious but playful, content, and eager to try new things.

He's steady and fun, and I can't believe I am wearing his ring on my finger.

"You're all I've ever wanted, Noel. I love you."

"I love you, too." He lifts me up, and I laugh. My legs are around his waist as he carries me to the bed and sets me down.

I'm aching so much for his touch. I reach for him; my hands run along his muscular back. He laughs as I fumble at his waistband.

"Impatient?"

"You know this about me."

"Yes, I do, and tonight, I'm not going to make you wait another second." He shucks off his pants, and the cock I love to taste so much springs free.

Grabbing him with my hand, I take it to my mouth.

He hisses, a growling, guttural sound emits from his lips.

I smile around his cock, taking in as much as I can. I twirl my tongue under his shaft. And I lick, feeling the shudders rake through him.

His cock is steel, and his reactions are soft; he's letting me see him vulnerable, and I love it. Slowly, I suck on his cock, playing with his balls as I sweep my tongue along his sensitive underside.

"Holly, I love you." He rocks back on his knees so his cock comes out of my mouth, and the next thing I know, I'm under his hard body.

He kisses me. Then kisses me again. He eats at my lips as if he can't stop tasting them, and I swoon with want, with need. Noel breaks off the kiss and skims his mouth along the hollow of my neck, down to my breast.

"Why is everything so different with you?" I mumble as he sucks in my hardened tip to the root of his mouth.

Pleasure rockets through me as he works his mouth over my nipple, sucking and tasting.

He grins at me as he comes off my breast, switching sides.

"Because we're meant to be. You're mine, Holly."

Ripples of pleasure break across my skin at the touch of his tongue on my nipple. I press his head against my flesh, wanting to be closer to him.

My body is all soft and needy, ready for him to manipulate it how he will.

No man has ever made me feel so loved, adored and treasured.

Noel grazes my nipple with his teeth before coming off of it and fusing his lips to mine.

His lips are slightly swollen and feel like electricity as they touch mine.

"I love you."

"I love you too."

He shifts himself so he's lined up with my pussy, and gently grabbing my legs, he places them around his waist.

"You're so soft and ready for me. I love looking at you like this."

"I need you inside me."

He laughs. "Yes, my present, anything for you."

His cock slides into me, deep and as he rocks his hips, even deeper.

He stays like that for a moment, poised above me, his eyes meeting mine as if he's remembering every detail about this moment.

"Please."

"I love hearing you say that." He kisses me as he rocks his hips, drilling into me.

He is all I need. He's filling every single inch of me, consuming me with need and desire, and I moan.

He groans in reply and moves his hips like a slow dance, intent on driving my pleasure. It starts to spiral upwards as he sinks deeper and deeper, pulling me to him with each thrust.

My head explodes with fierce want. We're skin to skin, and I breathe in his familiar, rich scent.

"I need you."

"Not as much as I need you. Come, Holly, come with me. Now."

He thrust long and deep, once, twice, before he drills right into my core, his gaze locked with mine, as if he's taking me into his soul.

"Noel!" I cry his name as the crest of pleasure rises even higher, feeling him tense above me.

"You're my heaven, Holly."

It's the naked love in his voice that breaks open the orgasm, sending me diving off the crest, falling into the abyss.

"Oh...oh!" I pant all my words, my breath gone.

One more thrust, and he's released right in me, making me cry out as his hot cum pumps out in a long sprut.

We both catch our breath. Noel slowly dislodges, wrapping me in his arms.

"I want to stay here forever."

"For five days?" He says against my ear.

"You're mine forever, no matter where we stay." I brush a finger along his lips.

"You got that right, my present. Never forget it." He nibbles my ear and chuckles as I squirm against him.

My heart is so full, and I know he'll love me forever.

***

Keep reading! The next book in the Sinful Delights Series is *Five Days to Be Mine* and *Five Nights of Yes, Ma'am*

www.ingramcontent.com/pod-product-compliance
Lightning Source LLC
LaVergne TN
LVHW091042080826
845145LV00002B/589

* 9 7 8 1 7 3 8 0 9 1 4 2 3 *